Blood

of the

Ràej

The Magic of Omneth Series
Book One

Hayley Rae Johnson

Published by Raw Magic Publishing, 2021

BLOOD OF THE RÀEJ

Second edition. Nov. 2021.

Copyright © 2021 Hayley Rae Johnson.

Written by Hayley Rae Johnson.

A Note From the Author

I was in the fourth grade when my teacher read us *Harry Potter and the Sorcerer's Stone*. Everyone knew I was already a fantasy fanatic, and this didn't help my obsession. As this series grew in fame and popularity, becoming a 'household' name, I became determined to write a fantasy that did NOT use wands.

And Pebble Pinching was born.

Unfortunately, I created Pebble Pinching in the very first draft of this series when I was thirteen. After life knocks you down and runs you over a few dozen times, your perspective on things change. As did mine. I still enjoyed the idea of Pebble Pinching, using 'borrowed' or 'gifted' magic, but I wanted MORE.

More POWER. More RAGE. More uncontrolled EMOTION. I didn't want my heroine to rely on a tool. I wanted her to feel it deep inside herself and I wanted her to throw it at anyone who got in her way.

And Ràej magic was born.

There's nothing better than having something to fight for with that forbidden-due-to-fear asset you possess. Imagine having a government saying you were wrong because they feared you? When there is war due to differences, people (or creatures in Omneth's case) are able to find what similarities they do have so they can fight the big battle and have a chance -- a chance at survival. The enemy of my enemy is my friend, right?

Just remember this:

NEVER trust a Pebble Pincher.

♦ ♦ ♦ Prologue ♦ ♦ ♦

The rain was torrential. Lightning forked across the sky, sending brief respites of light to the hundreds of soldiers huddling closer and closer together, trying to make room for more in the Great Hall. Thunder reverberated through the stone walls and underfoot. The head table was occupied by only two people: High King Mason and his lord chancellor, Gerald. The only thing separating them from the growing mass of armed men was the three-foot dais where the head table stood. As more people entered the Great Hall, the darker it became. The restlessness was increasing, as was the nervous chatter.

Gerald walked in front of the head table and put his hands out in front of him, as though he were holding a large, invisible ball. An orange and yellow sphere of fire grew between his outspread hands. Once it was almost touching his fingers, he spread his arms out wide. The flame dispersed to six torches on each side of the Great Hall.

King Mason stood next to his chancellor, who bowed his head slightly and stepped back. The king looked out over his soldiers, stopping to look at one face here and one face there, blood-soaked bandages wrapped around their heads. Their uniforms were caked in mud, rain, and tears, which made paths down their bruised, bloodied, and disheartened faces. They stood quiet and attentive.

He needed more time. But he didn't have it. He had only one more chance to give those loyal to him hope, to give them courage and a reason to fight. One more speech that could be the difference between life and death for the men before him.

"I know you are tired. You have been beaten down and wounded. You may not see the light through this storm but-"

"We cannot win, Your Majesty! The queen is gone. We need to surrender!" Shouting erupted, getting louder and louder until the king couldn't hear the storm outside.

"We will win!" King Mason's voice boomed. Holding his index finger at his throat, he projected his voice over the din, commanding silence once again. "Yes, Queen Mellony has been captured. And, yes, she is carrying the heir to this throne. We don't think they know about her pregnancy. If they did, our queen would already be slain instead of held for our surrender."

"They will kill her if we do not surrender!"

2

"We will not surrender!" King Mason shouted, enraged by the challengers. "We will never surrender! We are the Ràej! You are all Blood of the Ràej! We do not back down, we do not surrender!"

"Blood of the Ràej!"

"Blood of the Ràej!"

"Blood of the Ràej!"

More and more soldiers joined the chant until everyone in the Great Hall, and those who had not yet entered, were chanting together. The walls shook, making the torches go out, one by one. The chanting grew until it could only be described as an indiscernible noise. The roof and walls exploded outward, falling like dust on the shoulders of the soldiers.

The Blood of the Ràej were united. They had regained their fighting spirit, and their blood boiled with the taste of war and victory.

◆

Queen Mellony was riding through the forest, not daring to look back as wet branches whipped her face and snagged at her cloak. Shortly after she had been captured, man-handled out of her chambers by a group of Binders, she was shackled and put atop a horse to be pulled swiftly away by a hooded man. Ràej soldiers had stood in silence, listening to their queen's pleas and watching her be led away. Through pure luck her captor's horse had reared when the storm started.

When the thunder boomed, Queen Mellony felt it ripple through the air. She had watched the lightning streak through the sky in the dark, liquid eyes of her captor's horse. The horse had shrieked and lifted on its hind legs in fright, making the hooded man fall off his horse and lose hold of the reins to her own.

Though she wore both anti-magic gold and iron handcuffs, her hands were bound in front, allowing her to hold onto the pommel of her horse's saddle. The horse didn't need any coaxing, but she kicked her heels into its sides anyways. As soon as it broke into a run, she felt a sudden warmth between her thighs. Lightning flashed and thunder quickly followed, an unbroken chain that mimicked the pains intensifying in her abdomen. Queen Mellony held to the saddle for dear life, and for the life of her unborn child.

When she felt she could no longer hang on, Queen Mellony slowed the horse to a trot and then a walk. The rain had become a sprinkle with the thunder just a murmur in the distance. They had outrun the storm and ended in a clearing. A small, hunched woman stood in the middle, holding the reins of a donkey in one hand and a basket in the other. Queen Mellony licked her lips and blinked. Before she could ask for help, everything went black and she fell from the horse.

◆

"I can't believe it has come to this," King Mason said and put on his war helmet. "We used to be the protectors of all Omneth. I fought hell demons and power-hungry warlocks. Damn it all, I took down Berrien when he was siphoning magic from young witches! But this..." He looked at his lifelong friend, now chancellor, and shook his head. "These bastards are trying to eliminate magic! They turned most of the lower magics, and I know they have at least one Great Seer. They have my wife."

Gerald waited for the armsmen to finish ratcheting his greaves and straps and those of the king's before he spoke. "We are going to fight this battle like we have all others."

"No thoughts of failure, just victory and wine."

The two men gripped arms, thinking of better days far behind them, and nodded.

◆

Mineka was rumored to be a great sorceress. Her shrunken appearance and blindness had halted those rumors decades ago, but Queen Mellony had known it was her in the meadow before she had fainted. She awoke in a little cabin, decorated with dried plants and bottles of this and that and knew she couldn't be in a safer place.

"Don't sit up." A surprisingly young voice came from the old woman. "Your body has been through a lot. You

5

lost a lot of blood."

Queen Mellony tried to relax on the straw-filled bed. Her riding pants were hanging by the fire along with her cloak. Both were stained with blood, and her pants looked as though they had been cut off her. It was a wonder Mineka had bothered to hang them up at all. After a quick inventory of bodily injuries, Queen Mellony sat upright with a heavy ball of fear inside her.

"My baby! Where is my baby?" she screamed as she felt rough stitches instead of the bulge of her pregnancy. Her baby had been taken.

"Lie down, my queen," the sorceress said, putting a gentle but firm hand to Queen Mellony's shoulder, guiding her back to the pillow. "Your baby lives. She called a great storm, that one."

"What do you mean?"

"Who else do you think could have wielded the power to control that storm? Your magic was bound, was it not? I may be a sorceress, but I am not Blood of the Ràej, nor are my Sisters," Mineka said matter-of-factly and began dropping herbs and flowers into a pot of boiling water. "It was your little one that called the storm. I felt her power and called your horse to find me."

Queen Mellony took the cup Mineka shoved into her hands and stared gape-mouthed. How was it possible? Her daughter hadn't been born yet. Her husband was powerful, but men of the Ràej didn't wield that type of magic. She held the mug with two hands so Mineka could pour the hot liquid into it. Bruises on her wrists showed where the power-binding cuffs had been.

"I'll go get your babe while you drink up."

" *The queen has escaped. She has given birth.*"

King Mason slammed his sword into the chest of the man in front of him. He hesitated before kicking the slain man and ripping his sword out. The woman's voice was unfamiliar but sounded so close. He turned in circles. On all sides, there were men in armor with gore hanging off their plates, swords swinging, and blood spurting, but there was no woman.

"She is dying, Your Majesty."

The king's heart skipped a beat.

"Watch out!"

Mineka swaddled the baby princess and returned to Queen Mellony. The air had been warmed by the fire and smelled of herbs and flowers. The queen was slumped over, her untouched mug of tea spilled across the floor. Mineka shook the young woman's shoulder, but the queen was as still as her open eyes, staring blankly at the floor. Humming a soothing melody, Mineka proceeded to make a tea of lemon, chamomile, and lavender for herself.

"Let's just sit and wait, little babe," she said quietly to the bundle in her arms. "Doo dum, doo dum. Your father should be along shortly."

"Be gone with you! I need to find my wife!" King Mason attempted to push off a surgeon holding needle and gut.

"Your Majesty, we will send riders out to find her," Gerald said. "You will not be much help to anyone if you bleed to death at her feet."

The king tried to relax so the surgeon could do his job. He had been so distracted after hearing that voice he'd let his guard down. A sword had been thrust up behind his back plate, just under his ribs. It was hard to breathe. The surgeon was sewing closed a shallow wound on his stomach where a sword had sliced him. If he told the surgeon or his chancellor about the other wound, he might never see his wife again.

"All done," the surgeon said and wiped his hands on a cloth before walking over to his next patient. He looked back at the king. "I know you won't listen to me, but you shouldn't be riding for at least two weeks or you will tear your stitches."

"You're right," the king said. "Get me a horse! I'm going to find my queen."

◆

The storm had stopped. Only a lingering smell of rain betrayed the fact one had occurred at all. The princess, with the Ràej blood coursing through her veins, was sleeping peacefully in a wooden cradle by the crackling fire—and her dead mother.

◆

"She's over here. I know it!" King Mason kicked his horse forward through the clearing. The King's Guard followed close behind him. A tiny hut emerged at the end of the clearing. His head throbbed and blood was gushing out of both his wounds, but he had to see his wife before she died. Or before he did.

◆

The princess woke when the wood plank door was kicked down. Armed men rushed in and searched the home. One man sat by her dead mother, clasping her hand in his, and let out a howl of rage and despair. The princess followed suit with her own cries of rage for being rudely awoken, though pathetic in comparison.

◆

King Mason jumped when he heard the baby cry. She sounded as upset as he felt. He scooped the baby up gently and kissed her forehead. Rain was falling again. The king let out a sigh, full of broken dreams and hopelessness.

"My baby girl," he whispered. "Your parents loved you with all their hearts. Never forget where you came from. You are Blood of the Ràej."

◆

After completing a search of the house and surrounding area with the King's Guard, Gerald returned to the hut. He found King Mason holding his baby girl and the hand of his beloved wife. Dead.

◆◆◆ Terhese ◆◆◆

Chapter 1

"It's not fair," I said to Aunt Chloe. "Everyone knows he is terrible at Pinching Pebbles. He can barely Pinch a Play Pebble!"

The wind was whipping around us as we hurried to pick the remaining tomatoes before the first freeze of the season. We would need to dig up a few plants and transplant them into pots; these would be stored in the greenroom at the back of the house until they ripened. Doing anything with tomatoes had quickly become my most-hated chore. Aside from the row upon row of tomato plants that led to hours of backache and days of pricked fingers, it had kept me from playing with other kids throughout my childhood. Now, it kept me away from the few social gatherings that happened for the young adults in the community. As we picked, I knew my best friend, Natalie, was at a tea social, mingling with others from our primary school who would be moving to the Academy soon.

"Terhese Marie!" Aunt Chloe stood up from grabbing a low-hanging tomato. "You need to watch that tongue before it gets you into trouble. Pebble Pinching is for everyone."

"*House* Pinching is for everyone," I said as I spat out the dozenth strand of hair that had been swept into my mouth by the relentless wind. "You know what I mean."

"I know what you mean." Aunt Chloe nodded. "But others may not."

I understood her subtle warning. It was slanderous to speak of someone not having magic, and more so to refer to someone as being a true slate by calling them a slate. There was a tiny, blurred line that could affect a person's entire life depending on which side they fell.

We had learned early in primary school that the Slates had rescued Omneth, and all its people, from the Ràej tyranny. They didn't have their own magic, so they had brought Pebbles filled with donated magic from their land across the East Sea. The higher magics of Omneth had been conquered and the lesser magics were liberated.

The Slates brought their beliefs of magical equality and helped the people rebuild Omneth upon them. A new government was created to keep the balance and order. They supplied each household with Pebbles for daily use, as well as specific types of Pebbles for different jobs. Most of the Officials that worked at the government were Slates, but a few open positions were available each year for the skilled lesser magics: divination, healing, necromancy, conjuring, and illusions. Each of these lesser magics were derivatives of a higher magic.

The Officials were always looking for more Pebble Pinchers. Though everyone was supposed to be able to use this magical tool, some excelled at it. As long as you didn't have the forbidden higher magic, you were given an equal chance to work towards being an Official by going to the Academy.

Aunt Chloe had absolutely no magic in any one drop of her blood. She frequently referred to herself as a slate and made light of it. "Come help your dear Aunt Slate," she would call when she needed help with chores.

I was never very helpful. If I pinched anything other than a House Pebble, a minor explosion resulted. Like the guy I was making fun of, Travis, I had heard the same idiom about my ability for years, but he had already received his acceptance letter into the Academy.

"I belong at the Academy, Aunt Chloe."

"You belong in the place that fits you best." Aunt Chloe smiled and looked up at the sky. The sun was setting behind the hills, painting the low-hanging clouds in shades of yellows and oranges, then pink-lined purples and blues.

"That's the best comfort you can give me right now, huh?" I raised my eyebrows in a challenge.

Aunt Chloe started whistling, out of tune and offbeat.

I knew what she was really saying—the Officials know best. Those who had magical potential would be chosen to go to the Academy. Though you didn't need magic to pinch a House Pebble, you did need it to pinch the higher levels, like Fighting Pebbles. It didn't matter what type of lesser magic you had; any type would have a positive reaction to the magic inside the Pebble. If you did well in your specialty at the Academy, you could be selected for an Official internship. This would, generally, result in an offer to work with the Officials at one of the capitals.

When someone didn't have an affinity towards a certain lesser magic, they would focus on Pebble Pinching at the Academy. Each student was given the first term to choose a specialty. If they were unable to choose a specialty or succeed at Pinching, they would be dismissed from the Academy. It wasn't uncommon for a guy to return home and learn the family business, or for a girl to hope to wed and start a family.

I didn't want any of the latter. I didn't want to pick and wash and blanch and peel and stew and smash and store tomatoes for the rest of my life. Nor did I want to put my name on the list of eligible bachelorettes. I had kept my current beau a secret for half a year. Hiding my relationship hadn't been my idea, but I didn't mind being portrayed as a strong, independent woman. To the utmost annoyance of Aunt Chloe, it had only added to how "stubborn and opinionated" I was. I told her I was tenacious and assertive.

Aunt Chloe's whistling had turned to humming, but it wasn't quelling the resentment slowly building inside me towards my peers. My father, like many more of that generation, had been killed during the Ràej War, fighting the Blood for Omneth's freedom. Within hours, and miles away from each other, my mother had died while giving birth. When the Ràej Kingdom fell, the Officials had to find relatives, or generous couples, for hundreds of orphaned children. Aunt Chloe had been holding my mother's hand when she died and had adopted me instantly. I knew how fortunate I was to be with family. For them all, I pushed down my frustration and started humming along.

I resumed plucking the firm, red fruit from the vines. After years of practice, I had developed a flawless rhythmic pattern. *Twist, turn, place, twist, turn, place.* In between plants, a little *shuffle, shuffle* broke up the chorus as I stepped to the next plant. One by one, I quickly placed them in my basket, surrounded by different shades and shapes of their own. Though they would all be mashed up at one point or another, I was always careful not to bruise them.

"Where did you get this?" I asked Natalie. We were down by the river, the spot where we had been meeting since we were young. The morning was quiet and still, vastly different from the night before. It was a day of rest in my house, which meant I didn't need to do any chores. Natalie's family didn't have crops or any type of trade to run, so she never had many chores and was always thrilled when we had time outside of primary school to ourselves.

Our chosen spot, halfway between our two houses, was close enough to each that we could hear if we were being called for lunch or supper. An old cottonwood had fallen over during a storm one year, caught by the branch of another. The tree was partially uprooted, leaving a space between the ground and the base of the tree. We used to be able to sit comfortably in that space, side by side. Now we used it to leave objects we wanted to hide from our families or notes for each other. That is where I had found the newest item.

"Same as you," Natalie said sheepishly. "I asked a ... a guy for one."

I felt the warmth of the Pebble in my closed fist. It buzzed and called my name, like it was trying to tell me its purpose. I knew my purpose; I was to be a Pebble Maker.

I wanted to tinker with the spells and charms that could be put into these little things. Help defend the realm, like my father had done. I had so many ideas but lacked the magic to make them work.

Aunt Chloe had told me, at a very young age, that she wouldn't be able to help me grow in the ways of magic and that I would have to work harder than others to prove myself. All through primary, when I wasn't helping Aunt Chloe with tomatoes, I was studying some sort of magic. Being told I couldn't do something only made me want it more. I had the highest grades in primary and aced all my final examinations, but those were on numbers, reading, writing, and history. Good grades didn't stop children from calling me a slate.

As we grew older, the teasing of being magicless turned into the teasing of being an old maid, like Aunt Chloe. While other girls were at dances and picnics, I was studying, harvesting, or making food for the dances and picnics. Though I knew it was in jest, it didn't make the sting any less. People started joking that I needed the Academy so I could learn to charm a man. All I wanted was to prove everyone wrong and prove I could be valuable to the Officials, to Omneth.

"I think, when you say you got this from a guy, you mean you stole it from your brother's drawer." I laughed, more at the self-doubts that always emerged when I held a Pebble than at my friend.

"No, I didn't!" Natalie tried to grab the Pebble back. "I got it from Travis."

"Natalie, do you even know what this Pebble is?"

"No," she said. "Do you?"

"Yes." I pretended I was going to pinch the Pebble at Natalie but tossed it in the air and caught it again instead, rolling it between my thumb and forefinger. "It's an Ignorance Pebble."

Though I hadn't learned to pinch a Pebble correctly yet, I had read several books about the different kinds of Pebbles. When I saw the magically engraved marx, it took me a moment to place it. When I did, I knew Natalie didn't know what it was; she never would have touched it if she had.

"An Ignorance Pebble? It makes people dumb?"

"Not really. I haven't read too much about it. I can't even remember which book I saw this in, but I think this is a Fighting Pebble."

"No, no," Natalie said, shaking her head and crossing her arms. "Nathan wouldn't have a Fighting Pebble."

"During the war, they used this against the Blood to make them forget about the Ràej," I recalled the entry I had come across during my search for knowledge, ignoring my friend's insistent denial and admittance of getting it from her brother. "The spell was supposed to make one forget not only a certain bit of information, but everything related to it. The Slates had used the Ignorance Pebble to make the Ràej soldiers forget about their kingdom, forget about the tyrannical rule they were fighting for. When they did, they forgot about the higher magic they had been using to rule Omneth and the Slates were able to turn them to fight on their side, on the side of good.

"The Pebble was found to be faulty, though. Instead of affecting a specific target, it could affect anyone in the area, including the person who pinched the Pebble. It was more powerful than anyone had expected it to be. They outlawed it and stopped making them. I can't imagine how your brother found one of those," I finished abruptly, realizing how odd it was for her brother to have had this Pebble. He'd shown me dozens of Pebbles he'd brought home from the Academy, most of which he had made. It would make sense for him to get more advanced Pebbles as he progressed through his internship as a Pebble Maker, but this Pebble had been illegal since before I was born.

"That can't be right," Natalie said with pursed lips.

"You really think I'm wrong about a Pebble?"

"No, no," Natalie said and closed her eyes for a moment. "I don't think you're wrong about what the Ignorance Pebble is. I just don't think this is it. Maybe part of the marx wore off or ... or you're just wrong about the marx."

I wanted to object, but I didn't want to be right either. If I was right, that would mean my boyfriend had an extremely dangerous, illegal Pebble.

"Maybe we won't try Pinching this one," I said. Natalie's shoulders instantly relaxed and a smile spread across her face. "Here."

Natalie waved the offered Pebble away as though it were contagious. "You can keep that one for your collection."

I rolled it between my fingers again and shoved it into my pocket.

◆

"How dumb do you think I am?" I scoffed at Nathan and rolled onto my stomach, completely taking over his one-person bed. He had just led me up the stairs and closed the door quietly behind us, though no one should have been home at this time.

"I'm not calling you dumb," Nathan said and sat beside me, stroking my calf. "I'm just saying you aren't in the Academy and you don't know about these things."

"Wow." I flipped myself into a sitting position, almost violently. "You say that like I'll never be in the Academy."

"No." Nathan tried to grab my hand. "No, I didn't."

"Yes, you did!" I yanked my hand away from his and

crossed my arms. "Kind of ironic. We were arguing about an Ignorance Pebble, and now you're calling me ignorant."

"Rhesey, I didn't say that."

"Please, define *ignorant* for me, and then tell me how you didn't just say that I am!" I shifted my weight so one leg was dangling off the bed, preparing to run out of the room if my anger stoked his. "And don't call me that!"

"Come here," Nathan said softly, trying to put his arm around me.

I shrugged him off but turned to face him.

He rolled his eyes and tossed his hands up. "Fine. Well, what I meant was, you won't know as much about anything unless you-"

"Unless?" I almost shrieked.

"Rhesey, the Academy Ball is in just a couple of weeks," Nathan went on as if he didn't notice the tension I felt growing between us. "And everyone should have received their acceptance letter by now. Natalie got hers a few weeks ago. If your Aunt Chloe is a slate, odds are you won't get an invitation."

He put his hand on my knee, as if consoling me, and looked at me under a furrowed brow of engineered concern. I stared back at his stupid blue eyes. The same eyes that used to carry me away and make me think of the majestic sea he told me about. Those eyes were making

22

mine sting with unwanted tears. Everyone was supposed to receive an acceptance letter.

"*Stop calling me Rhesey!*"

I jumped off the bed and slipped out of his reach. He called my name, but I didn't hear him coming after me. He never did. He never had to. I always faltered, going down the stairs, before I calmed down and went back to him. Not this time.

My entire future was at stake, and I needed *somebody* to believe in me. It was as if the entire community thought I was oblivious of my situation. I was neither blind nor dumb. I knew Aunt Chloe had no magical ability and she struggled to pinch a House Pebble. Did that really matter, though? She grew the best tomatoes on this side of Omneth and sold her foodstuffs at every market from the North Shores to the Southern Harbors. Some of her recipes had even made it to River Country.

"Damn it, Terhese!" Nathan shouted from the window.

Without turning around or slowing down, I raised the Pebble we had argued about in my forefinger and thumb. I knew he wouldn't come after me; it would jeopardize our secret relationship if he chased me through town. The importance of the secrecy was becoming as hazy as the reasons for our relationship.

I didn't want to go home, and no way in Omneth would I go back to Nathan. It was unfortunate that the Ramos house was where I went when I was upset, immediately telling everything to Natalie. The past six months had been excruciatingly difficult. Nathan had made it quite clear I was not to tell anyone about us, least of all his sister. Everything about him was fueling the irritation and impatience I had been feeling about the acceptance letter, still yet to come.

Chapter 2

The wind was starting to blow, forcing me to tie my hair back, but it didn't force me to walk home. I wandered aimlessly around the outskirts of my little town. I followed one of the many streams that appeared after a rain or snow melt from the higher hills, then followed a black-tipped, lacey winged butterfly up an animal path. It took me a few minutes to realize where I was going, but no one could mistake Center Hill.

Being at the top felt like being in the center of the world, able to see the summits of the other green, rolling hills as far as the eye could see. Center Hill was far from being the center of Hill Country, but it was the tallest in Hilltown.

This was where the First Pebble had been erected. It stood at least ten feet tall and ten feet in diameter. The base was sunk into the ground a foot or so to keep it from rolling away. Thick grasses and shrubs had grown around it, further anchoring it to the hill. Deep green moss clumped under one side, like a pillow for the lichen covered stone. The marx were engraved at equal intervals on four sides, starting at the ground and reaching over my head.

"Of course," I muttered to myself. "I wasn't following the beautiful babbling brook or the fluttering butterfly. I was coming here."

This was the whole basis of the fight I'd just had with Nathan. I took the Ignorance Pebble out of my pocket and compared it to the First Pebble, so many times its size. When I had confronted him about the Ignorance Pebble, he told me that I was wrong, that it was a Bliss Pebble. Until that moment, I had been convinced the First Pebble was a Bliss Pebble. When I saw the marx, my mood dropped, and I felt a pang of guilt over our fight. He was right.

The First Pebble was, as Nathan said, a Peace Pebble. I stared at the two vertical lines and the single concave line at the top, like a bowl being held up on two poles. It was missing the second concave line that Nathan's Pebble had at the bottom. He was right.

I couldn't figure out why I would have thought the First Pebble was a Bliss Pebble, but it had been a long time since I had learned about the history of Hilltown. I was only seven when I had started primary school; a lot of knowledge could have faded and evolved over the years. Someone must have misinformed me at some point and I had continued to believe it.

Before I'd lost my temper, Nathan had retold me the Pebble origin story, as if I were a child.

When the Slates were about to surrender to the Ràej, a brave and selfless man named Berrien had spent five days and five nights baking the Peace Pebble. It was so large it took fifty men to haul it by rope, sled through the battlegrounds and up to the tallest hill they could. They were fatigued and unsure if they could go any further. But each person the Pebble passed had been overcome with a sense of peace and well-being. The Ràej recognized their evil ways and surrendered. A Peace Pebble was erected in every capital around Omneth as a tribute to Berrien and a reminder to everyone that peace had been accomplished without more bloodshed.

"The Pebbles probably accomplish the same thing, but the Bliss Pebble has an extra line because it is one step further than peace," Nathan had tried to explain.

"I don't know." I continued talking to myself in front of the giant First Pebble. "How could I have been wrong about this for so long? No one even thought to correct me? No wonder people think I'm ignorant."

"Who thinks you're ignorant?"

A young man came out from the other side of the Pebble. He was dressed in tan shorts, a dark button-up shirt, and sturdy boots. The stone canteen in his hand made me thirsty. I thought I recognized the voice, but the sun was behind his head, leaving his face shadowed.

"I was hoping just the ignorant," I tried saying lightheartedly and realized who the man was. "Do you think I am?"

"Following your deduction, unfortunately, I do not know the topic we are referring to, thus making me ignorant," the man said as he walked closer and sat with his back against the First Pebble, looking up at me with a wide smile. "Which should make me think you're ignorant. This, of course, is just following your weird logic."

I couldn't help but smile.

"Sounds like you took a logic course with the Officials." Of all the people I could have run into today, it had to be Nathan's biggest nemesis. "What are you doing up here, Jensen?"

He looked comfortable on the ground, leaning against the stone behind him. I wasn't sure if peace still emanated from the Pebble or it was the familiarity of an old friend I had been unknowingly missing, but I had a yearning to sit down next to him.

"Maybe I heard your anguish," he said seriously. His dark hair was curling up at the ends. It looked like he'd been hiking for some time; a drop of sweat glistened on the side of his neck and one at his hairline. What a perfect hairline he had. And those black eyelashes only made his green eyes more captivating. I couldn't help but stare into them. And stare.

"I'm sorry," I said. I shook my head and pretended to look out at the horizon to regather myself. "What anguish are you referring to?"

"I hike to the First Pebble when I have time," Jensen said. "I had just left the summit when I thought I heard your voice, so I came back up. I figured if you were talking to yourself, then maybe you wanted a friend."

"Are you still a friend?" I asked. Everything had been upside down since I had started dating Nathan.

"You tell me."

As children, we had all lived next door to each other, until a fire burned down Jensen's father's dairy farm, forcing them to move across town. Though we were less than three miles away, it was too far for any of us to walk back and forth and see Jensen as often as we used to. Shortly after he moved, he graduated from primary and was accepted at the Academy.

"I hope so." I returned Jensen's smile and sat down next to him. I hadn't known about the rivalry between

Nathan and Jensen until Jensen was given the Officials Investigator Internship, given to only one person each year.

I had been sitting next to Natalie when Jensen burst into the Ramos house, waving his acceptance letter at Nathan and talking about the great future the two of them would have together. Nathan had applied for an Investigator Internship too but had been given one of the ten Pebble Maker Internships. Nathan's face turned as red as one of Aunt Chloe's tomatoes when he heard Jensen's news. I thought he was going to cry. He simply shook Jensen's hand and feigned not feeling well so his friend would leave.

It was never the same after that. Nathan tried to hold it in, but little things would set him off. If Jensen mentioned anything about his internship, Nathan would leave the room or rudely interrupt him and change the subject. Finally, he cut out everything from his life that reminded him of not getting the Investigator Internship, which included Jensen, and threw himself into Pebble Making. He pretended he never wanted to be an Investigator. He touted how important and crucial Pebble Making was. Lately, he was lording himself over anyone he could to make himself feel better.

He lorded himself over me. I wasn't allowed to talk to Jensen or ask about Jensen. If I ever talked about my aspiration to go to the Academy, he would throw doubt my way. I used to want to be a Pebble Pincher and learn how to fight, but Nathan would put me down and tell me I would be lucky to be accepted as a Pebble Baker.

"I'm sorry, Jensen."

"For what?"

"You know," I said, looking down and chewing on the inside of my cheek. He probably had no idea why I ever stopped talking to him, why I threw away our friendship. He must have thought I was a bitch. "I'm sorry I haven't seen you or…"

"Or talked to me," Jensen finished my sentence. "Or acknowledged me."

He laughed genuinely, and I hit his shoulder playfully. I felt a little at ease that he didn't seem too upset.

"I wish I hadn't…" How could I apologize without telling him about Nathan?

"You wish you hadn't blown me off to have your secret relationship with Nathan?"

My mouth almost dropped with the speed that I whipped my head around to stare at Jensen. His eyes were not as cheerful as his laugh had sounded a moment ago. The deep, peaceful green from earlier seemed darker, too. I felt my mouth open and close, but nothing came out.'

"How did—"

"Stop fooling yourself, kid." Jensen was holding one wrist with the other, propped up on his knees, looking at the darkening hills before us.

"Don't call me that."

"You're only hiding this relationship from Natalie," Jensen said and looked back at me, but I couldn't read his expression. "And yourself."

"What do you mean by that?"

Jensen shook his head. "It doesn't matter, Terhese," he said with a ruddy flush in his cheeks. "If you're happy, that's all that matters."

I wasn't sure if I was going to cry or simply explode, but I settled on looking back and forth between Jensen's eyes. They looked calm again. Strong, stable, and reassuring.

"You really don't like him, do you?"

"It doesn't matter," Jensen repeated. I tried not to watch as he lifted the stone bottle to his lips, spilling water down his chin and chest. "I just want you to be careful. I don't trust him."

With that, Jensen stood and waved goodbye. I stayed where I was, feeling a bit dejected. The First Pebble was surprisingly cool on my back. Though I felt a calming tug, like something willing me to relax, I couldn't ignore what Jensen had said.

◆

I woke with a start. My bed was cold and hard.

"You've got to be kidding me!" I stood up, looking to the left and right to make sure I wasn't dreaming. The walls of my room would have morphed into being if I had been. Alas, I had fallen asleep at the top of Center Hill. "Stupid Peace Pebble."

The sun was setting and, at this time of year, it would be well behind the hills by the time I got home. I thought of what excuse I could give Aunt Chloe. She was more nervous than I was about the dark, probably because she remembered the dangers that used to live in the dark when the Ràej reigned. Whether there were giants or the common Hilltown gopher, I knew Aunt Chloe would be worried sick if I was out past dark, so I picked up my pace.

Going up to the First Pebble, I had taken an animal trail that had zigzagged across the hill. I chose the faster route this time. Moving between a jog and a fast walk, I couldn't help but think of the creatures Aunt Chloe had told me about over the years.

The tree in front of me looked like it could have been a small ogre. It was gnarled and stunted, not much taller than me. To kill my burning curiosity, I touched what would have been its nose, protruding out like a beak.

Something grabbed my arm. I turned and threw my fist out in front of me, closing my eyes in case it was a Ràej monster from Aunt Chloe's stories.

"Woah woah, woah." That deep, pleasant voice I had heard not long ago was coming from my presumed monster. "It's just me."

I relaxed and opened my eyes. The moon was yet to rise and the thick trees hid the last rays of light, but I knew it was Jensen. His hands were holding my arms, just below the shoulders. I was holding his forearms. I'd never realized how muscular they were.

"You trying to give me a heart attack?" I released him and continued my trek down the hill, though at a much slower pace.

"Your Aunt Chloe has been looking for you. I figured you were still on Center Hill somewhere. You fall asleep at the Pebble?"

"No," I said.

"That's a yes." Jensen's stride was much longer than mine, and he easily caught up to me. I could barely see the ground beneath my feet, let alone his features, but I imagined he was smirking and smiled. We continued talking about nothing important as we descended the hill and walked into town. He talked to me over his shoulder, and I responded as I stared at the ground, trying not to trip on any dislodged rocks.

When we reached the outskirts of town, Jensen stopped walking and turned to look at me. He scratched the back of his head and looked around, as if making sure no one was watching us.

"Okay, I think you can make your way home from here." He motioned with his head. "I live on the opposite side of town anyways."

I nodded and returned his awkward wave. It was weird he would leave me at the edge of town in the dark. He wasn't the kind of man who would leave any girl unattended. After our brief talk at the First Pebble, Jensen had no reason to pretend he didn't know about my relationship with Nathan. He must have been letting me keep up the charade, and stay clear of prying questions, by walking home alone.

"Terhese Marie!" Aunt Chloe came running out of the little white house, leaving the porch door swinging in the dying wind. "Where have you been?"

I let Aunt Chloe usher me inside. She wrapped a blanket around me and sat me down at the kitchen table. The worry on her face started to make me worry.

"I'm fine," I told her. "I went up to Center Hill and decided to watch the sun set. I'm sorry I worried you."

"Why were you up there? You never go up there." Aunt Chloe shook her head and breathed out deeply. "Well, no more staying out at night. Or going in the woods. Or going anywhere. Just," Aunt Chloe paced back and forth with a dishrag in her hand, "stay home."

"Aunt Chloe, what's going on? Are *you* okay?"

"Of course I'm okay." She tossed the dishrag at me and sat across from me at the little table. "An Academy student was found dead at the lake."

"What?" My stomach flipped. Names and faces of Academy students flashed through my mind. "Who? What happened?"

"Lucy Linden." Aunt Chloe shook her head. "Her mother is inconsolable. She is blaming the Academy for not letting Lucy take a defense class. She wanted to be a Pebble Maker, like you do. I'm just so glad you're safe."

Aunt Chloe walked around the table and gave me a big hug, squeezing me until I pushed her off.

"What happened?" I repeated, imagining different scenarios and picturing made-up Ràej beasts with piercing eyes, sharp talons, and spiked tails.

"They are keeping the details about this incident quiet." Aunt Chloe pulled items from the pantry: measuring utensils, bowls, spices, herbs, a wooden spoon, a cooking dish and a jar of homemade tomato sauce. It was her way of saying the conversation was over.

I trudged up the stairs to my room and lay on my bed, resigned to staring at my ceiling. We had painted the split-tree boards above a shade of pink when I was younger. The paint was blistering, but I refused to repaint it. Staring up at the bubbles had become a sort of pastime for me when Jensen had moved across town. It now seemed forever since the last time I had noticed it.

A rock hit my window and snapped me out of my reverie of painting with my aunt. I knew who it was and wasn't sure if tonight was worth the risk, but I swung open my window.

"Natalie." I tried to shout in a whisper. "It's not a good night. Didn't you hear about Lucy?"

"Of course I did!" Natalie shouted.

I winced at the volume of her voice. "Shush." I put my finger up to my mouth. "Aunt Chloe is in the kitchen making dinner. You should go. We can talk tomorrow."

"But it's about Lucy!" Natalie shouted again.

I rolled my eyes and stared down at her with exasperation. It would be a miracle if my aunt hadn't heard that one.

"Oh, good evening, Miss Chloe. I have a sweet bread for you. Mother made it."

"Dear Omneth, Natalie!" Aunt Chloe said. "You get in here right this instant. Didn't your mother tell you to stay inside? Terhese!"

I had started walking down the stairs when I heard Natalie talking to Aunt Chloe and was already in the kitchen when she called my name. She ushered Natalie to sit down at the table and grabbed another plate and placement setting. As was customary with Aunt Chloe and any company, she put a kettle on for tea, but for Natalie,

I knew she would make hot chocolate.

"You will have to tell your mother thank you for the sweet bread," Aunt Chloe said with a warm smile on her face. She bustled around to get cups and saucers.

"I heard that—"

"Are we talking about poor Lucy?" Aunt Chloe was holding a silver spoon in front of me as she craned her back to look at Natalie. "We shouldn't be talking about that incident. The Officials are trying to keep it quiet."

"Aunt Chloe, she's going to tell me down here or upstairs in my room," I said, hoping I wouldn't have to wait until we stole away upstairs after dinner.

She didn't respond but gave a slight nod and continued setting the table.

"Okay, what did you hear?"

"I heard it from the peephole." Natalie leaned on the table with her elbows and started her story.

The peephole was from a misadventure we'd had last summer when I tried to pinch a Pebble in Natalie's bedroom. Instead of imploding and releasing whatever spell or charm inside, it had turned hot to my touch. I dropped the Pebble, and it scorched the wooden floorboard. Natalie dropped to her knees to pick it up, but it burned her fingers. We tried grabbing the Pebble with a piece of clothing and then a towel, but the Pebble was burning anything it touched, like the hot blue flame of a fire would. Before we could pour water on the Pebble, it had burned a perfect circle through the floorboards. We ran downstairs and found a steaming pile of gelatinous muck. Fortunately, it missed the living room rug. We found a square shovel from the garden shed to scoop it up before it could do more damage.

The peephole was in the center of her room. If her parents saw it, they would question us about where we got the Pebble. We had stolen that specific Pebble from her father, who was a Pebble Pincher for the Officials. It took us a few hours, but we managed to bribe a carpenter apprentice to cut a circle of wood for a free month of tutoring service, trade half a dozen eggs for paint from the pottery, and grab an old rug from Jensen, who was living at the Academy. We had painted the circle of wood and shoved in the hole just as Natalie's mother entered the front door.

"No one knows I was listening so, as always, *don't say a word.*" Natalie eyed Aunt Chloe.

"Oh, of course!" Aunt Chloe sat down in the chair across from Natalie. She poured hot water from the steaming kettle and put a ceramic pot with a spoon in front of Natalie.

"The Officials came to our house, just after Lucy was found." Natalie was talking quickly and quietly. I leaned in. "They were questioning Father about where he was today and what he had done. They questioned Mother and Nathan, too."

"Did you have to talk to them?" I asked. It was not the best of circumstances, but I would never turn down a chance to talk to an Official, and I found myself inappropriately jealous.

"Not really." Natalie scooped out some brown powder from the little pot and dumped it slowly into her cup of still-steaming water. "I think it was because I was the only one with an alibi."

"Where was Nathan? Were you two not at home?" I followed my initial question quickly with another so I wouldn't sound too concerned about Nathan. I knew Natalie hadn't been there while I was there. His alibi should have been home.

"No." Natalie hesitated and took two more scoops of the chocolate, again dumping them slowly into her cup and stirring even slower. "I didn't tell you because I didn't want you to get mad at me. I was accepted into a Junior Internship for Healing. I'll be studying under the Officials Healer two nights a week. This afternoon was orientation."

"Congratulations, Natalie." Aunt Chloe stood up to give her a hug. "That is a great accomplishment."

"That is amazing!" I said with genuine excitement and joined in on the hug. "Why would I be mad at you?

I'm so happy for you!"

"Well, after not getting the ball invitation." Natalie shrugged and finally drank her hot chocolate. "Oh, this is divine."

Aunt Chloe smiled triumphantly and checked on the dinner in the oven before sitting back down.

"Okay, what happened next?" I asked eagerly, trying to forget about the missing ball invitation, wanting to hear about Nathan's alibi.

"It sounded like the Officials came to my house because they found remnants of a Pebble with my family's magicprint on it!" Natalie said. Aunt Chloe stifled a gasp.

"A magicprint?" I remembered our primary teachers mentioning them, but they had always said we would learn more about them at the Academy. "I thought we each had our own?"

"Pebble Pinchers and Pebble Makers use magic differently." Aunt Chloe nodded up and down as though urging me to agree."

"Yes." I nodded and winced. "Kind of."

"The Pebble Pincher needs to use a little magic to compress the Pebble correctly," Aunt Chloe explained, putting her thumb to her fingers. "I have no magic. I can only pinch the Pebbles provided to me by the Officials, the Household Pebbles and others of that level. People who have magical ability are able to pinch more powerful

Pebbles.

"The Pebble Maker uses the lesser magic of conjuration to place spells and charms, even hexes, inside the Pebbles." Aunt Chloe glanced at the oven. I could smell the roasting meat, onions, and garlic, but it wasn't done yet.

"Magic is a part of us." Aunt Chloe smiled and spread her arms out wide. "We exude it, like a scent.

"You can trace the magic of a Pebble to the Pebble Maker only if you find sediment from within the shell. Though there are fewer Pebble Makers than Pinchers, it is very rare to find sediment and even more rare to find enough to make a magicprint from."

Aunt Chloe grabbed an oven mitt and pulled out the loaf of meat she had been cooking. The jar of tomato sauce made a satisfying pop when she twisted it open. She generously poured the sauce over the loaf, and I was mesmerized by the transformation from dull brown to rich red. Aunt Chloe put the baking dish back in the oven and sat down again.

"Where was I?" She closed her eyes.

"Terhese," Natalie interjected. "I'm surprised you don't know more about this. Your nose is always in a book about Pebbles."

"Mostly I read about the marx and what they mean." I shrugged. "I've never been patient enough to read about how they are made."

"I had hoped reading about how to use them would have stopped you from making fires in the backyard," Aunt Chloe chided good-naturedly, and Natalie laughed.

"Yeah, yeah." I brushed off their teasing. "So, how is a magicprint found?"

"If you have magic," Aunt Chloe pointed to Natalie, "then it is like an aura around you. It is very faint until you use your magic. For most people, they will never need to worry about their magicprint. But it is a way for the Officials to track down those that misuse magic." Aunt Chloe paused and swallowed. I wondered if she was thinking about Lucy Linden.

"When the Pebble Pincher uses magic to pinch, they are leaving their magicprint in an amount that could be found. Expert Pebble Pinchers know how to pinch well enough that the shell of the Pebble should be all but destroyed."

"Which means a magicprint won't be found?" I asked.

"Correct," Aunt Chloe said. "An amateur, or someone with a lower ability, may not be able to pinch well enough and fragments can be found."

"Whose magicprint was found?" I turned to Natalie once the information had sunk in. "Why don't you seem more concerned?"

"It was part of my family magicprint."

"And that is?"

"Think of it as looking like your parent or grandparent." Aunt Chloe made a whoosh sound and stopped. I didn't have any of those.

"My magicprint will resemble both of my parent's magicprints, as does Nathan's," Natalie explained. "Everyone has a slightly different one. If we pass our exams in the first term, then our magicprints will be registered and we can continue into our next term at the Academy."

"Do you have one Aunt Chloe?"

"I do not." She emphasized the last word and stood up. "Slates do not have magicprints." She opened the oven and grabbed the baking dish in her mittened hands. "Can you grab the trivet from the cabinet, please."

"Thank you for dinner, Miss Chloe," Natalie said as the dish was placed on the simple piece of pottery I had set down. Aunt Chloe scooped out a serving for Natalie, then one for me and herself. "I heard the Officials ask my parents why they weren't at my orientation. They were supposed to be. But I think the Officials were really there for my brother."

I choked on my first bite, tried to pass it off like I didn't, and choked harder.

"Here, Terhese, drink this." Aunt Chloe gave me a

glass of water.

I nodded, gasping with my eyes watering. My throat was finally clear, but I continued to drink the water. I had been with Nathan, but I hadn't stayed long and had left early in the afternoon. Was he really a suspect in Lucy's murder?

"Why do you think that, Nat?" I managed to say without coughing.

Natalie washed down her food with a long drink of hot chocolate. I couldn't tell how Natalie was feeling or what Aunt Chloe was thinking. She had never liked "that Ramos boy." My heart was hammering.

"I think they questioned Father and Mother because they were supposed to, but they questioned Nathan for a long time. It was like they were trying to trick him to say the wrong thing." Natalie pursed her lips. "Nathan said he was home alone all afternoon and evening. They asked if he had anyone to back up his story, and he said I had been home all evening with him. That is when things got worse. They told him that I wasn't home, that I was at the Official Building for my internship orientation.

"Nathan said he didn't pay attention to my comings and goings and he had been in his room studying. When the Officials said they would need him to go in for a magicprint test, he said if they were looking for someone who had been outside, they should go find Jensen

Dontane."

"Jensen?" I stopped eating this time so I wouldn't choke. How could Nathan do that?

"Nathan said he took a smoke break in the tower, and when he looked out the window, he saw Jensen walking away from the woods at the bottom of Center Hill. That's not far from the trail that goes to the lake where Lucy was found."

I shook my head, trying to make sense of all this. It couldn't be Jensen.

"Then how did your family magicprint get there?" I asked. The Officials wouldn't accuse someone of being a suspect if there was no evidence.

"That's the part I cannot understand." Natalie sighed. "I have some cousins that live further out in Hill Country and scattered around Omneth. We should all have some similarities in our magicprint, but none of them would know Lucy."

"How is this even related to Lucy?" I cut a bite-sized portion with the side of my fork, more out of angst than a desire to eat it.

"Oh, right!" Natalie leaned on her elbows again. "They said it looked like a Pebble Pinching gone wrong. Her throat was crushed, like she was strangled, but there were no marks on her throat. They said it was done by magic. Parts of the shell *and* sediment were found on her body. The sediment was found to be from a Pebble to stop speech."

"A Tongue Hold Pebble," Aunt Chloe said. "Those were used back in the wars. Pebble Pinchers and the Slates used them to prevent the Ràej from casting magic. Most Ràej needed to speak to use their power, and those Pebbles stopped their voices."

"Instead of stopping her voice," I spoke slowly, "the Pebble was pinched wrong, and it crushed her windpipe, suffocating and killing her."

Natalie nodded. I was glad I hadn't attempted that last bite. The three of us sat in silence for a moment. I couldn't stop thinking about how likely a suspect Nathan was. If I had been right about the Ignorance Pebble and then he had a Tongue Hold Pebble, it sounded like he was trying to stop Lucy from telling something he didn't want told.

"That was delicious, Miss Chloe." Natalie stood up and collected everyone's plates; mine was mostly bits of meat that had been flattened and smeared around while I had been listening. "I'm going to return home now. I just had to tell you what I heard. I know you and Jensen don't talk as much as you used to, but you should go check on him tomorrow."

I nodded and walked Natalie out. After Aunt Chloe had told her we could walk with her to make sure she got home safe, several times, she settled with telling her to be safe and have a good night. I washed the dishes, preoccupied with my thoughts of Nathan and Jensen. If the magicprint hadn't been found, it could have been either one of them. I had slept for a decent amount of time, so there was no telling what Jensen had been doing.

But the magicprint had been found.

It was a couple weeks before until the ball, and I wasn't able to talk to anyone. Natalie wasn't allowed to visit while her family was under investigation. Both Nathan and Jensen were under house arrest with constant supervision. I still couldn't understand how Jensen could be a suspect. The worst part was that everything was being kept a secret. Most of Hilltown went about their normal business. They either pretended not to know anything or they really didn't.

I was going stir-crazy. The ball was in two weeks, and I needed Natalie. I still hadn't received my acceptance letter, but I hadn't received a rejection either, so I refused to be turned out before I could even try. Most classes at the Academy were only taught at the Academy. How would I know if I had the lesser magic of healing if I didn't have a family member who had the mystical waters to use?

It was a silly paradox. The higher magics hadn't needed tools or totems to use their power, but the lesser magics did. It was a never-ending conversation between Aunt Chloe and me. Though the higher magics were gone, and we had been made equal through monthly allotments of magic for all, the socioeconomic status still had many levels. Even if someone could pinch or heal or see, it cost money to get the items needed to use those magics. All I wanted was a chance. If I couldn't pinch, then there must be something I could do.

"Aunt Chloe, how do you know so much about everything?" I asked after an hour-long conversation about what the Junior Intern Healers learn.

"I was much like you when I was younger." Her smile reached her eyes before they glazed over with memories of her past. "If I couldn't do something, I would just try harder. And I tried many things. Before the Academy was, well, the Academy, it was the summer castle for the Ràej family. That is where I was training to become a seer."

"I thought..." I tried to think of how to phrase my question without offending her.

"You thought I was a slate?" Aunt Chloe raised a thin, dark eyebrow. "You know your dear Aunt Slate has less magic than a child's Play Pebble." Aunt Chloe laughed and sipped her tea.

"And?" I urged. "What happened with becoming a seer?"

"I wanted so bad to be a seer." Aunt Chloe looked up as though she were watching her dream come true. "I had no ability for that though. I went from trying to see to working in the gardens, which is when I found I had a green thumb. I met my husband, your uncle, at the castle, too. He'd been drafted into the Ràej army and was in training. That's where the First Battle was."

"I remember learning about that in primary." I wanted to ask more questions, but Aunt Chloe already wore the vacant look she had when thinking of her long-lost husband. They had been married shortly before being separated by the war, and she never saw him again.

Throughout the days following up to the ball, I had many long talks with Aunt Chloe about anything that came to mind. This was the most time I had spent with her in years, the longest I had ever spent away from Natalie and, more recently, Nathan. It was a new pastime for us. We were not picking, washing, mashing, straining, preserving, or doing anything else with vegetables, and it was great. It almost took my mind off the missing invitation.

We were just sitting down for a cup of afternoon tea, a few days before the ball, when a knock on the door interrupted us. Aunt Chloe got the door, exchanging pleasantries with whoever was standing on the porch, and led them back to the kitchen. I almost dropped the half-eaten scone out of my mouth when I saw the two Officials enter behind Aunt Chloe.

"She's right in here," Aunt Chloe said. "Would you gentlemen like a cup of tea? The kettle is still hot."

"That would be great. Thank you, Miss Chloe," the Official wearing glasses said. He looked kind enough. "Good afternoon, Miss Terhese."

"Good afternoon," I murmured, shaking his hand with my clammy one, then cleared my throat and said it louder.

The other Official was staring at me with unwavering eyes, making me look everywhere else when I shook his hand. His neck was as thick as a tree trunk, and his arms were bulging through his uniform. I wasn't sure if it was truly a uniform, but they were both wearing dark, long-sleeved shirts that went high up their necks, dark pants, and utility belts I presumed were full of Pebbles.

"Do you know why we are here today, Miss Terhese?" Muscles asked. His voice was softer than I'd expected. It didn't put me at ease, but it made me feel a little calmer.

"No, I do not, sir," I said, trying to sit up straight in front of the Officials.

"Let me start by saying this is all confidential," Spectacles said. "We have two young men in custody as suspects for the murder of Lucy Linden."

Both Officials stared at me expectantly.

"Uh, yes." I nodded slowly and looked back and forth at them, trying to get a sign of what I should be doing. "I heard about Lucy."

"And we have some conflicting stories about your whereabouts on the day of her murder."

"My whereabouts?" I wished I could be shocked into silence. "Why mine?"

"Let's start slowly, here," Muscles said. "What did you do on the day of Lucy's murder? Specifically, between midday and dusk?"

"Is this confidential?" I asked.

"To an extent."

"Well." I tried to think quickly. As far as Aunt Chloe knew, I was with Natalie for the first part of the day, and then I went hiking by myself. If there were different stories already circulating, I could get myself into trouble by adding another one. My alibi might be the only thing saving Nathan. Or Jensen. I was never good at lying though, and I had been thinking for too long, so I told the truth. "I spent the morning with Natalie. Natalie Ramos. I went to see Nathan Ramos in the afternoon."

Aunt Chloe made a sound, and I couldn't help but wonder if she was disappointed in me for keeping that secret from her.

"What is your relationship with Nathan Ramos?"

Spectacles asked.

"We have been in a romantic relationship for about six months. We didn't tell anyone."

"You were in a romantic relationship with this man, but you didn't tell anyone?" Muscles asked.

"Yes, sir."

"Why would you not say anything about this relationship? Tell your friends or family?"

"I'm best friends with his sister, and I knew she wouldn't like it. I was waiting for the right time. Still waiting." It wasn't entirely true, but I hoped they wouldn't probe further.

"Okay," Muscles said. "Go on. How long were you at Nathan's house?"

"I wasn't there very long." I shifted my weight in my chair, getting more uncomfortable by the minute. "We had an argument and I left. I went to Center Hill."

"What kind of an argument?" Spectacles asked. "Was he violent? Was it about adultery?"

"What? No." These questions were getting ridiculous. "He wasn't violent. Nothing about adultery. He just likes to belittle my apparent lack of magic. I am passionate and determined that I will get to the Academy so I can work with the Officials!"

I realized my passion was overflowing and filling the room. Spectacles was stoic, but Aunt Chloe and Muscles were looking at me like I had just sprouted extra limbs. I hadn't realized how pent up these emotions had been the past few weeks. Seeing how awkward Muscles looked made me want to laugh.

"Sorry, about that." I dropped my head, trying to hide my mirth and embarrassment. "I went for a walk and ended up at the First Pebble. I know there isn't any higher magic anymore, but Nathan makes it seem like I'm below even a lesser magic. The First Pebble makes me feel better. I like to go there to relax."

That had been the first time I had gone to the First Pebble in years. I couldn't tell the Officials why I had really gone. I didn't know who killed Lucy, but I wasn't about to say I thought Nathan had an Ignorance Pebble, which was hidden upstairs in a dresser drawer.

The Officials were nodding. Spectacles was smiling like he was watching his child walk for the first time, and Muscles was scribbling on a piece of parchment.

"That would bring us to mid-afternoon?"

"I believe so." I tried to focus on my thoughts so I wouldn't reveal too much. "The sun had a couple hands left before setting. Not long after I reached the top, Jensen came up from the South Trail."

"You saw Jensen Dontane?" Muscles's head popped up. He looked intrigued.

"Yes." I kicked myself for letting my mouth run

again. Why was I blabbing so much?

"How long was Mr. Dontane with you?" Spectacles asked.

"Not long," I said bluntly. I thought back to the last day I'd seen him. It was easy for me to bring his face to mind: his lips and eyes and chin. I couldn't recall Nathan as well. "When he left, I leaned against the Pebble and fell asleep. It was dusk when I woke. I started down the South Trail and ran into Jensen."

"Jensen Dontane?" Muscles asked, perking up again.

"Yes, he said that my aunt had been searching for me so he came to fetch me." I watched Aunt Chloe nod and put her hand over her heart.

"Why didn't Jensen tell anyone that he knew where you were?" Spectacles asked.

"You would have to ask him." I shrugged, forcing myself not to go into details. Spectacles didn't look pleased with my lack of answers for that question.

"Why didn't you, Miss Chloe, reach out to the Ramos residence about Terhese's whereabouts?

"Oh, I did." Aunt Chloe nodded, wiping her hands with a dish towel as though she had just whipped up a pie. "That was the first place I went. No one was home."

"What time of day was that?"

"I'm not sure." Aunt Chloe wiped her hands again. "It was before dusk. Mid-afternoon, perhaps. It was before I had heard about Lucy. When I heard about the incident is when I started looking for Terhese again."

"Really," Muscles stated smugly. I could have sworn on Omneth that these two Officials had a wager on who killed Lucy.

"Let me see if I have this right, Miss Terhese." Muscles looked over his notes before speaking. "You left Nathan Ramos early afternoon and did not see him again that night. Miss Chloe, you went to the Ramos house at mid-afternoon and no one was there. No one knows where Nathan Ramos was during that time. Unless, Miss Terhese, you have more information you would like to share?"

I shook my head. This was becoming a strange nightmare. As little as I had wanted to say, and as much as I had said, everything seemed to point at my boyfriend being the more likely suspect. They hadn't even mentioned the magicprint.

"Last part, Terhese," Spectacles said, sounding resigned. "What happened after you saw Jensen for the second time at Center Hill?"

"He told me my aunt was looking for me," I repeated. My brain was stuck on Nathan and how Jensen had warned me about him. "When we got to the bottom of the trail, he said that I could walk the rest of the way home."

I almost told them the details about how Jensen knew about my secret relationship and about how he and Nathan used to be friends but no longer talked. My mouth wanted to flap open and explain how Jensen had tried to help me and my relationship by having me walk alone. Through sheer effort, I didn't say anything further.

"It all checks out." Spectacles closed his pad. "Terhese's statement makes everything fit together."

"What do you mean?" Aunt Chloe asked before I could.

"Both suspects are saying they didn't see Terhese all day." Muscles leaned back in his chair. "We have a couple witnesses saying they saw Terhese leave the Ramos house, but Natalie hadn't seen her since the morning. Ramos accused Dontane by saying he saw him walking through town from the direction of the woods, but he said it was near the North Trail, which would be closest to the lake where Lucy was found.

"We have witnesses saying they saw both Dontane and Terhese, here, at the South Trail, which Terhese confirmed," Muscles continued. "There are ways to forge a magicprint, easier for an Investigator to do, so we may still need your statement in court."

"What?" My heart stopped for a moment thinking of how angry Nathan would be if I betrayed him like that, even though it would be the truth. I could barely hear

Aunt Chloe talking to the Officials in the background.

"I thought you said this was confidential? If Nathan *did* kill Lucy, won't that put my niece in danger? He's a killer!"

"Don't worry, Miss Chloe," Spectacles said. "If Mr. Ramos is guilty, he will be guilty of misuse of magic, magic without a license, and accidental homicide. This was not done with malicious intent, but he would have a sentence and Miss Terhese would be protected. These are still hypotheticals."

I nodded. My head felt like it was full of a thick, heavy pudding.

"We will contact you shortly," Muscles said.

Aunt Chloe led both Officials out the door and returned to the table to serve the afternoon tea.

We drank in silence. I wasn't sure if I should broach the subject of my secret relationship or let it lie. If I believed Jensen, then Aunt Chloe already knew. As I battled with myself on what to say, she grabbed my hand and squeezed it, sending comfort through her warm touch.

If all went right, I would be moving to the Academy in a couple of weeks. I felt the heavy weight of not having these daily teas for much longer.

The day before the ball, I was staring at the Pebble in

my hand for the dozenth time that day. I wasn't sure what it was. Not long ago, I would have staked my life that it was an Ignorance Pebble. After the past few weeks, I concluded that I didn't know as much as I thought I did about Pebbles. Unfortunately, I wasn't able to find the Bliss Pebble or the Ignorance Pebble in any of the books I had at home, not even a note or subscript. I was tempted to pinch it, but I couldn't be absolutely sure that the Pebble wouldn't backfire and wipe my memory. A rock at the window stopped my wild thoughts.

"Natalie!" Though it was far from necessary to throw the rock in the middle of the day, it was tradition and a very welcome announcement that she was there. After shouting her name with uncontrolled glee, I ran down the stairs to let her in. "I can't believe you are here! I've missed you."

We exchanged a hug, one I felt Natalie needed more than I did. If I was feeling emotional turmoil and confusion about my boyfriend being a murder suspect, I couldn't imagine how she was coping with her brother being a murder suspect.

"I've missed you too," she said and started up the stairs instead of going to the kitchen. She carried a large, canvas bag with her. "I wish I could tell you everything that has happened in the last few weeks, but I really can't this time."

"That's okay. I understand." I had so much I wanted to tell her but couldn't risk it. "How are you here? I thought your parents wouldn't let you out until the case was solved?"

"The Officials said that the ball is too important, so Nathan and I are allowed to go!" Natalie was clearly looking forward to the ball more than I was, but this cheered me up too.

"That is great news." I beamed. "I still haven't received my acceptance letter. Maybe it's best if I don't go."

"You're going!" Natalie plunged her hands into the bag and pulled out a dark purple bundle. After standing up and letting her bundle unroll, she revealed the most beautiful dress. "And you are going in this."

I couldn't help but touch the dress and run my fingers down to the bottom where I felt three layers of tulle under the silk of the dress. It was long-sleeved with a simple, scoop neckline and would hang slightly off each shoulder. The bottom portion of the dress was adorned with tiny silver beads sewn in no particular pattern. Natalie turned the dress around to show the plunging back.

"Okay," I said, in awe of the dress. "I'll go. This dress is amazing! I knew you said you would make me something, but I thought it was going to be much simpler or plainer. This ... this is gorgeous, Natalie. Thank you."

"This is the biggest night of our young lives!" Natalie said after I released her from another hug. "I needed to make sure we are dressed the best so we can enjoy the night to our fullest."

We spent the next few hours practicing for the ball. Natalie gave me tips and pointers on how to wrap my hair, curl my eyelashes, paint my lips, and bring out the colors of my eyes with different colors on my lids. Natalie had colors on her cheeks, lips, and eyes, and she had curled her lashes and dyed and curled her hair. By the end, I had taken the makeup off several times, reapplied different colors or different amounts, only to take it off again. Nothing came off as easily as it went on, and it easily smeared on other parts of my body.

"This was a learning experience." I huffed as I scrubbed my cheek raw.

Chapter 3

The evening of the ball, Natalie came over and we did it all again. She brought a mixture of ash and elderberry juice to make our eyelashes look darker and longer. We rubbed our lips with colored beeswax. Natalie's mother had sent several colors for us to experiment with.

"I'm only going to do my eyelashes. This is too hard." I poked myself in the eye with an applicator.

"Here." Natalie knelt in front of me. "Let me do it for you. Mother has been teaching me how to do this for years."

It took Natalie just a few minutes to apply my makeup in a satisfactory way that looked natural.

"Great job, Nat." I smiled at my reflection in the wall mirror. I watched Natalie purse her bright red lips and make other faces at the mirror.

"I think you look great." Natalie grabbed our dresses.

"I don't think we have time to do your hair again. The curls fell out, but your hair is beautiful as it is."

Once we were dressed, me in purple and Natalie in gold, we went downstairs to where Aunt Chloe was sitting in the kitchen with a cup of tea. She stood up to hug each of us, tears in her eyes. It didn't seem long ago that we were both wearing buckle shoes with pigtails and playing hopscotch in matching jumpers. Now we were fully grown women wearing fashionably cut dresses and makeup.

"I am so proud of you." Aunt Chloe dabbed at her eyes. "Both of you. Now, how are you getting to the ball?"

"Nathan should be here any moment with a carriage," Natalie said, looking out the window.

I saw Aunt Chloe stiffen and hoped my reaction wasn't as noticeable. In my mind, Nathan was the most likely person to have murdered Lucy, and it scared me. I couldn't figure out what Natalie thought about it all.

"Oh, he's pulling up now!"

"You two be safe."

"We will." I grabbed Natalie's arm and ran out the kitchen door. As confusing as my feelings were towards Nathan, he was still my boyfriend, and I felt the happy butterflies in my stomach when I glimpsed him out the window. I made sure to walk slowly down the porch stairs so I wouldn't trip in my heels and make a fool of myself. When I knew he was watching, I strutted to the carriage.

Nathan stood by the door of the one-horse carriage, smiling at me as I walked over. Smiling like he'd forgotten we had fought the last time we saw each other. Smiling like he wasn't the prime suspect of murdering a classmate.

He leaned over and kissed my cheek and helped me into the carriage. I was afraid Natalie had seen that, but he kissed her check as well. She held her dress up with one hand and took his offered hand as easily as if she had done it a million times. The little pitter-patter he'd given my heart flatlined. The kiss seemed to be just a formality. Something you learned when you grew up with Officials as parents, who had the money that required etiquette be learned.

The carriage ride didn't take as long as I thought it would. Aunt Chloe had been to the Official Building a couple of times. She said it was a half day's walk but not worth taking the carriage she used for market. We didn't have a passenger carriage like the Ramoses did. I felt like royalty, sitting in the comfort of the furnished carriage while Nathan drove.

There was little silence in the carriage as we rode to the ball. Natalie was nervous about what the other girls would be wearing, especially the upper years. I was thinking of Nathan and how I should act around him. Was I supposed to dance with other men? Or be a wallflower? Did the other students know about Lucy? Did they think he was guilty? It could have just been an accident, like the Officials said.

"Terhese?" Natalie whispered. "Are you okay?"

I nodded, biting the inside of my cheek, wishing I could tell her about my dilemma.

"We're here. I can't feel my hands. I can't feel my feet. I'm going to drop my drink and step on my dancing partner's feet!"

"You will be fine." I squeezed Natalie's hand. "We are here to have fun and we will! Don't worry about anyone else."

I was having trouble breathing. What if they wouldn't let me in? I'd never received the invitation. Would they ask for an invitation? What would I do if they turned me away? Would Nathan bring me home or would he stay at the ball?

Nathan opened the carriage door. He helped Natalie step down from the carriage and took my hand after helping me down. He pulled me close and stole a kiss in the cover of the carriage. I blushed with the semi-public attention, nervously looking around to see if anyone had seen us. He squeezed my hand and nodded at me to go catch up with Natalie.

"You girls have fun." Nathan waved.

"Are you not coming in?" I flustered as I heard my accusatory tone. "It just looked like you were dressed for the occasion."

"I will." Nathan smiled and looked around. "I'm going to have a smoke and then come in. Save me a dance."

I smiled and felt warm all over. There was no way he was capable of doing what they said he did.

I caught up with Natalie, and we walked up the front stairs to the Official Building. The kiss from Nathan had given me confidence, but that was extinguished when I heard an Official call my name. All my hopes and dreams flashed before my eyes. How did they already know I was here without being accepted? I didn't know what to do, so I stood still.

"Terhese Neems." An Official shoved his hand in front of me. "I am Professor Milsby. I have heard so much about you, and I am very excited to work with you in the coming years."

Before I could form a response, Professor Milsby shook my hand furiously and then was off to greet another student.

"Did you hear that, Natalie?" I nudged her excitedly. "That professor said I would be at the Academy this year. I must have been accepted!"

"I knew it!" Natalie smiled, and we both laughed. She seemed as relieved as I felt. The night was already starting to be better than I had anticipated.

Now that one of my worries was no more, I took a moment to look around. We had just entered the ballroom. Unlike Natalie, I didn't come from a family that frequented the Official Building nor did I have an internship. Everything within eyesight was magnificent. The pillars of the room were white with intricate carvings. While Natalie talked to a group of first years she had met through her internship, I walked over to further inspect the pillars.

The carvings were detailed but not as beautiful as I had thought. They depicted the Ràej War, and they were grotesque. Scenes of butchery and battle, pillage, and rape. I walked around the room until I found the last column to the story. It contained scenes of the First Pebble. The column was the same size as the others, but it seemed to be the focal point. The First Pebble started at the bottom of the column, then grew as it progressed up the column until it was sitting at the top on a carved hill.

"Punch?"

I started at the voice and turned away from my study of the column. "Excuse me?" I turned around. I had walked the perimeter of the ballroom, and the First Pebble column was at the front with the refreshment table. It was Jensen.

"Would you like a glass of punch?" He was already

offering it to me, standing in his pressed navy suit.

I took the offered glass of blood red punch, realizing too late that I was looking him up and down with a goofy smile.

"Don't let your boyfriend see that smile."

Jensen was smiling himself. No doubt enjoying my embarrassment. I couldn't help but wish he looked at me like he did the other girls at the ball. They displayed all the colors Natalie's mom had sent us to use. I wasn't showcasing myself like the other girls did either; they made it a point to walk across the room to say hello to a friend, holding their dress with one hand and holding out the other arm, almost dramatically, to accentuate the curves of their bodies, wrapped in rich fabrics decorated with sequins, jewels, embroidery, lace, and buttons and string to fasten them up. Their hair was curled and teased and pinned and bowed.

"What if he sees you talking to me?" I countered, smiling out of sheer awkwardness. I couldn't copy these other girls if I tried. We'd curled my hair several times, but it wouldn't do anything more than wave over my shoulders. I had fallen in love with the dress when I was upstairs in my room, but even the fashionable cut and spatter of sparkle at the bottom didn't compare. I was the dirty blonde in purple silk.

"He'll keep up the charade you two have." Jensen

touched the tip of his glass to mine and raised it slightly in the air before taking a sip. "We've been friends since before I went to primary. Everyone knows that. If he wants to keep up appearances, then so should we."

I appraised Jensen and thought on this proposition as I took a drink of my punch. I almost spit it back into my cup but managed to gulp it down. My eyes watered, and I stifled a cough.

"This is not punch," I finally said, taking a smaller sip of the spiked beverage in my hand. "You should have warned me."

"I'm sorry," Jensen said sincerely. "I didn't even think of it. Do you want me to get you a glass of something else?"

"No, no." I took another sip. "It's fine."

The drink wasn't as strong as I had first thought, though it had shocked me on that first mouthful. A subtle burn went down my throat and settled warmly in my stomach. When I finished my first glass, Jensen took it to bring back to the refreshment table for a refill.

It wasn't long before a small group of girls surrounded Jensen as he stood in line for the punch bowl. I felt a pang of jealousy. I knew he wouldn't make anyone hide a relationship with him. It was becoming almost ridiculous how many times Nathan had told me to wait longer before we could go public. *Where was he?*

"Terhese, I'm sorry I left you for so long!" Natalie appeared at my side. She was flushed, too, and I guessed it had more to do with the punch than the makeup. "I was talking to some girls that are in my internship program and then someone asked me to dance. Did you see us?"

"No, sorry, I missed it," I apologized. I hadn't even noticed that dancing was happening. "That is so exciting! Who was it?"

Natalie surveyed the room, and her face lit up when she spotted the man she had danced with.

"He's right there." She pointed and whispered, though no one was near us to hear. "To the left of Nathan."

"Nathan?" I jerked my head to where Natalie was pointing. He was standing with a tall brown-haired man and a few girls, all of whom were wearing glamorous dresses with jewels on their bodies and pinned in their hair. One of them kept touching Nathan's chest. "Let's go say hi. I want a closer look."

My fists were clenched as I started to lead the way, but Natalie grabbed my arm. I thought she had lost her nerve, so I turned to give her encouragement. It was a man's hand on my arm. Jensen had caught up to me.

"Hey, sorry for the wait." Jensen pushed a glass into my hand and stood comfortably between me and Natalie. "That line was long. Good evening, Natalie. I heard you got a junior internship. Congratulations!"

Jensen gave Natalie a friendly hug, and she talked animatedly about her orientation day. Though he was giving her a nod and a word here and there, he was staring at me. I tried to be discreet, but I was shooting daggers at Nathan with my eyes. It didn't take long for Jensen to see what I kept looking at.

"That is great, Natalie," Jensen praised her again. "Terhese, I know you haven't been to the Official Building before, so would you like a quick tour?"

Natalie pushed me into Jensen. She had always thought there was something between the two of us, though she never had an inkling about me and her brother. Before we walked a foot away, a man was already approaching Natalie, who was posing for him with hands on her hips and a smile plastered from ear to ear.

I couldn't provide an excuse in front of Natalie, so Jensen took my arm and steered me through the ballroom, making sure we would pass Nathan. I tried to lead us a different way, but Jensen put his arm around my waist and bent his head to my ear.

"Don't you want to know what he'll do?" Jensen whispered. "You shouldn't be with him if he treats you like this."

"He won't do anything," I whispered back, noticing Nathan had seen us and was trying to catch my eye. "He won't do anything here. He'll just yell at me later."

"Don't you see how wrong that is?" Jensen's voice turned to an angry whisper. "You won't have to worry about that this time."

"What do you mean?" I looked up at Jensen. His eyes were stuck on Nathan. "Jensen?"

"Jensen! Mate, come over here," Nathan called when we were about to pass him and exit into the corridor. "Glad we could both make it tonight."

Jensen gripped Nathan's hand, making him flinch slightly. They smiled at each other. Nathan's smile was full of bitter contempt, and his eyes were cold. The group of people stood awkwardly for a moment, and Jensen placed his arm around my waist again. Nathan's eyes dropped to where Jensen's hand was holding me and then passed over me.

"Everyone, this is Terhese," Jensen introduced me. "Terhese, this is everyone. Danielle, Evan, Tilly, and you know Nathan."

Everyone exchanged pleasantries. I eyed Tilly for a quick moment; she was the girl who had been putting her hands all over Nathan. The conversation was at a standstill as we stood there. I couldn't figure out where the tension was stemming from. Perhaps their rivalry was a well-known thing. Or Nathan's friends believed he was innocent and believed his accusation about Jensen.

"Cheers, everyone." Jensen lifted his glass and led me out of the ballroom.

Couples speckled the hallway, small groups here and there. I kept my ears perked, waiting to hear Nathan come up behind us, but he never did. Jensen pointed out every portrait on the walls and described why that person or place was notable. Everything seemed to be post-Ràej War, nothing from before the Slates had come to Omneth.

We went down one hallway and then another, up a flight of stairs, and then down another hallway. When we ran out of portraits and statues to see, Jensen led us into a room. It looked like it used to be a small bedroom or a large broom closet, but it was furnished with a single wall sconce making it impossible to tell. Jensen grabbed the metal fire-starter, hanging on the sconce's lower hook, and lit the candle stub.

"Damn it, Jensen," I said as soon as the door was shut. Since there was no furniture to throw myself on, I settled on pacing in my frustration. "Why did you do that? You know I couldn't say anything in front of Natalie, and Nathan isn't going to do anything in front of others. He's going to be furious with me!"

"Terhese." Jensen grabbed my shoulders gently. My neckline was cut so that his thumbs were on my bare skin. "Terhese, he shouldn't treat you like that. He doesn't even acknowledge you. You're his sister's best friend!"

"He's just playing it safe," I excused Nathan. Jensen's touch was warm.

"Playing what safe? Why?" Jensen was emphasizing his frustration with his hands. I knew he didn't trust Nathan, and I knew Nathan hated Jensen, but I hadn't known how much hostility he had towards Nathan.

"Jensen," I looked at the floor, nervous about the answers I might receive if I asked the question. "What did you mean when you said I won't have to worry about Nathan being angry this time?"

I looked up when Jensen didn't respond. It looked like he was fighting with himself over what he should say.

"Nathan and I have been on house arrest for Lucy's murder," Jensen said. "The only reason I am a suspect is because Nathan accused me. Think about everything you know. About me and about him. Tell me, who do you think did it?"

I leaned against the wall and slid to the floor, kicking my flowing dress out from under my feet. My heart hurt, and I felt ill.

I tried to speak. Nothing came out. A tear from each eye slid down my cheeks.

"Tell me."

"I can't."

"You can say it, Terhese."

"No. It can't be." I shook my head, releasing a sob. "How could he do it? Why? I just don't understand."

Jensen sat down next to me and took my hand in his. He kissed my fingertips and sat with me in silence for a moment. My heart quickly turned from broken to yearning. The feel of his lips on my fingers, the tenderness, the silent companionship...

"What will happen after tonight?" I murmured through a sniffle.

Jensen let his head drop back to lean on the wall. "I'm sorry, Terhese." Jensen squeezed my hand. "You might have a rough year."

"What does that mean?"

"I told you I don't trust Nathan. Over the past couple weeks, I've learned some ... things ... and most of my assumptions were true." Jensen pushed a piece of hair out of my eyes. "I didn't think it was my place to tell you."

I stared at him, looking back and forth between his eyes, looking for some sign of flinching or faltering. When we were younger, I could always tell if he was lying. It had been some time, but I hoped I would still be able to see the difference. Unfortunately, I thought he was telling the truth.

"Wh-what do you think happened?" I barely heard my voice. It came out small and quiet, like a last breath. "With Lucy?"

"Why don't I take you home?" Jensen stood and reached his hand down to help me. "I can tell you later if you still want me to."

"No! Tell me now." I swatted his hand away, zapping both of us with a small, static shock.

"Terhese, I promise I'll tell you after the ball." Jensen put his hand on my shoulder, as if a gentle touch would convince me. His hand was freezing cold this time, almost uncomfortably so. "Let's go back to the ballroom, or I can take you home."

"Tell me now, Jensen Dontane!" I shouted, jumping up and stomping my foot. The little flame that had been above us went out, but it didn't faze me.

"Okay, fine." Jensen snapped his fingers with annoyance, and the flame flickered back to life. I stared at Jensen's fingers, wondering if that had been coincidence or something more. "I don't think he meant to kill her. I think he pinched a Tongue Hold Pebble. Nathan has never been a good pincher, so it makes sense it didn't work correctly and he left his magicprint."

"That's what the Officials told me, too." I nodded, caught between curiosity of the flame and my emotions. The latter won. "Why did he do it?"

"She wanted their relationship to be public," Jensen said bluntly, not taking his eyes from mine. "From what I've heard, his family doesn't want him to marry a slate.

76

From what I know, Nathan needs to feel like he has power, so he only dates people who, in his mind, have less magical ability than he does.

"Lucy couldn't pinch well enough to be accepted into that specialty and had no other magical abilities. Tilly has yet to be accepted into a specialty," Jensen continued, though I was no longer looking at him.

"Tilly?!" I said in disgust.

"I think that was Lucy's last straw," Jensen said. I could see his head in the corner of my eye, but I refused to look at him.

"Last straw?" I felt my voice waver, fearful of what he could possibly say next.

"Lucy and Tilly are cousins," Jensen said as though it were a reminder. "When Lucy found out, she confronted Tilly then was going to confront Nathan."

All the emotions I had been feeling were gone. There was nothing.

"Somewhere along the way, Lucy found out he was seeing someone that hadn't been accepted to the Academy yet. She wasn't the only one that knew." It seemed Jensen couldn't stop talking once he'd started. "There was a rumor it was you."

"*Wasn't the only one?*" I blinked my eyes several times, bringing myself back to the room. "There are other girls? And they *know* there are other girls? If I am just *another* girl, then why would I matter to them?"

"Nathan's dad is up for a big promotion with the Officials. People will fight for power," Jensen explained. "At the Academy, Nathan told people he was dating a girl from a different academy that had an internship with the Officials. This appeases his parents, and he can sleaze around with any girl that hopes to be his mistress when they get dismissed from the Academy. They are all vying for that spot."

Jensen shrugged.

"It's a weird system," he said. "There is a fine line between too little magic and too much magic."

"So how many girlfriends does he have?"

"Oh, no," Jensen said and snickered. "He doesn't have any girlfriends. He tells them that his girlfriend is the one with the internship."

"They don't mind the polygamy?"

"His dad is an Official and Nathan has an internship. It's not the best internship, but people will fight for power. If these girls don't get an internship, they'll try to marry someone who does. Or, like I said, get paid for being a mistress."

I knew what adultery was and I had heard about it being more prevalent in Official households, but I never knew I would come face to face with it. It seemed much more political than romantical.

"Gross."

"Yeah," Jensen said. I could feel him staring at him. "When the rumor started spreading that his girlfriend was not in the Academy, and may have no magical ability, the rivalries and jealousy rose. They seemed to think it equaled the playing field."

"He didn't want Lucy to tell me or to tell his parents?" I was starting to understand the phrase "blind anger". Nathan had made me the butt of a cruel joke.

"I don't know about that part." Jensen shrugged. "Most of this is just from what I've heard."

"That's why he had an Ignorance Pebble." I told Jensen about the Pebble Natalie had found in Nathan's drawer and my confusion.

"Yeah, that sounds like the marx of an Ignorance Pebble." Jensen nodded, rubbing his eyebrow. This validation made me want to run downstairs and shout "I was right" in Nathan's face.

"It makes sense. Except one part." I nibbled my bottom lip as I thought. "He told everyone he was dating someone, which turns out to be me. Yes, he is cheating on me, but I'm the only one he was truly dating. It sounds like he wanted to be with me."

"That's what you got out of all of that?"

I shrugged.

"Your relationship with him is a secret!"

79

"*Was*," I corrected.

"What?" Jensen looked bewildered.

"I'm done." I had no feeling left. I was numb.

I walked out the door and down the hallway. Jensen followed half a step behind me. Though I was slightly surprised he didn't try to stop me or to say anything, I was grateful. I'd just found out that my boyfriend, my best friend's brother, accidentally murdered a woman he was sleeping with to keep her from telling the truth about his adulterous ways. Secrets and lies.

We walked towards the main entrance where there was a gurgling fountain. I wasn't sure how I missed it on my way in earlier. It was made of white stone like the pillars of the ballroom and had gold inlaid around the edges and the bottom where the water pooled. We were the only people in the room, so I sat on the edge and put my fingers in the water. It looked like steam was rising from the wakes of my fingertips crossing the water, back and forth.

Jensen sat down behind me, both of us watching my fingers dance on the water. My hair dangled in front of me, frizzy and lifeless. I felt Jensen's fingers trace the low-cut back of my dress, from the small of my back up to my shoulder. A string tied at the top, keeping the shoulders from falling down. I felt his thumb flick it, like a string instrument. Before he fiddled with it too much and it came undone, I turned to face him.

I wasn't sure who started it, but our lips drew together. Jensen's hand went from my chin to caressing my cheek, pulling me into the kiss. His other hand was against the bare skin of my back. I didn't want him to let go.

When we took a breath, we both hesitated. I leaned my head against his and let it fall to his chest. He kissed my forehead, and we stood up, his hand lingering on my wrist.

"You want to dance?" His eyes were bright and cheerful. I smiled and nodded. We walked into the ballroom and found an opening on the floor. The song started with a slow, high whine from an instrument. It almost made me feel like crying, but Jensen twirled me around and I was smiling again.

Nathan hadn't left his spot on the wall. He had a new group of girls surrounding him. Evan was still there, flirting shamelessly with Natalie. She blushed with every comment or joke, probably wishing her brother would go talk to other people.

The Academy Ball was my first dance. Jensen taught me where to put my hands on him and how to dance the steps to different songs. As we danced and laughed, my anger dissipated. After a few upbeat songs full of twirls and dips, the tempo slowed, and I rested my head on Jensen's shoulder, catching my breath. It was comforting to be around him again.

"A dance, Miss Terhese." Nathan slipped his fingers under my hand resting on Jensen's shoulder and stopped us from dancing. Jensen stepped back and nodded. It seemed etiquette was everything at the Academy. "Thank you ... Jensen."

My heart was racing as I danced the steps Jensen had taught me not an hour earlier, but with Nathan, and it was not a good racing of the heart. I didn't know if I wanted to fight or flee. His voice was as smooth and controlled as ever. I smelled the fragrance of the sweet grass he chewed after smoking. It was so familiar and brought with it good memories. I was at a loss for how to feel.

"I've missed you tonight." He didn't try to hide his words but spoke in a normal volume. "I didn't miss how jealous you were trying to make me though."

He pushed me gently away with one arm holding my arm out, guiding me to walk under his other arm before he pulled me close again and dipped me.

"I don't know why I waited so long, but I'm ready." Nathan held my face close to his as he kissed me. It was a long, deep kiss that everyone saw, but I felt the harshness behind it. His lips mashed into mine so hard it hurt. It wasn't like the sweet kiss he'd given me before entering the Official Building, and it was nothing like the passionate kiss I had shared with Jensen.

The song ended, and the musicians took a break. Everyone was clapping. I wasn't sure if the applause was merely for the musicians or if it was a derisive gesture towards Nathan and me. Jensen was bowing to a first year as they ended their dance. His eyes were on Nathan, full of scorn.

Before I could respond, in any way, to Nathan's abrupt show of public affection, I felt the hard blow of a hand across my face. Stunned, I blinked and staggered back. My head was spinning, and the three girls in front of me slowly merged into one.

"Tilly!" Nathan shouted. "What the hell was that?"

"I knew it!" she shrieked at me with her fists curled by her sides. Her pinned curls were loosening and falling down. "You are the little no-magic tramp he's been lording over all of our heads. What's so special about you?"

Tilly shoved me, making me stagger a few more steps. The crowd had made a circle around us, watching us.

"Tilly, stop!" Nathan shouted.

Other girls were squeezing to the inside of the circle, their eyes filled with hate. I couldn't tell if the hate was directed towards me, Tilly, or Nathan.

"Your time to talk is done, Nathan." Tilly smirked and looked at him. "It's time to hold your *tongue.*"

This comment caused a wave of unease through the ballroom, students and interns alike. That was the final sign that I needed to believe Nathan had killed Lucy. Before I could turn and confront him, Tilly ran at me, tackling me to the ground. I screamed but then gasped for air when the ground knocked it out of me. Tilly straddled me, making it doubly hard to squirm with my layers of dress stuck under her bodyweight.

"Get off me, you crazy bitch." I grunted as I tried to get my arms back from Tilly's grip.

"You are the reason Nathan can't be with me, and *you* are the reason my cousin is dead!" Tilly backhanded me. I heard people shouting above and around me. Nothing was coherent, but I heard her refer to Lucy as cousin. *Gross.*

Someone was trying to pull Tilly off me. Her legs were squeezing my torso. I closed my eyes and clenched my teeth. Everything happening was Nathan's fault. My first time at an Official Building, my first ball, was ruined because of this pathetic man. A man who had always put me down and made me feel powerless. I wasn't the only one he did it to apparently. Anger filled me. I could no longer hear the voices around me, and I no longer felt Tilly's knees in my ribs. Memories fueled my rage until I thought I would explode. *I am not holding this in anymore.*

With an ear-splitting shriek, I released everything I was feeling. It felt like I had been holding my breath for years and I was finally able to exhale. I felt it release from every orifice of my body. When I opened my eyes, I was standing. Jensen was holding me up by the shoulders. Nathan stood a short distance away, staring at me in absolute shock. Tilly was lying on the ground with the same expression as Nathan.

"What is going on over here?" an Official chaperone of the ball pushed through the crowd. It was Spectacles. I couldn't make my mouth or brain work. That tended to happen around him. I looked up at Jensen and fainted.

✦✦✦ Jensen ✦✦✦

Chapter 4

I watched Tilly run into Terhese, knocking her to the ground. Half the ballroom had already crowded forward to see the spectacle unfold. Nathan was shouting at Tilly, but he wasn't doing anything. I pushed myself through the girls who had made a tight circle around the two on the ground. Tilly was swinging her arms like a wild animal, and I dodged her fists and tried to pull her off Terhese.

"Get off me, you crazy bitch." Terhese grunted from below.

I could hear her anger; it was almost tangible. Before I could pull Tilly off, I felt the ground shake. *Shit.*

I let go of Tilly in time to see her fly off Terhese and fall on the ground ten feet away. Terhese was on her feet, eyes glazed over and emanating heat. Nathan's mouth dropped, and he crab-crawled over to Tilly. The crowd seemed more confused than scared, which was preferred under the circumstances.

I wasn't sure if Terhese was fully aware of what was happening. It didn't look like she was blinking. I ran behind her and leaned forward to whisper in her ear.

"Terhese." I shoved my hand in my pocket, grabbed a Play Pebble, and pinched it. They were simple toy things, made of super thin clay that was harder to keep together than to break, but the sediment was fine enough that a magicprint couldn't be found, and I didn't go anywhere without a handful of them. I grabbed the soft dust and dropped it on the floor under Terhese. "Terhese!"

She seemed to come to her senses a bit. I grabbed her shoulders when she turned to look at me, a wide-eyed look of fright, and she fainted.

"You, you, you, and you!" An Official chaperone shouted from behind me. I turned around to see his stubby finger shaking in our direction, his round glasses falling off his reddened face. "To the magistrate's office right *now*!"

"I want to know *exactly* what happened tonight!" The magistrate slammed his fist down on the mahogany desk in front of us. I had laid Terhese down on a couch in an empty room by the ballroom, but the office was still crowded with Nathan, Tilly, and me. It was most unfortunate that we were meeting with the Head Official of the Academy before classes had even started.

Before anyone could answer him, I stood up from my chair and took the lead.

"It was me, Magistrate," I said firmly, looking him in the eye. "I pinched a Thunder Pebble."

"You did what?" The magistrate put his fingers to his temple. "Why in Omneth would you do that? Did you want to lose your internship? What were you thinking? With everything else going on right now!"

"It wasn't his fault." Tilly stopped his angry tangent. "I was fighting with a first year. He was trying to separate us."

I couldn't tell if Tilly knew what had really happened, but I wasn't about to rat myself out. If I'd had more time, I could have come up with a better story. As it was, I had blurted out the first Pebble I could think of that would have had a similar effect to what happened. To everyone in the crowd, it looked like there had been a disturbance in the air, like a heat wave.

"I didn't realize it would be so strong," I said, hoping I sounded more confident and collected than Tilly had. "I thought it would be a smaller pulse. I think I knocked Ter— the first year unconscious."

"Right." The magistrate didn't sound convinced. "Mr. Ramos. What do you have to say about this? It seemed you were in the middle of this scene as well."

We sat in silence, Tilly and me staring at Nathan, waiting for him to speak. I wondered if he knew what had really happened. He was so pompous that I doubted he would put it together. Someone could tell him the sky was blue, and he would argue until he was the same color being debated.

"Yeah." Nathan nodded slowly as if in a stupor. "What Jensen said."

"Okay, then." The magistrate shook his head. "Tilly, why were you fighting a first year? Why were you fighting at all?"

Tilly looked at Nathan, who was staring hard at the wall, not blinking.

"It was a fight over a boy," Tilly finally said. "I was jealous, and I didn't behave like I should have. I lost my head. I am sorry for my actions, Magistrate."

She bowed her head in deference and sniffled. I knew it was fake, but I was grateful she didn't say anything more.

"It's unfortunate this happened tonight," the magistrate said. "Tilly, you're starting your year on thin ice. You and Mr. Dontane will be doing community service the first day of classes. I don't know what it is yet, but it will have something to do with helping the first years." He sighed.

"Mr. Ramos." The magistrate looked at Nathan and

stood up. "You are all excused."

We walked out, not saying anything to each other, and headed back towards the ballroom. Nathan stormed out the front doors. Tilly gave me a pleading look and followed him out.

"Tilly!" I shouted after her, but she was through the door and gone. I couldn't follow her. I needed to go help Terhese. After making sure no one was paying attention to me, I slipped into the room I had left her in. "Terhese? Hey, Terhese, wake up."

Terhese woke slowly to me shaking her shoulder. She blinked her eyes lazily, taking in the room.

"Ugh, I don't know why people drink liquor if this is how it makes them feel." She groaned.

I laughed and helped her sit up. "You're not having a hangover, Terhese." I talked quietly, grabbing one of her hands. Using her power would have taken a lot out of her. "What is the last thing you remember?"

She closed her eyes again and took a deep breath. "I remember a lot of things I wish not to," she grumbled. "Like Nathan ignoring me at the ball. Then you told me about how *horrible* he is. And us. We kissed."

It had been an interesting night between the two of us. Of all the things that had happened, I was taken aback by our first kiss being put into the category of things she wished not to remember. It made me want to find Nathan

91

and punch him.

"Oh." Terhese shuddered. "I remember! I don't understand, but I remember. The last thing I remember was Tilly sitting on top of me, but then I managed to get up ... and that's it."

I nodded, waiting to see if she would say anything else. Maybe my silence would prompt her to say she enjoyed the kiss. This was Terhese, though. She was different than other girls, always had been.

She didn't say anything. It was hard to tell what she was thinking, but it didn't seem like she remembered using any power. If she didn't remember, then I wasn't going to tell her. If anyone else knew she had been the one who had produced the thunderclap indoors, with nothing but her inner power, then she would be taken by the Officials and executed for having Ràej blood. Only the Ràej had higher magic like she had used.

"It was my fault," I said. "I used a Thunder Pebble. I couldn't pull Tilly off, and it didn't seem like Nathan was going to stop her. The force must have knocked you unconscious. Tilly, Nathan, and I were taken to the magistrate's office. Tilly and I have community service on the first day of class. That's all you missed."

"Aren't you supposed to be an expert pincher or something? You have an Investigator Internship and all that."

"Uh." I scratched my head and looked at the ceiling, smiling at the simple question I didn't have a good answer for. "Heat of the moment, I guess.

"Oh." She rubbed her forehead. "Where's Nathan?"

"He left." I hadn't planned on telling her, but anything to denounce Nathan came easy nowadays. "Tilly went after him."

Terhese nodded. Even with everything she knew and everything that had just happened, she looked crestfallen. Nathan would be going to prison soon; I wondered how she would act then. When I had told her about his deceit, when we were upstairs, she had become listless and left the room.

"Jensen," Terhese said softly, twisting her fingers in her lap. "Tell me the truth. Did I do that?"

She remembered.

"Terhese." I looked at her eyes; they were big, blue orbs, trying to search mine for falsehoods. It wasn't the right time, or place, to discuss all of what happened, but I couldn't lie to her. "Yes."

Terhese stood and grabbed my arm. I followed her to the ballroom. She ran her fingers quickly through her hair, laid it over her shoulder, and flashed me a huge smile. "Let's go."

Everything was as it should be. The girls were in their beautiful gowns and the men were in their suits, everyone dancing and enjoying the ball. It didn't seem like anyone let the event from earlier distract them from having a great night; fights were not an uncommon occurrence at the Academy.

"I want to find Natalie," Terhese said as she weaved in and out of people.

"Terhese!" I grabbed her arm before she got too far and pulled her to a stop. "You cannot tell *anyone* of this."

Terhese shook her head but kept searching for her friend. I wasn't sure if that meant she understood me and wouldn't tell Natalie or that she disagreed with me and would tell the person she told everything to. As she searched the ballroom, stopping to ask people if they had seen Natalie, I was stopped by girls asking me to dance or guys asking me what had happened. I was halfway across the ballroom when I caught a glimpse of her dirty blond hair, followed by the swish of her purple dress as she exited.

I shoved people out of my way to try to catch up to Terhese. She had already left the Official Building when I reached the anteroom. It had snowed while we were inside; clouds covered the moon and left few stars. I saw her, walking through the snow with her arms crossed, head down, not too far away.

"Terhese!" I shouted through the dark and ran until I reached her. "Where are you going?"

"I'm going home."

"Let's take a carriage." I pointed my thumb over my shoulder towards the dozens of carriages we had passed. "This walk is further than walking to Center Hill and back from either of our houses."

Without responding, Terhese turned on her heel and headed towards where I was pointing. I took her hand as she passed by and weaved it over my arm so I could help her manage the footing in her heels. I was lucky her fatigue trumped her stubbornness; I'd see her do some crazy things just to prove a point while she was younger.

I led Terhese to my black carriage. It was the only one of that color, so always easy to find. The lack of embellishments made it stick out as well. I helped her into the carriage and climbed onto the front seat to drive. We seemed to be the only ones leaving. I snapped the reins, and my horse, Tasha, fell into a smooth trot through the fresh-fallen snow.

As we put distance between us and the Official Building, I scribbled a message on a scrap of paper and ripped it up, throwing pieces into the wind every couple of minutes. By the time we were down the road and at the outskirts of town, no more pieces remained.

I focused my eyes and ears on the forest around me, making sure no one was walking about at this time of night, especially a determined student who wanted to leave the ball without waiting for a carriage driver. Everything was silent. I threw my hand over my head and pushed the air back hard and fast. The snow behind us flew into the air and settled down as if it had just snowed, leaving no tracks as far as the eye could see. If I had been with other people, I would have pinched a Play Pebble over my shoulder, pretending it to be a Sweep Pebble.

After covering the road from the Official Building, we went down the more traveled road that already had tracks. This road led deeper into Hill Country. When I turned the carriage off the road and onto a trail, I didn't hesitate to sweep the trail behind us every few feet. Not many people came out this way, but I couldn't risk this trail being found.

The carriage ride had put Terhese into a dead sleep. She didn't wake when I tried to rouse her or when I scooped her up and carried her into the one-room cabin I had brought us to. I put her in the bed in the far corner and went over to the fireplace. Looking over my shoulder, I made sure she was still sleeping before I conjured a small ball of fire between my hands and shot it towards the stack of logs. The wood caught flame and roared to life, sending heat on yellow and orange tongues of light.

My shadow danced on the walls, making the silence unnerving. It had been quite some time since I had been here. I wanted to wake Terhese, but I knew I shouldn't. She was suffering from power fatigue. If this was the first time she had ever used her power, which is what I assumed, she could end up sleeping for days. I had sent a message to her aunt when we had left the ball, telling her Terhese was with me and was safe.

I may have gone to extreme measures to make sure Nathan had no way of finding Terhese, but it was the only way to make sure he didn't ask questions and find out about her powers. I got extra blankets and pillows out of a built-in pantry and made a bed for myself on the floor. I would stay with her, and protect her, for as long as needed.

Terhese slept for three days. While she slept, I sent messages to her aunt and attended court. I left the cabin only when I had to but came back with food and water each time.

◆◆◆ Terhese ◆◆◆

Chapter 5

"What's happened now?" I groaned after I looked around the unfamiliar room and spotted Jensen. The fear I had first felt dissipated when I saw him.

Jensen smiled and sat on the edge of my bed. "Not much, since you've been sleeping for three days." He laughed. "How do you feel?"

"Um." I sat up and rubbed my eyes. My mouth was parched. "I feel good. I'm starving. I have to pee. I'm thirsty, too."

Jensen pointed to the bathroom on the other side of the room. I ran across the room on my tiptoes, holding up the front hem of my dress. The bathroom was small. Just a toilet and shower. A few shelves above the toilet for towels and toiletries were bare. I knew this wasn't the house Jensen had moved to with his parents, but I couldn't figure out whose cabin it was.

When I returned from the bathroom, Jensen was

putting meats and cheeses on bread for a sandwich. A pail of milk sat on the table with a ladle and two cups next to it.

"If you need more to eat, let me know and I'll make more," Jensen said, pulling out a chair at the square table for me. I sat down and ate the whole sandwich before drinking the glass of milk. My stomach grumbled. It sounded like a woodland creature trying to scare a predator away from its young.

"Before I eat more, I need some answers."

Jensen nodded and sat down opposite me, inviting my questions.

"Okay, first, where are we?" I lifted my eyebrows and looked around.

"We are at a ... hidden cabin." Jensen smirked.

I could tell I wouldn't get more than that. "Fine." I smiled and rolled my eyes. "Why are we at a hidden cabin?"

"With what happened at the ball, I didn't think it was safe for you to go home." Jensen shrugged. "If Nathan had gone to your house, he could have confronted you about what really happened. He could use a Pebble on you. So many things could have happened. I'm not sure if Nathan knows or not, to be honest." Jensen shook his head. "Tilly backed up my story about the Pebble. I think she believed it. It's hard to believe otherwise."

"And what are we talking about?" I asked in exasperation. "What is it that I did? Why is it bad for Nathan to know? I'm sorry. Everything is kind of fuzzy, and I'm confused."

"Terhese." Jensen said my name in disbelief. "You have *power*. Not lesser magic but higher magic. You have Ràej power." He stared at me intently. "It's not just Nathan or Natalie. *No one* can know about this. Trust me, Terhese. I'm an Investigator Intern, and I know what they do with people who are Blood of the Ràej. You must *never* tell anyone. Do you understand?"

I nodded. "Are you sure it was me?" I asked. "Why can't I do normal magic like everyone else? Every time I try to pinch a Pebble, I create a catastrophe."

That was the thing that annoyed me the most in my life. Pebbles were supposed to be for everyone, but I was incapable of using them.

"The Blood of the Ràej don't use Pebbles because they don't need to," Jensen explained. "Even if they wanted to, the power the Blood of the Ràej possess is too strong for the Pebbles. Higher magic acts more like a catalyst than anything else."

I thought about the Pebble that had burned my hand and made the peephole in Natalie's bedroom. Every time I held a Pebble, I felt that call of magic, but when I tried using them, they would explode and the spell wouldn't work.

"Did you say three *days*?" I must not have heard him correctly the first time. "I need to get back to Aunt Chloe. Asleep or not, I don't think she would want me sleeping at a man's house."

"I've been sending her messages."

"Oh. You went to see her?"

Jensen grabbed the knife and cut more slices of cheese and meat, taking his time before answering. "I had to go to court, so I dropped them off."

I couldn't pinpoint what it was, but something made me think he wasn't telling me the truth.

"What happened to Nathan?"

"He's in prison," Jensen said. The vein at his temple bulged when he clenched his teeth. I could tell Nathan's name put him on edge.

"What happened at the trial?" I pushed. "What happened to you?"

"To me?" Jensen scoffed. "I'm fine, Terhese. Thank you for asking though." He stood up and walked around the room, his shoulders betraying his mood. "Your precious beloved pleaded guilty to third-degree murder."

I gasped and covered my mouth.

"For misuse of magic and cruel use of magic that ended in death, he gets five years." Jensen's voice turned steely. "You were dating an absolute slimeball."

Though Nathan hadn't been loyal, it didn't completely stop my feelings towards him. I had loved him. I thought I had loved him. At the moment, I was confused about my feelings and overall emotional intelligence.

"I can't believe it," I murmured. "He's in prison because of a horrific accident." I put my head in my hands. Tilly's voice echoed around my head. *You are the reason my cousin is dead.*

"He was convicted of murder, Terhese." Jensen was kneeling in front of me. His brows were furrowed and his voice firm. "Even if he didn't take the plea deal, all the evidence led to it. He had a motive. His magicprint was there. The sediment proved to be from a Tongue Hold Pebble. What more do you need?"

"And you brought me here," I stared hard at Jensen, "so I couldn't see him. I couldn't say goodbye."

Jensen stood up so fast the chair fell over. He pushed his fingers through his hair, making it stand on end like a crazy person that had been lost in Hill Country for the winter.

"Why in Omneth's *Hell* would I let you near him?" Jensen shouted.

I felt my eyes narrow and my own anger spike as his voice rose.

"*Let* me?"

103

Jensen took a breath, kicked the chair further across the floor, and stormed out of the cabin. I ran to the door and called after him, but he was gone. The horse was gone, too. I closed the door with a heavy heart and hurting brain.

The fire was warm, filling the cabin with the smell of pine. It was dusk, and the cut out window didn't prevent all the cool air from coming in. I grabbed a blanket and pillow from the cot I had been sleeping on and laid them down next to where Jensen had his. It was the closest spot to the fire. After waiting and pacing for what seemed like hours, I lay down on the makeshift bed.

◆ ◆ ◆ Jensen ◆ ◆ ◆

Chapter 6

I ran my horse up the hill and across the meadow at the top of the hill. I had been so careful, protecting Terhese's identity all these years. Then the very first day she visits the Official Building, she uses her powers. And after everything she heard and saw the night of the ball, she still felt loyal towards Nathan Ramos.

The bigger question, though, was why Nathan had picked Terhese. He told all the girls he'd been seeing that he was dating someone else. Her. Terhese was the only one he pretended to be true to. And he announced their relationship at the ball. What was he doing? Why Terhese?

So many questions were running through my mind. Terhese must have even more. She was a hard-headed, stubborn girl, but she used to listen to me. I just hoped she would listen to me again. Would choose me over the memory of that sleazeball. That was all he could be, a distant memory. Thinking of Nathan made me yank the reins, startling the horse.

"Sorry, girl." I leaned forward to pat her neck. "It's okay. We're good."

When Nathan had first started talking to Terhese, I had thought nothing of it. I did feel a small pang of jealousy when Nathan told me they were dating. At first, it felt like brotherly protection, but when Nathan said it had to be kept a secret until his dad got his promotion, I wished I could be the one to announce Terhese was mine. There were so many times I had thought about how Nathan was taking her for granted and how he could treat her better. I couldn't find an excuse as to why I never did anything.

As the months went on, Terhese didn't just stop talking to me, she seemed to go out of her way to avoid me. That's when I watched Nathan closely. I wanted to find something he was doing wrong. When I started seeing little things, here and there, I became suspicious. The little things added up, and right before Lucy was found dead, I had concluded that Nathan was sleeping with at least eight girls from the Academy.

Riding alone in the dark wasn't calming me down. I threw my arm out towards a tree, letting a blast of power hit it squarely in the trunk and breaking it in half. I turned the horse around and rode back to the cabin.

◆ ◆ ◆ Terhese ◆ ◆ ◆

Chapter 7

"You came back." I was relieved when Jensen came through the door. The fire had gone out, and I hadn't found anything to light the remaining logs with. Most houses had a little pot of Fire Pebbles, but I didn't find anything of the sort. I had wrapped myself in the blankets like a caterpillar in a chrysalis, trying to glean any remnants of heat.

"Of course I came back." Jensen rushed to my side and sat next to me. He took a Pebble from his pocket and pinched it as he threw it into the fireplace.

I sat up clumsily and pulled my hands out of their hiding place in the blankets, rubbing them together in front of the warm blaze. If Jensen hadn't come back, I would have slept on the floor and woken up half frozen. Nathan had left me at his own house on several occasional after I'd upset him and not returned. I was glad Jensen had come back.

"I'm sorry I ran out," Jensen said. "I thought I needed to get away, to think. Once I was gone, all I could think of was you."

I glared at him. "Of me freezing to death?"

He looked apologetic but didn't say anything. I continued to stare at him as he untied his boots and sat next to me, propping himself up on his hands with his legs stretched out in front of him. He still said no words.

The fire cast shadows on the walls, dancing figures that imitated the cadence of the flames. I saw it reflected in his eyes, throwing light and dark and mixing together. I couldn't take my eyes off his.

"Jensen?" I said, trying to sound nonchalant. "I'm still cold. Will you sleep close to me tonight?"

I heard it, the plea in my voice. I hoped it sounded more demure than desperate, but I felt my cheeks flush with embarrassment. Jensen stared into the fire and looked back at me.

"Of course," he answered quietly.

His voice was deep and sweet, like molasses. He stood and grabbed the blankets and pillow from the cot in the corner, tossing the pillow next to me and throwing the blanket over me, covering me like a child playing hide-and-seek. I giggled, pulling the blanket off and squirming out of the blankets I had already wrapped myself in.

Jensen took the blankets and cast them out so they

fell in a haphazard square. I lay down and pulled the blankets up to my chin. When he lay down, I turned to face him.

"You warm enough now?" Jensen asked, his voice a soft whisper that made me lean in closer.

"Almost," I whispered back. The fire was at my back, and Jensen was a couple of inches in front of me, sharing my cocoon of blankets. I was getting warmer by the second.

"Give me your hands." Jensen took my hands as he asked for them. His felt so much warmer than mine.

"That feels good." I closed my eyes and angled my face up towards his. His hands were much larger than mine. They were strong and dexterous as they massaged my fingers and palm. Warmth and relaxation spread throughout my body.

Then, lips. Jensen's lips were soft and tender, erasing the memory of my last kiss with Nathan. As I melted into him, Jensen kissed me deeper, one hand running up my arm. I put my hand on his chest, feeling the muscles beneath his shirt.

I inhaled quickly when he put his hand on my lower back and pulled me closer. Jensen didn't miss a beat though. He rolled me onto my back and swung his leg over to straddle me. It seemed like he had more than one hand, running up and down my arms, my face, my neck

111

and playing in my hair.

Seeing no point in restraining myself anymore, I put my fingers under the bottom of his shirt and slowly hiked it up, feeling his warm body at every inch. When I had it halfway up his torso, Jensen sat up and pulled it off. He smiled, just south of cocky, then leaned forward and pulled the shoulder of my dress down with his teeth, letting them graze my skin just enough to give me goose-bumps. His lips went to my neck, tasting it with his tongue before kissing up to my ear.

Jensen sat up and looked at me, fire in his eyes over a heaving chest. I swallowed but didn't look away. He put his arm around me and pulled me up to sitting. His lips claimed mine again wrapping his hand over both of mine, holding me close.

Then he untied the string at my back.

He kept his hand on mine, holding them down in my lap but sat back to look. My dress fell, slowly at first. Jensen took my hands and held them to my sides, allowing the dress to fall to my waist.

Aside from being in bed with a man for the first time, this felt completely different. I wasn't worried about doing something wrong. I didn't have to bow and scrape to earn his respect or attention. It had mere days since I had been smitten with Nathan, hours to my own recollection. That relationship had always been difficult. Tedious.

My heart was racing and my breathing was shaky, but I wasn't scared or uncertain. Being with Jensen was effortless.

His hands pushed mine to the floor, stuck in puddles of cloth from the long-sleeved dress. I had to brace my arms to hold myself up, arching my back for balance. Jensen took advantage of my posture, kissing up my sternum, spiking my heart rate with each one.

Jensen lay me down, freeing my hands as he did so. I touched his hard chest and abs, feeling something harder against my leg as he held my breast, squeezing as he moved his hips against me. He kissed across my breasts, making me arch towards him until they got what they wanted. His mouth enveloped each one in turn, making my core hurt with the need for more. I held his head to me, fingers in his wavy, brown hair as I panted for more.

He held my waist with both hands and started kissing down my stomach, making my heart gallop. His fingers slipping between the fabric of my dress and my hips, sliding it down a fraction with every lick or kiss.

A crunching noise outside made my body go rigid. I imagined Nathan at the door, then bursting in. His rage would be ignited and Jensen was already at the top of his shit list.

"What's wrong?" Jensen looked up at me and turned his head to the door when the sound came again. He pulled the blankets over me and grabbed his shirt. "Stay here."

The covers were up to my chin again. I was frantically trying to tie my dress while lying down. I had never disliked dresses more than I did at that moment, wishing I had a simple shirt and pair of pants. I had one ear towards the door, trying to hear better. It sounded like one person, or creature, and they were getting closer to the cabin. If it was Nathan, would he try to harm Jensen? Or me?

A sharp rap sounded on the door. Jensen put his finger to his mouth, shirt still clenched in his hand. Three knocks, then two, then four. Jensen's shoulders dropped, and he opened the door. The man who entered was unfamiliar. Jensen hugged the man but tried to keep him from entering the cabin.

"It's been a while, Uncle." Jensen scratched his head. "I thought you weren't due to be back for a few more months. What brings you?"

My ears perked up at this. Jensen's uncle was an elusive man. Though he'd helped raise Jensen, the man was often gone for Official business. He was an Investigator.

"What brings me?" Jensen's uncle scoffed and squeezed between the wall and the unmoving Jensen. "I heard you were a suspect in a murder trial! Aside from that, there are ... oh! You have company..."

The uncle turned around to face the door again. Jensen put out his hands in a good-humored shrug. He unfurled his shirt from his hand and pulled it over his head.

"Uh, yes." Jensen walked over to me and tied my dress back on. "I do. She is ... uh ... decent now."

I wasn't sure if I should be embarrassed or start laughing. I settled for wrapping a blanket around myself and meeting the uncle and nephew at the table. Jensen sat next to me, which left his uncle the seat across from me. I stared at his unkempt appearance and wondered if he really was an Investigator. The few Investigators I had seen had been at presentations during primary. The men and women looked the same; their hair was greased back, they wore black suits and black gloves, and they had black utility belts with their Pebble bags attached.

This man was different. He wore his hair long, tied in the back with a piece of twine, but some of it had strayed and was hanging loose. His face was covered with a thick, dark beard and bushy mustache. I couldn't remember the last time I'd seen facial hair. His clothes could be his travel attire, but I assumed he wore them daily. They were covered in dirt and grime.

The pants were dark canvas and well-worn. It looked like he wore sturdy boots, but the pants were long enough to brush the floor so I couldn't be sure. His shirt didn't look as old as the pants, though the button-up flannel showed a dark stain. The color of dried blood.

"Terhese, this is my Uncle Kevitt," Jensen said. "Uncle Kevitt, this is my friend Terhese."

"Uh huh." Kevitt raised his eyebrows and looked at Jensen, subtly avoiding looking at me. "Close friends I think."

I blushed and let out a nervous laugh. Jensen stiffened and made a noncommittal noise.

"Yeah, yeah," Jensen said. "What brings you back so soon?"

"Naturally, I heard about the trial, but I had someone keeping me informed so I wasn't too worried about you." Kevitt relaxed in his chair and faced both of us, including me in the conversation with his eyes. "As an Investigator, most of my information is classified, so I can't say too much. I will say it has to do with bonds and partners."

"Bonds and partners?" Jensen asked with urgency.

I looked back and forth at the two men. They had their eyes locked on each other. It seemed they were having a conversation of their own, one I wasn't privy to.

"Why are bonds and partners so important?" I finally asked. "It sounds financial."

Jensen gave me a sidelong glance and looked around the one-room cabin before his eyes landed back on me.

He took a deep breath and blew it out with exasperation.

"Do you want me to go stand outside or something?" I asked awkwardly. Both men looked towards the only window. It was dark. I really hoped I didn't have to go out there.

"No, no." Jensen shook his head and leaned back in his chair. "Well, I guess this needs to come out sooner than later. Uncle Kevitt, she knows a little bit about it. We can talk in front of her."

Kevitt lifted his eyebrow, a silent question.

"I know what?"

"Terhese is here because she used her powers at the Academy Ball a few days ago and I thought she needed protection from Nathan Ramos." Jensen quickly explained the past few days. "She had power fatigue and just woke up a few hours ago. Ramos is in prison now, so I think she's safe, but she'll be going to the Academy in a few days. I think you should give her some advice on how she can stay safe at the Academy, teach her how to hide her powers." Jensen caught my eye. "Like you did for me."

I stared at Jensen in shock.

Kevitt sighed deeply and stood up. He paced around the kitchen table and sat down again in the same chair. Slowly, he nodded and laced his fingers together.

"Okay, I'm agreeing with you, Jensen, only because

I'm taking you north with me." Kevitt held up his hand when Jensen's face snapped to attention. "We will be gone for a couple months, but it will be done as part of your Investigator Internship. You know I wouldn't bring you unless I needed you, Nephew."

Kevitt turned to me. "Miss Terhese, it may be a rough couple of months for you. I wish I could leave Jensen here with you, but we must leave at first light. Before I say anything more, do you understand that you cannot repeat any of this?"

I had begun to really hate secrets, but I nodded.

"The Blood of the Ràej possessed some of the highest magic in Omneth. The Royal Ràej reigned for hundreds of years, serving as protectors of the land for all magics." The rough-looking Investigator talked fast but clearly. As he spoke, my world expanded so quickly I felt dizzy. He explained the difference between my higher magic and that of lower magic, which is what the students at the Academy, and most Omneth, had. It was critical that I only use my magic to make it look like lesser magics were happening during my classes at the Academy. I found it ironic that Nathan had looked down on lesser magic when, really, he had the lesser magic and I had the higher magic. It would be hard not to tell anyone, especially Natalie or Aunt Chloe, but Kevitt described the danger of using my power vividly enough to scare me from wanting to even try it.

"You could pretend to be a slate." Kevitt tilted his head in thought. "But the power the Blood of the Ràej has is stronger with emotion. As a young Ràej, you could accidentally use your power when you're upset. Ràej women are stronger than Ràej men. Some of them can even control the weather. It would be wiser that you focus on controlling it than suppressing it.

"Jensen has always known he was Blood of the Ràej. When he started at the Academy, he already had control of his powers. Since the Blood cannot pinch Pebbles, he learned to use his powers to mimic a Pebble's intended use. He had a few close calls but," Kevitt paused, looking up at the ceiling, "we've been lucky."

"How long do I have to pretend?" I asked, feeling that this new power was worse than being a slate. At least I would have been accepted as the latter.

"Forever, Terhese," Jensen said. I heard sadness but didn't want to look to confirm. "The Officials will eliminate anyone they find with Ràej blood. There aren't many of us left. Right now, we're just trying to survive."

I pursed my lips and nodded. Everything I had learned in primary seemed to be false. We had learned that the Blood of the Ràej were evil, that they hunted and killed the lesser magics for sport. The Royal Ràej feasted while the people starved.

The next hour was filled with Kevitt talking and Jensen adding a tidbit here and there. They said the best place for Blood of the Ràej was to be working as an Investigator. They were the first to be given information about suspected Blood. Kevitt would be ordered to kill the supposed Blood, but he would save those he could and send them somewhere safe.

"If the Ràej were not evil, then why was there a war?" I asked, hoping I was confused due to the late hour. "What happened to them?"

Jensen looked at his uncle. It didn't seem like either one of them wanted to answer that question.

Kevitt stood up. "Maybe ten years before you were even born, something new came to Omneth. It had a magic that we were not prepared for.

"Through a single touch, it could control its victim." Kevitt looked as though he were living that time period again. "They called themselves Binders. We didn't know how they breached our first defenses, nor have we figured it out. Once they were here, they spread like wildfire in a drought.

"All of a sudden, half of our allies had been Bound to the will of these power-hungry monsters," Kevin spat out with contempt. "When they started Binding the sorceresses, that's when we started to lose the war. They turned them against us. They turned *everyone* against us."

I noticed the fire grow with his anger.

"Why aren't we taught any of this?" I didn't understand. "I've never heard of a Binder."

"There's a war coming, Terhese," Kevitt said, almost dangerously. "The Binders may have gone back to whatever hell land they came from, but they are still controlling Omneth. With so many people killed during the war, it's hard to know who to trust. I've probably said too much, but I'll tell you one more thing. Be wary of Officials and never trust a Pebble Pincher."

The conversation was done. Kevitt walked outside, leaving Jensen and me sitting at the table. The fire had died to embers.

"What do I tell Aunt Chloe?"

Jensen looked grim. "You tell her you were with me," he suggested. "Like I had told her before. Stick with the same story. Don't mention anything about what happened at the ball unless she specifically asks. Then you tell her that I pinched a Pebble. Just stay low until you go to the Academy."

"What do you mean *if?*" I laughed. "Aunt Chloe is going to ask me a million questions. She's not going to be too pleased that I spent several nights with you."

"It'll be okay."

Before I could complain more, Kevitt came back in the cabin, carrying an armful of chopped wood. After stacking the wood in the ashes, he waved his hand, like shooing away an annoying child, and the fire was ablaze. He hadn't bothered with the façade of Pinching. I was trying to understand this new world, but it was overwhelming. Kevitt bid us goodnight and slept on the bare cot in the corner.

Jensen and I lay on the floor by the fire. I felt his arm wrap around me and pull me close to his chest. It felt awkward with Kevitt there, but when the fire went out I wouldn't have cared if there were fifty people watching us sleep; his body warmth was welcome.

Chapter 8

It wasn't as hard as I thought it would be to keep the Ràej secret from Aunt Chloe since she was overly excited about me going to the Academy. She didn't even seem to care that I had been with a man for almost a week.

"I don't want to be liable for what you do in your spare time," she chided. "Just don't do anything illegal or stupid."

I had done both those things, but I couldn't lie to her either so I just smiled and joined in the enthusiasm of the Academy preparations.

We made a list of everything I would need and wrote down the costs. Aunt Chloe sold a few batches of tomato sauce at the local market and the market a town over. She used the funds to buy cloth to make me new dresses, a bundle of feathers to make quills, and a supply of inks and paper.

I sat in my room and stared up at the peeling pink

paint. My trunk was full, but Aunt Chloe kept trying to find ways to buy more new things for me to take: boots for inclement weather, heels for dances, a cloak, hair ribbons, hair pins, salves for dry skin, salves for dry lips, makeup, curling rods for my hair, and the list went on and on. At the moment, I would give away all of my belongings if everything could go back to normal.

"Oh, look what I got for you!" Aunt Chloe burst through the door without knocking. She carried a canvas bag full of different-shaped objects, some wrapped in thick paper. I sat up to observe the items Aunt Chloe pulled out. "I know you probably won't have too much time on your hands with all your studies and new friends, but I didn't want you to be without your afternoon tea. Look at this ceramic teapot!"

The teapot Aunt Chloe unwrapped was light grey with tiny purple flowers painted around the top. Tiny purple lines were etched on the bottom of the pot and the spout. One side of the pot showed a large intricate version of the purple flower. She unwrapped two matching teacups next and set them next to the teapot. She also pulled out a little satchel.

"Smell this." Aunt Chloe shoved the satchel under my nose. "It's lavender tea. Your favorite! Last thing."

Aunt Chloe pulled out what appeared to be a rock. It was two inches thick and eight inches on all four sides. I stared at it and then back to Aunt Chloe with absolute confusion.

"What is it?"

"It's a hot plate!" Aunt Chloe placed it on the bed next to me and put the teapot on top of it. "See? You put the plate over two logs in the fire, and you put your kettle or pot on top. This way, you can make soup, stew, or water for your tea in your room. Or on a cold night, you can wrap it in a thick blanket and put it at the end of your bed to keep your feet warm."

I was already overwhelmed by all the gifts Aunt Chloe had bestowed on me, but I responded with as much enthusiasm as I had with the first gift of new quills. Aunt Chloe's rationality of working harder to buy more things before I left was that she wouldn't be able to buy me anything for quite some time. We exchanged a long hug over the teapot.

"Tomorrow is the day," Aunt Chloe whispered as she squeezed me. "Do you want to come downstairs for a last afternoon tea with me? After you finish packing of course."

The packing had been finished, before these new items arrived. I rearranged my trunk so I could safely pack the teapot. The hot plate was heavier than I had expected, but Natalie had told me there were people to help move the trunks, so I shouldn't have to worry about the weight of it. I sat on the trunk to latch it closed and went down to the kitchen to meet my aunt for our last cup of afternoon tea.

As usual, the tea was piping hot, but it warmed my hands. I looked around the kitchen, staring at everything I was going to miss. In the end, it was the feeling of *home* I would miss the most. The kitchen is where I shared meals with Aunt Chloe, where I told her about school and my day as I grew up, and where we would simply enjoy each other's company and watch the sun set out the porch window. On good weather days, we would take our tea out to the porch.

The afternoon was a quiet one. We sat with our own thoughts, in comfortable silence together. Once the sun was gone, Aunt Chloe bustled around the kitchen to make dinner. She made a casserole that she would pack with me to take to the Academy just in case I got hungry.

Five academies were spread throughout Omneth, each in a different region. The Sandstone Academy was almost a full day's ride to the northeast, weather dependent. It was named for the sandstone castle it was made out of. The castle was on an island, connected to the mainland by a bridge. I had never been to the sea, but Nathan had made it seem amazing: a huge expanse of water that the sun would rise from, creating a sparkling canvas that covered the unseen creatures below.

The next morning, Aunt Chloe and I waited on the porch for Natalie to come in her carriage. We were both thankful Natalie had offered me a ride; it saved us a small fortune. When she arrived, it was a teary goodbye between Aunt Chloe and me, but the carriage ride to the Academy was full of non-stop, excited conversation.

"Do you think we'll meet some cute guys on the first day?" Natalie asked nervously, touching a hand to her hair. It looked like she had spent almost as much time on her appearance for this day as she had for the Academy Ball.

"Ugh, I think I'm okay without meeting a guy right now." I felt a pang in my heart at the thought of Jensen. I wished he hadn't left. "What happened to you and Evan?"

"Oh, that was just a one-night thing, I think." Natalie blushed and looked out the window. When she looked back, her demeanor had changed. "Speaking of that night, I heard what happened. A bit of what happened. Is it true?"

My heart stopped cold. I took a deep breath, thinking of what to say. *Do not tell anyone* is what Jensen had told me when he brought me home under the cover of dawn.

"There are so many rumors right now." I shook my head, trying to give myself a chance to think. "What did you hear?"

"Well." Natalie was fidgeting. "I heard my brother

announced you two are a couple, and it sounded like you've been hiding it for some time."

Relief swamped over me. I felt like I could melt like butter into the cushion I sat on, but I held myself upright and tried to hide it.

"I'm so sorry, Natalie." I feigned feeling bad. "I wanted to tell you, but Nathan kept wanting to wait for the right time. It was a horrible secret to keep from you. I kept it from everyone."

Natalie pursed her lips and looked out the window again. "I'm not sure what went on that night. You're right that many stories are circulating right now. I wish you had trusted me though."

Natalie was staring at me. It made me feel like a child who had been caught stealing a second cookie.

"I would have been on your side, Rhese," Natalie said, almost sadly. "I know what you found out that night. I knew about it."

"What do you mean?" My heart was in my throat. With so many different factors involved in the night of the ball, I couldn't be sure what Natalie was talking about.

"The girls."

I chewed my lower lip and clenched my fists. I hadn't thought about Nathan for a few days. Since I'd learned about my powers, and since I'd spent a night with Jensen, I'd had other things on my mind. Now, all the shame and humiliation came rushing back like a punch to the gut. I couldn't even look up at her. It infuriated me that Natalie had known, but I knew that was absurd. She had no reason to tell me about her brother's love life.

"Are you mad at me?"

"I want to be," I said. "I am mad at myself. If I had told you in the beginning, none of this would have happened."

"What do you mean?" Natalie's voice was gentle, as though she didn't want to scare off a frightened animal. "What happened? Aren't you two still a couple?"

I laughed. "Still together?!" I was too shocked to hide my scorn about the idea. "Natalie, I have never been more humiliated or ashamed in my life! Aside from that, he killed Lucy! What kind of crazy person would be with Nathan?"

"You believe all that?" Natalie's body stiffened, and she was no longer fidgeting. "He was framed. Nathan would never kill someone."

"Accidentally, but he did it," I said firmly. "Lucy wanted her relationship with him to go public. Nathan was going to pinch the Ignorance Pebble you took from him, and I refused to give it back to him. He pinched a Tongue Hold Pebble instead." It all came together as I said it out loud. "His magicprint was found! How can you think he's innocent?"

Natalie looked out the window. I couldn't be sure, but I thought she was crying.

"Thank Omneth, we're here," Natalie said curtly.

I looked out my window, but the castle was on the other side. All I saw was dense forest. If Natalie hadn't been fuming, I would have scooted over and shared her window. I waited for her to beckon me over with a little jerk of her head.

The castle was breathtaking. Towers of all different sizes thrust themselves into the sky. It was made completely of sandstone, bleached white from years under the sun, made more spectacular by the blue sea surrounding it. I caught a glimpse of a watchtower on the east side, standing on the precipice of a high cliff. The whole island looked as if it ended in some level of cliff.

"I thought your brother said there were beaches," I said, feeling a little deceived by his descriptions.

"I think it's high tide."

"High what?"

"High tide." Natalie seemed to have forgotten her anger; she loved to be able to tell me something I didn't know. "The tide is the level of the sea. When it is low tide, you'll be able to see some sand right there." Natalie leaned into her seat and tried to point out the window for me. "There is a beach the students go to somewhere, but I don't think it's that one. It must be on the other side.

I've heard the undertow can bring you all the way to the Devil's Trench! I've only been here a couple times for Family Night and Official proceedings," Natalie said, making her sound more pretentious.

As we got closer, I saw the bridge that would bring us from the mainland over to the island. It looked mostly man-made, huge rocks and boulders pushed together with wooden planks on top. It was wide enough for just one carriage to go across at a time. Four or five carriages followed the descending pathway, waves splashing at the wheels and hooves of the horses. They trudged more slowly as the wooden planks turned into an ascending causeway before becoming level with the rest of the island.

We waited for carriages to go and come back before it was our turn. I felt as nervous as the horses had looked walking over the creaking boards that teetered on the rocks beneath them. It wasn't until we reached the narrow, but solid, causeway that I was able to let go of my breath.

"Does that ever get covered in water?"

"Oh, of course!" Natalie exclaimed. "This castle was very strategically placed. The Ràej were evil, but they were smart. At its highest tide, the castle is completely cut off from the mainland. At low tide, there's a sand bar between Devil's Trench and the island, so ships can't get to the island."

That was strategic. If they saw ships and needed to run, they could flee to the mainland at low tide before the ships could make it across.

"Sounds like they trap themselves if it's a land attack at low tide," I mused.

"I think we're going to learn a lot here." Natalie beamed. "I remember flipping through one of Nathan's books when he was a first year. The Ràej were able to control almost everything! The causeway used to go from the mainland all the way to the island. The Ràej used to call earthquakes to make it crumble and fall if they had a dispute with someone."

Natalie pursed her lips and was giving me the slow nod that she did when she thought something unbelievable.

"I know," she continued. "They had to make the bridge once they destroyed the causeway too many times, but they could make that crumble at any time they wanted. They could control the tides when they wanted to. What horrible people! Or creatures. Whatever they were. They probably crawled right out of the Devil's Trench."

That was how we had grown up, hating the Ràej. But I might be one of them. I could understand why Jensen and Kevitt were so stern about their warnings to me. The Ràej were not just a territory we didn't trade with, like Tree Country or North Shore. They had committed genocide, enslaved thousands, and behaved tyrannically in all other matters.

When our carriage parked, I opened the door, glad to hop out and away from thoughts of my possible ancestors. Natalie waited for someone to open the door and help her out. I waited awkwardly outside the carriage, wondering what to do next. From the window of the carriage, it had looked like someone was helping with luggage. It turned out to be some upperclassmen.

"Thank you so much," Natalie said sweetly and walked up the steps with her dress held in one hand. She walked by me without a glance. I clicked my tongue with annoyance and went to ask for assistance.

"Excuse me?" I tapped the shoulder of the first person. Tilly turned around. "Oh, um. Hey Tilly. I was just wondering what I'm supposed to do ... here?"

I folded my arms across my chest, trying to look casual. If I had known I would be running into Tilly, I would have spent more time on my appearance. Instead, I had argued with Aunt Chloe until I didn't have time to change out of my baggy pants and plain t-shirt before Natalie had pulled up. I was just glad I'd let Aunt Chloe make me new dresses; it seemed the Academy was more similar to the Official Building than primary.

Tilly was wearing a high-collared, button-up dress that swung around at her calves. Her strawberry-blond hair was slicked back and pinned in place. She looked put together and every bit the Investigator she was training to be.

"Good day, Terhese." Tilly's voice and smile seemed authentic, but I was wary. "Show me your trunk, and we'll get it taken to your room. Do you know your room number?"

It was interesting to think of how many stories were circulating the town and the Academy about the fight we'd had at the ball. I wondered what Tilly remembered.

"How do I find my room number?" I asked, leading Tilly to the back of the carriage. Natalie's trunk had already been removed.

"Follow me. I have a list." Tilly took a Pebble from the black bag at her waist; it blended right in with her dress.

Foolishly, I tensed, thinking she was going to curse me for her cousin's death. I saw the hint of a smirk on her face before she pinched the Pebble and the trunk rose into the air.

"Grab it!" Tilly shouted, jumping for the trunk when I didn't reach for it. "You don't want it to fly away."

"What was that?" I grabbed hold of my floating trunk.

"Oh, just a Weightless Pebble," Tilly said. If she hadn't had her hair greased back in the Official style, it

134

would have flipped with the sharp turn of her head.

I followed Tilly to the open gate of the castle. It looked so small in comparison to the whole. I couldn't stop looking at the stonework. In Hilltown, most everything was made of wood. Those who had stone in their house were very rich or very lucky.

The gatehouse could fit my house, roof and hall. Inside the outer bailey was a field larger than all of Aunt Chloe's crops. The stonewall surrounded the field and went further to surround the castle, which loomed higher and larger than I'd expected. It was breathtaking. Unfortunately, I had no idea where I was going, so I couldn't stop and chance getting lost.

The next doorway was between large glassless windows that started at about chest level and were at least the height of a tall man. This led us into the inner bailey. It was an intimate courtyard with tables set out here and there. On the west wall were three large windows, like the ones that flanked the portcullis. It was pulled up high and held with stone supports. I was surprised to see the gate was made of wood. It was reinforced with black metal, crisscrossing across the timbers, and ended with barbs. Each window had a similar contraption above it, but not as intricate. The battlements were at the top of these, perfectly shaped. The east wall had four doorless apertures, but I couldn't see what was through them.

Tilly was at the door of the keep. It was a plain, wooden door with a string to pull it open. A metal ring had been stuck into the wall so someone could tie the door open. Inside was a podium, almost too close to the doorway, that she stopped at.

"Okay, last name, Terhese?" Tilly was looking down at a pile of parchment.

"Neems." It was hard not to look over Tilly's shoulder. Though I had finally received an acceptance letter to the Academy, I was still worried something would go wrong since I'd never received the Academy Ball invitation.

Tilly flipped through the pages, using her finger to run down the list of names and then place the paper face down. She was meticulous. When she found my name, she ran her finger to the far side of the paper to find the room number.

"Got it!" Tilly turned around. She tied a length of string to my trunk and let it rise over our heads before she started walking with it. I wished she had told me about that trick. I'd traipsed across the first courtyard trying to keep the trunk down by my side, but it kept bumping my knee or hip, so I'd walked with my arm raised through the second courtyard. I'm sure Tilly found it humorous.

I followed Tilly up a set of stairs, down a corridor, up a few more stairs, over a corridor, and down more stairs.

As we walked, Tilly pointed out different rooms and areas. Little lounge rooms and practice rooms were scattered everywhere, but it seemed like most of the space was underutilized.

By the time we reached my room, I had no idea how we had gotten there or where in the castle we had ended up. Tilly opened the door, walked to the center of the room, unleashed my trunk, and sat on it. She spread her hands out to encompass the room. It was about the same size as the cabin Jensen had taken me to. Instead of a kitchen, two beds were placed at the far side of the room and a desk was pushed up against the foot of each. A wardrobe was on either side of the door I had entered. There didn't appear to be a shower, but I found a washstand and basin when I opened the wardrobe.

"You should have a roommate by the end of the day." Tilly started giving me the speech I was sure she had done several times already. "Sometimes you do not get a roommate, but do not remove any furniture. A faculty member or a Helper will do that if needed. If you do not get a roommate by tonight, you probably will not have one. The tide will cover the jetty in a couple of hours.

"This is your room key." Tilly opened a desk drawer and pulled out a small, iron key. She took out a slip of paper that had several lines of script on it. "This is important information you may need. The showers are down the hall, and there is a shower schedule. This will tell you your time slot. It will also tell you what time meals are. Your class schedule will be given to you tomorrow when you are in homeroom. Your homeroom location is here as well."

Tilly handed me the paper and the key. "Any questions?" she asked.

I shook my head. I was sure I would have questions later.

"Okay. Well, I wanted to talk about Nathan..."

I stopped walking towards the window and turned slowly, folding my arms across my chest. "What about him?"

"Just that ... I'm sorry." Tilly stared down at the floor. "You didn't know anything. I should have fought Nathan, not you."

That took me by surprise. I wasn't sure what to say, so I didn't say anything.

"Okay, see you around." Tilly stood up and awkwardly left the room.

It was nice to be alone. I unpacked my trunk and set my room up, making sure not to touch the half that was reserved for my roommate. I wondered if Natalie was supposed to be my roommate and that was why it was still empty. Maybe she was off meeting people or she had to do something with her Junior Internship. If her silent treatment couldn't be broken with an apology, I wasn't sure if we would ever talk again.

Chapter 9

According to the slip of paper Tilly had pointed out for me, it was almost time for dinner, which would be served at the bottom of the Keep. It made me feel more comfortable when I left my room to see a dozen other first years trying to navigate the halls. Older students had been appointed to act as signs and point us in the right direction.

I wasn't as far away as I had thought from the Keep, just a few corridors from the grand staircase. At first, I wondered why Tilly hadn't taken this route, but I realized why when I saw the staircase was filled with people going up and down. The Great Hall was directly across from the little door with the string. The podium Tilly had been at was gone. Students were everywhere.

The Great Hall was packed. I tried to look for Natalie, but it was as busy as a beehive. Sparkling letters and numbers hovered over each table. They looked like fireworks that wouldn't fizzle out. The upperclassmen were shouting out the numbers they stood under.

"Sit here! I saw you earlier today," a girl called over to me. "You didn't have a roommate yet when I passed your room. Did she ever show up?"

Although I was unsure if I wanted to sit down next to this bubbly first year, I saw no other option of where to sit, so I sat down at the long table. The girl had a black bob with a silver barrette holding the hair from her face.

"No, she didn't show up."

"I'm Maisy and this is my roommate, Suzette." Maisy introduced at least ten other people at the table. I quietly introduced myself. It had been years since I'd needed to make new acquaintances, and it pained me not to have Natalie by my side.

"What specialty of magic are you going to focus on? I know we're encouraged to try everything, but we all know what we want to do, right?"

"Uh, yeah." I hesitated. Until a few weeks ago, I had been telling everyone I wanted to be a Pebble Maker. It had sounded fun, when Nathan explained it, to select the magic and put it into the Pebbles. A successful Pebble Maker could progress to making new Pebbles. Prior to dating Nathan, I had wanted to be a Pebble Pincher or an Investigator. If I had to hide my newfound magic, I wasn't sure what I should declare. Everyone from my town thought I was a slate. "I'm not sure yet. I've always been fascinated by Investigators."

"An Investigator?" Maisy looked intrigued and impressed. "That takes a lot of studying. From what I hear, it's mostly strategy and logic rather than magic on the tests. You need to know everything about magic. That's awesome!"

Maisy reminded me of a child with a new toy. She even had the rosy cheeks of one.

"I don't have a great affinity for magic, but I *really* want to work for the Officials," I said. I used to want to work for the Officials to protect people, but now, I wanted to work there for a different reason. It was going to be important for me to keep up the façade.

"Well, you just let me know if you need anything," Maisy said. "My dad is Chief Investigator, and he'll do anything for me and my friends."

My mouth dropped. "That's awesome! And thank you," I said when I regained my composure. "What are you declaring?"

"I'm a Pebble Pincher." Maisy made a pinching motion with her fingers. "Oh, do you hear that? I think the food is here!"

If the noise hadn't distracted us, the smell would have. It was a mixture of the best smells I had ever experienced. My mouth watered as silver dishes and baskets of bread were placed on two long tables at the back of the room. The lids were removed, revealing food I had only had on special occasions. Pitchers of milk and dishes of churned butter were set at a separate table with rows of mugs. I followed Maisy to fill our plates with food.

Roasted pig and smoked turkey were being sliced at the start of one table followed by dishes of vegetables: fluffy mashed potatoes, orange squash and yellow turnips, roasted brussels sprouts, and corn on the cob. The second table had garden fresh tomatoes, peppers, carrots, cucumbers, celery, and lettuce. The breads were brown and gold, all of them warm and soft. At the end of the table were pots of soup and stew: vegetable stew, meat stew, corn chowder, and a tomato bisque. I filled a bowl with the latter, though it made me homesick.

"My aunt has a few acres of vegetables," I told Maisy after a bite of tomato bisque–dipped bread. "Her largest crop is tomatoes. I thought I would be thrilled not to have anything tomato for the rest of my life, but I couldn't help myself. I spent my weekends, and hours after class, helping her pick tomatoes. Then, after we picked them, we had to wash them and prepare them in the right way."

"There are different ways to prepare a tomato?" Maisy asked.

"Well, it depends on what you want to do with it." I turned to face her and wanted to laugh at myself for being so passionate about tomatoes. I would have to write about this to Aunt Chloe. "You can make salsa, sauce, soup, bisque, paste, or even just jar them for later. My aunt sells her tomato products all over town and to other towns, too."

I hadn't realized how proud I was of Aunt Chloe until that moment. It was a great accomplishment I wished I had acknowledged before I left for the Academy.

"That is really cool!" Maisy said animatedly, as she did everything else. "I grew up with an Official." Maisy's mood went from cheerful to sullen in the blink of an eye. "If I wasn't at the Official Building being told to sit still and be quiet, then I was at home being told to sit still and be quiet because we had Officials over."

"I would have been in trouble constantly at your house." I laughed, trying to make light of the conversation again. "My aunt couldn't keep me still or quiet for the life of her. If I wasn't causing mischief, I was planning it. Poor Aunt Chloe."

The two girls laughed. Though Suzette was Maisy's roommate, it didn't seem like they connected as well as Maisy and I had. On the outside, we looked very different from each other. Maisy had shiny black hair that matched her curled eyelashes, her collared dress was free of wrinkles, and she was overflowing with Official etiquette. I hadn't changed out of my travel attire, my dirty blonde hair was thrown up into a very messy ponytail, and I knew almost nothing about Official etiquette. Though I excelled in my studies at primary, Aunt Chloe did not favor the formalities of the Officials, so we did not follow etiquette in our home.

"Are you going to the mixer after dinner?" Maisy asked. "I heard about it from a second year I met earlier. They said the interns are throwing one at the North Tower. It's super close to our hall too!"

I had planned on finding Natalie after dinner, but I couldn't say no to my first invitation. We finished our dinner and brought our trays to a corner where a line of students left their trays in a hole in the wall. When it was my turn, I saw some sort of conveyor belt that the trays were going on.

"We have one of these at home," Maisy said. She must have seen my curiosity. "Everything on the conveyor belt gets pushed into a big tub. When the tub is full, a servant pinches a Wash Pebble into the tub. They push the tub to the next servant who puts away the dishes."

"I'd rather be the Pebble Pincher," I said, looking at how easy washing dishes could be. Aunt Chloe very rarely used Pebbles. The magic was available to all, but we still needed money to purchase it or goods to trade for it. Aunt Chloe only sold her foodstuff at the markets at the Southern Harbors or if she made it out to River Country, but she traded it in town for meat, dairy products, eggs, and clothing. "They have the easy job."

"Sort of." Maisy shrugged as she led us back through the corridors and up a few flights of stairs. "It takes a little magic to pinch more complex Pebbles, and magic takes energy. You could end up feeling quite drained from Pinching Wash Pebbles for an hour."

We walked down short corridors and then up a couple of stairs and down a few and through an empty room. I wasn't sure if I would ever find my way around this castle. We were following some other students, and I could hear people behind us. If anyone was watching us from above, we would have looked like ants on a long trail.

A guy ahead of us stopped at a wall and looked over his shoulder. He tapped his thigh, winked at me, and walked through the wall.

"*What?*" I ran up to the wall and stared. "Was that normal?"

Maisy looked equally confused. "What the crap was that!" she shouted. "If this whole path was a trick, I'm going to be so mad!"

I wanted to laugh. We had only known each other for a couple of hours, but I didn't expect this cherub in buckle shoes to know how to raise her voice. She looked at me and laughed.

The students who were following us caught up and looked around. Everyone felt the wall for a secret door or hinge. They were all discussing what could have happened.

"Could a Pebble do this?"

"Was it a ghost?"

"This is definitely a prank!"

I looked around slowly. We were at a dead end in the hallway, and I did *not* believe in ghosts. After a few minutes of pushing on the wall, the other students walked back, scanning the walls to see if they'd missed anything. I thought of what the guy had done. Aside from winking at me, he'd tapped his thigh. Was it twice? That must be it. It had something to do with the tap. I stared at the dead-end wall and looked over my shoulder like he had done.

There it was!

I saw what made the disappearing act happen. Lodged high on the ceiling, just a few feet down the corridor we had come, a little mirror was angled towards the door. I assumed someone was watching the mirror, waiting for the correct signal. When I tapped my thigh twice, I held my breath, hoping I was right.

The wall wavered, like it was about to collapse. We stared at it and each other, daring someone to do something. I reached my hand out to touch it; I could feel everyone else holding their breath. My hand went through

147

the wall. I felt open space, like a hidden room. If I'd had someone to wink at, without looking insane, I would have done it. I settled with grabbing Maisy and pulling her through with me.

For the split second it took to pass through the wall, the temperature dropped by several degrees. I thought we had walked outside, but it was the same hallway. A room at the end of the hallway poured out warm light, cheerful chatter, and raucous laughter.

"Wow!"

"What did we do?"

I was smiling from ear to ear as our little group moved forward down the hallway. All smugness dissipated as I led us into the room, where whispers ignited like dry brush all around.

"That's her! The first year."

"What first year?"

"You didn't hear?"

"I heard she's the reason Nathan killed Lucy."

"No, I heard the first year killed Lucy."

"No way!"

My heart jumped from my stomach into my mouth and back down at such a rapid rate it was making me feel sick. Was *everyone* talking about me? The rumors were becoming more outrageous by the second.

"She tried killing Tilly at the ball."

"No, Nathan tried killing Tilly, but the first year saved her."

"I heard Jensen saved her."

Maisy wasn't perturbed. She grabbed me by the wrist and pulled us through the throng of people. We finally stopped squeezing between people when Maisy found the second year who had told her about the mixer. Already flustered with everything I was hearing, it took a moment for me to recognize the man kissing Maisy's cheek.

"Terhese, you made it to the Academy after all," he said jocularly. It was Evan. Of course, it was Evan. A good-looking, upperclassman who just happened to be a shameless flirt.

"Oh, hey, Evan," I murmured and glanced around at the faces in the circle I had been pulled into. No one else looked familiar so it wasn't the same group he'd been with at the ball. That didn't mean Tilly and her posse weren't there. Though she had apologized to me, I wasn't sure how much I trusted her.

"How do you two know each other already?" Maisy feigned betrayal. "Should I be jealous?"

Enough rumors were already flying around about me, and I didn't want one about me and another man. Just a couple of weeks ago, people had found out I was dating Nathan, which was enough to wag anyone's tongues while he was sitting in prison. If anyone had seen me and Jensen kiss, that would make everything even worse. I had no room for yet another man. I would have to set the precedent that I was no longer with Nathan and that I had ended it due to the Lucy incident.

"Of course not," Evan answered for me, playfully touching a tip of Maisy's hair. "I told you, that black hair of yours has me completely enthralled."

I couldn't help but stifle a laugh and roll my eyes.

"Isn't he a charmer?" Maisy didn't stifle her giggle but leaned into him with her hand on his chest, claiming him for all to see. It occurred to me that she was not as innocent as I had thought. "Aren't you glad we came?"

"Yeah, I'm going to go find a drink." I excused myself and followed the gesture of one of Evan's friends. No one had made introductions, which I was glad for.

As I squeezed back through the crowd, I had every intention of leaving, but I couldn't find the exit. It was probably another hidden door. On our way in, I'd noticed a little basket of Pebbles. Someone was probably supposed to watch for the sign and then pinch whatever Pebble was used to make the door passable. I couldn't find the hallway, and I didn't see any Pebbles lying around to give me a hint of how to get out.

"How do I get out of here?" I muttered with frustration as someone backed into me and spilled some of their fragrant cocktail on my shoulder.

"Are you leaving already?" A man's voice interrupted my anger-fueled thoughts about the girl in velvet next to me. A voice as smooth and comforting as velvet. I looked up and my words stuck in my mouth. The man's smile was more charming than Evan's puppy-dog affection for Maisy. "Let me get you a drink, and you can tell me why you're leaving so early."

"I wasn't planning on staying for a drink." I smiled coyly.

He let out a pearly white laugh, grabbed my hand, and kissed the top of it. "It would please me very much if you stayed for a drink with me."

"Wow." I giggled like I had heard Maisy do, not ten minutes ago. "You're putting on all the airs tonight, huh?"

He was no longer bowed down to my hand, but he didn't let it go. His thumb stroked my hand gently. The smile was not stretched across his face anymore but was perfectly calculated.

"One drink?" he asked.

I pursed my lips to the side, pretending to think hard about this proposition. "Oh, all right." I smiled. "One drink."

I let him lead me to a large, round table that held all sorts of bottles, cups, plates, utensils, and containers with different kinds of foods and dips. Though we had all just come from dinner, it didn't seem to stop anyone from

151

filling up a plate or a cup. I didn't see any bottles that were not already half empty. I was hesitant to try anything, but I'd learned at the ball to take small sips. He poured at least four different liquids into my cup.

"You look nervous," he said as he handed me the cup.

I took it and sniffed at the contents. Something sweet and something strong made my nose wrinkle. "This is not the punch they had at the ball." I tried not to grimace.

He nodded, grabbed a bottle with bright green liquid in it, and splashed some into my cup.

"This should help." He tapped his cup against mine, lifted it up to his lips, and urged me to do the same.

My drink should have been a dirty dishwater color, but it was an enticing emerald. After taking a small drink, I still couldn't identify what was in it, but it was drinkable. He smiled, grabbed me gently by the elbow, and led me to a wooden bench.

"So." We sat down. His drinking hand rested on his knee, touching my knee just enough for me to wonder if we were skin to skin or not. "Here we are with drinks in hand, but it seems we have skipped the introductions."

I smiled and shook my head, looking down at my drink. Would he still be this charming without that smile? It wasn't like the intriguing smile Jensen had, where the slight curl of his lip had me wanting more. I was never sure what his smile meant. This was a fun-loving smile that matched the sparkle in his eyes. It was as though he felt pure joy at what he saw. Pure joy at looking at me.

"Terhese." I offered him my hand awkwardly, sitting side by side. He took it in his, though he made it seem eloquent and natural as he lifted it to his lips with Official etiquette.

"Pleasure." He released my hand and looked across the room nonchalantly.

"Hey!" I playfully leaned into his shoulder with mine. "Don't let me be the girl who drank with a stranger all night."

With deliberate and exaggerated hesitation, he bumped me back and turned to face me.

"Mark."

From the very start, Mark's humor had me feeling comfortable and enjoying myself. His smile was contagious, and I couldn't make myself leave the mixer that I had wanted to leave as soon as I had arrived.

We didn't get up from our bench, in fear someone would take it if we did. When my drink got low, he would call over to a friend at the drink table to bring us each a new one. It became apparent that just about everyone knew and liked Mark. For the second time that night, I felt myself feeling a little smug at having early success at the Academy.

Our conversation moved as quickly and erratically as lightning. We started with the normal conversation of what specialty we wanted to focus on. Mark wanted to be an Investigator with an Official Investigator Internship. I told him about Jensen and his internship and then brought up Natalie and how proud I was that she already had an internship.

Talking about Natalie reminded me about our fight and how I hadn't seen her since we had pulled up in the carriage. I didn't mention that situation, or anything about Nathan, but it made me talk about Maisy.

"Maisy said she grew up in an Official household," I said. "And it sounds so different than where I grew up. I wonder if I'm going to do poorly at the Academy because I don't have any experience with the Officials."

Though I voiced my superficial worries, I was more concerned about how I would fare at the Academy with my powers. A few people could already have suspicions about me.

"Did you hear me?" Mark stroked my hand with his forefinger, dipping his head to try to make eye contact. I blinked and looked up, getting rid of my inner dialogue.

"I'm sorry." I smiled and pointed at the drink, which was only half to blame for my scattered thoughts. "What did you say?"

"I said you'll do great." He gave me that smile again,

but his eyes still held some concern.

From there, I learned that he, too, was brought up in an Official household. His father was an Official Executive who directed Investigator campaigns, and his mother was the Official Director of the Seer Division. He said she had recently been succumbing to headaches that would leave her incapacitated for days.

"I'm sorry." I squeezed his hand for comfort. He said he'd spent most of summer break taking care of her and was worried he'd fallen behind in his studies. Most of the other students who wanted to be accepted into the Investigator Internship hadn't stopped their training.

When the conversation went back around to my childhood, it was more comical than Mark's. I told him I had always wanted to work for the Officials, but I had never had a great affinity for magic. At times I had taken a Pebble from the kitchen, just like any other child, and tried to use it without knowing how. The hole in Natalie's room was not the only disaster I'd created.

Aside from the damaged property and fires I had created with Pebbles, I told him stories of me growing up on a tomato farm. I shared how hard it was to get tomato juice and seeds out of long, braided hair. The longer out in the baking sun, the harder it was to get out.

"You cut your hair?" Mark exclaimed, laughing wildly.

"I did!" I nodded. My sides were aching from laughing. "I was only seven or eight, and I was so frustrated. It was a day without primary and there was a picnic at the top of Center Hill. All I wanted was to finish picking the darned tomatoes so I could go. My hair had half fallen out of its braid, so I was trying to replait and braid it, but the tomato juice was sticky, and the seeds were stuck.

"We had little knives to cut the tomatoes quickly off the vines, you know? I grabbed one and used it as a little razor blade wherever I felt tomato. When my aunt saw what I'd done, I thought she was going to yell at me."

"What did she do?" Mark's eyebrows were up his forehead, a laugh still playing on his lips.

"She laughed." I laughed at the memory. "And I cried. She hugged me and told me it was okay. She drew me a warm bath and even added bubbles to cheer me up. Then she fixed my hair."

Mark shouted at someone and waved two fingers in the air, asking for another round. When he put his arm down, he laid it across my shoulders. I felt like this should be my signal to leave. At the beginning of the night, I hadn't wanted rumors to be going around about me and another man so shortly after Nathan. It didn't seem too important anymore. I relaxed into the arm and continued chatting away.

Chapter 10

I woke up to the sound of a deep bell ringing outside my window. At that moment I realized I had no curtains nor any brackets to hang them. The result was blinding light from the morning rays and an instant headache.

"Ugh," I moaned, pulling the cover over my face. "What happened to *one* drink, Terhese?"

After scolding myself, I had nothing else to do. And not feeling up to Maisy's overly cheerful self, I fell back into a restless sleep.

I was walking by the lake with Nathan, then Jensen was there, warning me about what Nathan was about to do to Lucy. In the dream, I almost found the notion a joke, until I saw Lucy walking by. She was thumping her chest, sticking her fingers down her throat, and scratching at the white flesh of her neck until red streaks appeared. In strangled gasps, she tried to tell me something, but her lips turned blue and she fell at my feet. Nathan let go of my hand and knelt beside Lucy. He kissed her pasty forehead and placed a Throat Crush Pebble on her lips. I turned to look at Jensen, but he was gone. Nathan had vanished too, but I heard Natalie calling for me.

"Terhese!" She stared from me to the dead, already decaying, body of Lucy. "What are you doing?"

"I didn't do it, Natalie," I pleaded, tears stinging my eyes. "You know I would never do such a thing."

"What on Omneth are you talking about?" Natalie shook my shoulder. The world spun and spun, and I was in my bed at the Academy. Natalie was sitting on the edge of my bed, looking worried and perplexed. "Are you okay?"

Natalie stood up in the motherly fashion she adopted when doing something she deemed important. After straightening her knee-length skirt, she walked towards my desk at the other end of the room. I thought she was going to leave and continue her silent treatment. Instead, she grabbed something from my desk and sat down on my bed with it.

"What's that?" I asked groggily, though I was very interested in what had mysteriously appeared in my room. "I don't remember seeing that before."

"Well," she said matter-of-factly and handed the piece of parchment to me. "If you hadn't been irresponsible on your first night at the Academy, you would have made it to homeroom when they handed them out. When I didn't see you, I asked if I could bring it to you. This is your course schedule."

I glanced at the schedule and jumped out of bed. According to the brown parchment floating to the floor, I was already late to my first class. Natalie stood calmly and watched me run around the room trying to find underclothes, an appropriate first day dress, matching socks, and hair pins. I dug through my unpacked bags, and my room looked like a tornado had hit it.

"Okay, I have to ask." Natalie's look of calm had turned quizzical. "What are you doing?"

"I'm already late for my first class!" I snatched the parchment from the floor and shoved it into her hands. I caught the side of my dress in my peripheral vision and noticed the hem was on the outside. "Drat! My dress is inside out."

The laughter started slow and then became hysterical. Both of us were sitting on the bed, sides hurting when we finally stopped. It felt as if we had never quarreled.

"Don't worry, Rhese." Natalie patted my knee. "You weren't late for that class. You completely missed it. Lunch should be served any minute."

Natalie convinced me to spend a few minutes to get ready. I made sure my dress was right side out and the pleats were all folded the right way. Aunt Chloe and Natalie had ensured my wardrobe would be in style for the year. This dress was a short-sleeved baby blue that ended just above my knees. Navy stripes went down every other pleat, starting at the hips.

"Your biggest fashion accessory is your socks," Natalie had explained months ago when we had applied to the Academy. Over those months, Aunt Chloe had made and bought over twenty pairs of different colored knee-high socks with designs that varied from simple stripes and diamonds to flowers and stars.

For the simple blue dress, Natalie threw me a pair of crimson socks with thin, crisscrossing navy lines. I laced up my brown ankle boots and was about to walk out the door when Natalie tapped me on the shoulder with a brush. Aggravated, I brushed the knots from my hair, pushed the strands framing my face out of the way, and pinned them to the top of my head.

"Can we go now?" My stomach grumbled as I walked slowly through the door.

"Don't forget these." Natalie handed me my course schedule and the key to my room. I locked my door with the iron key. It was long and circular at the end with just one small blade on either side. I slipped it into my pocket and read through my schedule again as I walked down to the Great Hall with Natalie.

I asked her about every class to see which ones we had together. Though we had a lot of the same classes, we had only a few at the same time. Aside from homeroom, I'd missed my first day in Healing. I didn't think I had missed much, but she said homeroom had been a vital class with Q&A for new students and a tour of the Academy. She thought the first day of Healing would be equally important, so she would share her notes with me when she went to that class later.

The course schedule had the same four classes on Silver days and two classes on White days. The days were staggered with a day off after three Silver and three White days.

"We only have three classes together, and one is just homeroom. That's not even a real class. We only go once a week," Natalie complained. "What else do you have again?"

"My Silver classes are Healing, Baking Pebbles 101, Telepathy, and Astronomy." I turned over the parchment to see my White Day. "And then I have Cauldrons with you in the morning and Pebble Pinching in the afternoon."

"Is that your schedule?" Maisy came out of nowhere, grabbing the schedule from my hands and looking it over before handing it back. "Why don't you have any fun classes? Like Demons and Devils? Or What Walks

Amongst Us?"

"What are those?" Natalie asked, her eyes wide.

"Oh, Natalie!" I'd almost forgotten introductions again. "This is Maisy. Her room is in my hall. Maisy, this is Natalie. We came from the same hometown."

"*And* we've been friends since before we could walk," Natalie said. She sat down at the table, and Maisy sat directly opposite her, already talking about the classes she had mentioned.

I looked at the line for food, but it was snaking its way around the hall. With my stomach still growling and my head pounding, I sat down beside Natalie and tried not to be bitter. The two most talkative people I knew had met. They seemed like fast friends, though neither one took a breath while talking. It was almost astonishing they didn't pass out.

"Is this seat taken?" The voice from behind me made me blush, smile, and blush deeper. I looked up over my shoulder and saw Mark. He had a fully laden tray with two plastic cups full of an amber liquid. I couldn't help but lick my lips.

"There's a high price for this seat, you know." I tried to use my sweetest voice.

"I'll pay anything."

"And who is this handsome charmer?" Maisy leaned across the table with an open-mouthed smile from ear to ear, batting her eyelashes.

Natalie seemed to be taken by him as well. Without verbal permission, Mark swung his leg over the bench and sat next to me.

"This is Mark," I announced to the table, though I was staring at the steaming sausage, yellow eggs, fluffy biscuits with gravy, and fragrant apple cider. "I met him last night at the mixer."

Maisy gave a satisfied smiled and told Natalie about the mixer she had missed. I could hear them talk in the background, but I was fixated on Mark. It was as if we were in our own little world. He passed me the apple cider and pulled out a little flask from his coat pocket.

"Oh no." I sniffled my nose at the smell of whatever was coming out of his flask and gave him a face. "What is that?"

"This is your hangover cure." He put his arm around me and squeezed my arm a little.

I drank the cider, and it was more refreshing than I could have imagined. The liquor Mark had poured in didn't make it worse either, just different. I could feel my dehydration ebb as I drank the cider. I set the empty cup down, and Mark nodded with a small laugh.

"That was easy."

I laughed and joined him with eating his overflowing tray of food. He said he didn't know what I liked, but it was his fault I'd drunk too much the night before, so this was his way of making it up to me. I told him I'd missed my first class and had put my dress on inside out.

"It looks great now, though." He held my eyes just a second longer than usual and looked away. I could feel his fingers playing with my sleeve and fluttering over the skin of my arm.

"Thanks to you," I broke the sexually charged tension I was feeling when I noticed the silence around us, "I missed the tour of the Academy too."

"I can take you around," he offered.

"Rhese, I thought we were going to the bookstore after lunch?" Natalie said.

I felt like I snapped out of a trance. "Yes. Um, we are." I nodded at Natalie and looked back at Mark. "We're going to get our books and supplies, and then we have our next class together."

"That'll be fun." Mark smiled and rubbed his thumb up and down my arm near my shoulder. It was so comforting that I didn't want to move. I was falling into his eyes again. Natalie stood and stacked her dishes on her tray. With an echoing clatter, her bowl fell to the floor, spinning on its edge before lying still.

Mark's hand fell to my waist, and I could feel the weight of it as I tried to lean over and help Natalie. I didn't want to leave his warmth yet, but I squirmed out of his arm and went to the floor to help Natalie balance her dishes again. Waving bye to Maisy, Mark, and the other people who had joined the table without my notice, I walked with Natalie to dispose of her tray.

"Thank you," she murmured as we walked over to the line. I could see the flush on her cheeks and knew she was embarrassed by the spectacle; she hated being the center of attention, especially negative attention.

We dumped the dishes into the wash bin, and Natalie hooked her arm casually through mine, walking me out the only opening of the Great Hall. When both doors were open, two coaches would have enough room to pull through.

"It seems like you and Mark have a connection," Natalie said as soon as we were through the massive archway and heading down the hall. I couldn't tell if her comment was accusatory or pure curiosity, but it made me feel uncomfortable and a little guilty. It wasn't long ago that she'd found out I was dating her brother.

"He's funny," I tried to say lightly. "And very sweet."

"And super attractive!" Natalie exclaimed.

I tried to her hush her.

"He is! From what I hear, you'll be a lucky girl if you start dating him."

"No, no." I shook my head. "I want to focus on my studies, not boys."

I could tell Natalie didn't quite believe me, but she didn't say anything. In the back of my mind, I didn't believe myself. I had dreamed of going to the Academy for years, and I had always thought I would have to spend more time studying than other students. I had no idea what I was supposed to do now, except wait for Jensen to return.

As we walked to the bookstore, Natalie gave me her version of the tour she'd received earlier that day. The Great Hall had been used by the Ràej family to lord their wealth over the nation by throwing balls and fancy feasts. This was the summer castle, just one of many residences they had. We walked through the courtyard and into the outer bailey.

"They used to keep livestock here, but now it's just used for Pinching classes and such," Natalie explained with her hand waving it away. "Over there, on the far side, you can see what used to be the gatehouse. The towers are off limits to students, but you can travel through when the gate is open."

"Do they close it often?"

"They close it at night. There are guards on watch though, so if you get locked out they will let you in," Natalie said. "There are a lot of off-limit areas for students. Don't worry," Natalie reassured me, "I'll tell you about all of them."

We didn't go any further but turned around and went back to the courtyard. Students were walking in all directions, some holding books and papers, others holding hands with their current love. The weather was fair, and it looked like some students had chosen to spend their lunch lounging in the grass or sitting in the windows. Natalie waved at a person here and there and told me their names, where they were from, and what they were studying.

Had I missed only one class?

Though the castle hadn't been repaired after the war, it was still an impressive structure. The stones had been cut from the cliffs that the castle stood next to. It was a vast contrast in style to that of the Official Building where the ball had been. Natalie said rumors had spread of tunnels that ran from the castle, under the sea, and through the cliffs on the mainland, but no one had found them. The cliffs were another area restricted to students.

When we reached the bookshop, I was more lost than I would have been if I had given myself the tour. Natalie had taken me back to the Great Hall to show me the entrance to the Meeting Chambers. She said it used to be where the king and queen would hold private meetings. Then we went back the other way, crossing in front of the Great Hall to go up a flight of stairs. She took me down a hallway, down three steps to a hallway perpendicular to the first one, and then another step up and down another hallway that ended in a boarded-up door.

"There are doors like this all over the castle!" Natalie pointed at the door as if I didn't know what the boards meant.

"Did you bring me all the way over here just to tell me I can't go in there?" I asked and laughed. "You are ridiculous, Natalie! Can we please go to the bookstore now?"

"Don't you think it's fascinating, though?" Natalie was a step behind me as we backtracked our steps.

"Well," I contemplated, "why are they off limits?"

"Booby traps."

"What? Why are there booby traps?" My interest was piqued.

"The Ràej, of course," she said with a slight roll of the eye. "They didn't have the courage to fight against the Slates, so they set traps all through the castle. Some areas still have active traps."

Hmm. I didn't know what to think about the Slates and the Ràej anymore. I had been brought up believing the Ràej were power-hungry tyrants that ruled only by wielding their power against others. The Slates came to Omneth to liberate the people from the Ràej rule. But how could I continue to hate a people that I came from? That I was?

"Terhese, where are you going?" Natalie's voice burst through my thoughts. I had been walking down the stairs towards the Great Hall, but she had continued down the hallway.

"I don't know." I shrugged. "Where's the bookstore?"

"I want to show you some other places first. It won't take long." Natalie's energy was almost too much. I was still suffering from a headache and wasn't sure if my breakfast was sitting well anymore.

The castle was like an anthill, full of corridors and chambers. The only room that looked like it could fit more than fifteen people was the Great Hall; it could fit an army if it needed, which it probably had. Every corridor was as confusing as the last. We went down a hallway, then up or down a few steps, and then did it again.

In some rooms we could enter but not exit through the same door. The only way to get out was to exit on the opposite side of the room. Natalie said we could be assigned a Helper that would take us to our classes for the first semester if we needed. I would rather get lost every day than use a Helper, but I didn't tell her that. She would probably take every offer of help.

"Last, but not least, is the bookshop!" Natalie announced with a flourish of her arms.

I tried not glaring at her, but I felt like I had been

169

dragged in circles for way too long. We were on the ground floor again, standing a stone's throw from the Great Hall, staring down a corridor with wooden doors on one side and the open doorways into the courtyard I had seen yesterday.

From where I stood, each door looked to be the same. They were plain, sturdy wood held together with wide, dark metal. More modern than the door to the Keep. The door handles looked like they used to be something discernible, probably a Ràej sigil. They had been reduced to ugly clumps of metal with a solid ring hanging down. A line of students was coming out of the furthest door.

"Please don't tell me that's the bookshop." I groaned.

Natalie hesitated and led me to the back of the line. "Don't worry," her optimism sounded strained, "these lines go really fast. We have plenty of time."

The line did not go fast, but our class was at third bell, and I hadn't heard second bell yet. It was well worth the wait once we stepped inside the bookshop. From the outside, I'd expected to be walking into a dimly lit pantry.

"Wow," I murmured as I tried to take everything in. Similar to the hallways above, this room made use of steps going up and down at random. I saw cubicle-like shelves almost everywhere I looked. Everything was stocked full: books, quills, inks, parchment, aprons, folders, twine, slates, and other odds and ends. The rest were items I could only guess at.

Some shelves held jars of different colored sands, slimes, and less viscous substances. One jar was overflowing with what looked like snake skins. A shiver slid down my spine as I imagined the real-life creatures and grimaced.

"It's not that bad," someone said. "There are a lot of weird looking things, but the scarier items are under lock and key."

I turned to see an old woman holding a slate with a stack of parchment on it. She looked up at me expectantly through small, round spectacles. If her back weren't so slumped, she could be a little taller than me. It was hard to tell with her sweeping traveling cloak.

"Your name, hun," the lady prodded.

"Oh." I stifled a laugh of embarrassment. "Neems. Terhese Neems."

"Neems. Neems. Neems." She flipped through the pages and browsed through the names with her finger. "Ah, there you are!

"Follow me to your books and mailbox. We do not gather your other supplies because, well, most of them have to be fresh." She laughed as though she had made a joke and bustled away. Natalie and I shared a look of mild amusement.

We followed the shopkeeper to the back of the room. It was much larger than I had imagined. When we reached the back, she took us under a staircase and down a short hallway where we went up a few steps and down another hallway. I would never be able to find my way around this castle!

"Here it is." She stopped so quickly I almost ran right into her frail, hunched body. Natalie didn't stop fast enough, and I felt her grab my shoulders so she didn't fall backwards. I wanted to laugh but didn't want to be rude. My Official etiquette was already lacking enough.

"This is your box, so please have your friends and family use this number because I will never remember every student's name, let alone which box number they are." She took a key from the square opening and handed it to me. "This is your key. Don't lose it because it will be annoying for me to get you a new one. Your books are in the box. Any questions?"

I shrugged and shook my head, not trusting myself to open my mouth without laughing hysterically. It was hard to tell if this lady was serious or if she was trying to be humorous.

"I'm almost always somewhere in this shop. Have a good day, ladies."

When her footsteps disappeared down the hallway and into the din of the several dozen students that were wandering the bookshop, Natalie looked at me with her eyebrows high on her head. I couldn't hold my laughter in anymore.

"She was an interesting lady," I said. "I didn't catch her name though."

"I didn't want to ask." Natalie was taking my books out of the box. "I was afraid to annoy her."

One by one, Natalie pulled a book out of the rectangular prism, read the title, and handed it to me. I was going to need to buy something to carry them. One book was the size of two or three of the other ones.

"Why do I have ten books for six classes?" I couldn't remember all the classes I had, so I couldn't tell if any of the books were wrong. It seemed like a lot for one semester.

"I think some of them are workbooks."

"Of course they are." I sighed. A book to read and a book to write down what I read.

Natalie wanted to look around the shop more, but I felt mentally drained from the past couple of hours. I had heard second bell not long ago, and I wanted to find my classroom and wait for it to start rather than be late. It didn't sound like Baking Pebbles 101 would be a super interesting class, but it was a requirement.

Chapter 11

The tour Natalie had given me didn't help me find the classroom for Baking 101. I was thankful we had this class together. The room was up a flight of stairs and then down a few different corridors with steps that wound downward. When I thought of our path, it seemed like we were halfway down the height of the Great Hall, possibly over the Meeting Chambers.

"I think you're right," Natalie said when we were sitting at our desks and waiting for class to start. "It's probably because of the chimneys on this side of the Keep."

Before I could ask about the chimneys, students started filling the room. I sat back and watched them come in. This was a first-year class, so we were all new to the Academy. It made me feel a little less overwhelmed knowing that.

As the students took their seats, it looked like there

was a division between Official students and not. Natalie was an Official student because her father worked at the Official Building, but she was sitting next to me. I was glad I'd let her and Aunt Chloe take over my wardrobe selection for the Academy. I was still different from the Official students but was at least wearing the same style.

When it was my turn to introduce myself, I had to say my name, where I was from, and what I wanted my specialization of magic to be. It wasn't as awkward as I had thought it would be; plenty of other students had not been raised by their parents due to the war, but most of them sounded like they had more experience with magic than I had.

Aunt Chloe was as close to a slate as they come, like I thought I was. Neither one of us could pinch a Pebble correctly. The only magic we had in the house were the small Fire Pebbles that Aunt Chloe kept in a clay pot on the kitchen counter. She always said she could make a fire *just fine*, but I knew she would pinch a Pebble or two when she was too tired from working on her crops. Small House Pebbles, like the Fire Pebbles we had, only required pressure to be pinched. These were part of the yearly Pebble stipend each household received.

I thought I sounded like the least practiced student there, but then Natalie gave her introduction. She fully acknowledged the fact that she couldn't pinch a Pebble without it exploding on her and she was thankful she had a knack for healing. In the back of my mind, I was wondering if she had brought attention to her extreme inability to pinch a Pebble for her brother's sake, like she wanted people to think it ran in the family and it wasn't his fault. She had gained everyone's full attention the moment she announced her name.

It didn't seem like many of the first years had heard of my debacle at the Academy Ball or my relationship with Nathan Ramos. I didn't have girls sending daggers at me with their eyes or have guys looking me up and down, wondering why Nathan had thought me so precious to hide and kill over. I felt bad for Natalie. She was getting everything from sympathetic looks to questioning.

I was glad we didn't spend too much time on introductions; I'd already forgotten most of their names. It seemed everyone in there was enrolled because it was a mandatory class. I wished I hadn't missed homeroom; I had no clue why it was mandatory or what else was mandatory. No one *wanted* to be a Pebble Baker.

"Take one and pass it around." The teacher set a stack of papers on a student's desk. Her name was either Angela or Angelina. "This is your supplies list for next class, so make sure you don't lose it. I am Official Kane."

This was not a class I had expected an Official would teach, but she looked the part. She wasn't wearing the student fashion of pleated skirts and high socks. Hers was a very strict and formal fashion. Black pants, white shirt, and everything as stiff as her demeanor. I couldn't stop staring at the little curls on either side of her face, like they were pasted down.

Official Kane had us take notes on the elements of the different materials we were to get from the bookshop. After I had a complete page for four different substances, we went back to the beginning and broke it down even further. I had a lot to learn about dirt.

"We do not use *dirt*," Official Kane reiterated every time someone used the *d-word*. "Pebbles are not made from *dirt*."

Every time she said the word, it looked like she was tasting a mouthful of it. She said it was not dirt because dirt has all sorts of matter in it. Pebbles are made from pure substances, like clay or sand. If a soil, to use the acceptable word, is too loamy or silty, the Pebble can lose its structure before it is pinched. The power within can even eat through the soil if it has any air pockets.

"Next class, you will be mixing, rolling, and kneading out ten types of soil. Don't wear clothes you are attached to because the clay can be impossible to remove."

"Um, Official Kane?" a man behind me spoke up. "I only have five things on my list and one is an apron. Did you say ten soils?"

"Don't start a sentence with *um*," Official Kane said as if she were chastising a child. I was glad I hadn't felt well enough to ask any questions. "The list is correct. Read your syllabus tonight, Mr. Burske."

The teacher opened the door on the other side of the room, indicating it was time for us to leave. As students went through the doorway, Official Kane walked back in and sat at her desk. I couldn't believe I was intimidated by the Baking 101 professor who had spent the afternoon teaching me about the moisture levels of soil.

Yes, I was intimidated and eager to leave the classroom. With Natalie in tow, I practically had us run into what appeared to be another classroom.

"What is this?"

"I think this is for the baking part of class," Natalie guessed. The room had little stone ovens lining the walls. Down the middle was a long counter with wooden stools pushed under on either side.

"Hm." I gave it a once over as we walked through to the door on the other side.

"I have to go to my Healing class now." Natalie hiked her bag strap higher on her shoulder. "Where's your next class?"

I opened my top book to where I had folded and stashed my schedule. Each class had a time, professor name, and room code next to it. Unfortunately, I had no idea where any of those rooms were or what any of those codes meant.

"This says I have Telepathy in room NE022." I shrugged and closed the book. "Do you know what that means?"

"I wish I could take you, but my class is by the West Tower." Natalie looking genuinely apologetic. "I don't know where that specific room is, there were way too many on the tour this morning for me to remember, but NE is the northeast part of the castle. The numbers tell you the floor number and the room number.

"Your room is actually NE-0-22," Natalie explained quickly, trying to make me walk faster with her. "That means it's on the ground floor and is room twenty-two."

With that, Natalie waved goodbye and hurried down the flight of stairs before us. At least she led me to the staircase. I made it to the bottom and wished I had signed up for a Helper. Being at homeroom would have been beneficial.

I had no idea which direction was which when I was outside, let alone inside this maze of a castle. At home, I could tell direction by the First Pebble on Center Hill. Having a landmark wasn't really useful here, as the towers were too tall to see past.

"Excuse me?" Someone tapped on my shoulder. "Do you know where NE022 is?"

"No, but I'm looking for the same room," I answered the girl standing before me. She was a couple of inches shorter than me with curly, brown hair. She didn't seem to be an Official student by appearance, but Natalie didn't always either. "I'm Terhese."

"Shannon."

The two of us asked the normal introductory questions about each other as we searched for the classroom. Neither of us had declared a magic specialty yet or really knew what we were going to do. It was nice to finally be honest with someone about that. I didn't reveal my secret or let slip any details, but I told her that I would take my time and see what the best fit for me would be.

We found a door with *21* etched into it. Next to it was a door that said *23*. We both stared, confusion clearly marked on our faces.

"Are you girls looking for NE022?"

"Yes, we are!" we said in unison.

When I turned around to face the owner of the voice, it was Mark. My knight in shining armor. He gave me that smile again, like I was missing out on something fun and he wanted to show it to me.

"Oh, hello, Miss Neems."

"Oh, hello." I found myself blushing and batting my eyelids as he grabbed my hand teasingly. "Mr ... Mark."

"You can call me Mark." He laughed at our exchange

and offered his hand to Shannon for an introduction. She smiled, almost nervously, shook his hand, and looked at us back and forth like sparks were literally flying between us.

I awkwardly asked Mark if he could direct us to the classroom we were looking for. He had us follow him to the end of a hallway and through a door that couldn't be seen until we were right on top of it. After this we went down a hallway that led us to a corridor with more doors. These doors were numbered *20*, *22*, *24*, and so forth.

"The odd numbers are on one corridor and the even are over here. You'll see that a lot here." Mark confirmed my assumption. "Have a good class, ladies." He kissed my cheek. "I'll see *you* at dinner."

I didn't know I could feel like this. I couldn't even find a word for this feeling. I couldn't hide my smile, and it made me want to laugh. My toes were curling in my shoes with how much I wanted to hold onto this feeling. The thing that exhilarated me the most was that he showed his affection for me in front of other people.

Shannon raised an eyebrow at me with a toothy grin.

"He's ... a ... I met him last night," I muttered, half with embarrassment. It had been less than a full day since I'd met the man who was kissing my cheek!

"Lucky girl." Shannon bumped her shoulder with mine and laughed. Despite myself, I joined in, feeling better about the situation. As soon as we entered the NE022 classroom, our excitement was squashed by the dim lighting and overly fragrant, heated air.

"Find your assigned seat, please." The professor stood right inside the entrance of the classroom. The room wasn't just fragrant, it was filled with smoke from an active burn. The heat could have warmed half the Great Hall. I could barely see the name tags on the individual square desks through the thickness filling the room. The names were written in a curly writing that would have been hard to read in normal circumstances. After more time than it should have taken, I found my seat. I was one over and one behind Shannon.

The professor walked down the aisle to my left and stood at the front of the classroom. He looked much younger than I thought a professor would be. He couldn't be much more than ten years older than me. His hair was gelled but not slicked back like most Officials, and he didn't wear the Officials attire either.

Shannon turned around, shielded her mouth to others, and whispered back to me, "Talk about attractive!" I gave her a side smile. She was already growing on me.

"It looks like most of you were able to find your way here." The professor surveyed the students and an empty desk before him. "Sorry about any confusion. The backside is a little hidden. Don't forget you can still sign up for a Helper. This is first come, first served. I have a sign-up sheet on my desk.

"I am Professor Milsby." He paused while a small hum rose from the students around me. They must have recognized him at the same moment I did. He was the professor I had met at the ball, but he had been in Official garb that night. "No, you do not have to call me Official anything. Let's begin.

"Telepathy is something that takes focus, concentration, and a lot of practice, so we are going to jump right in. Open your books to page one and take out your workbooks."

Though I was taken aback by how quickly these classes started their lectures and coursework, I preferred it over studying the syllabus for the first class like we had done in primary. The Academy was already a far better place.

After going down each row of students, taking turns reading passages from the first chapter of the book, I felt like I was back in primary. It was more confusing to hear a different voice every couple of minutes read the same thing I was trying to read. The teacher would reiterate the main points on each page and tell us what to write in our workbooks.

Professor Milsby was not joking around about jumping right in either. After finishing the reading, he had us pair off to put what we read into practice. Shannon and I stood face to face with nervous smiles.

"Okay, you go first," I urged.

The teacher had told us to close our eyes and to hold hands. This would give us a better connection. Breathing in the herb-filled air around us would increase the telepathic ability by opening the mind. I felt Shannon's clammy hands take mine and immediately felt pressure in my head. This didn't feel like the headache from earlier or like any other headache I had felt before. It felt like someone was shoving their thumbs into my temples.

Shannon dropped my hands like she would a hot iron. I opened my eyes and stared at her wide-open eyes.

"What?" I asked slowly and quietly. "What happened?"

"Pain."

"It hurt you?"

"No." She looked sad. "I felt your pain. It hurt you."

This completely caught me off guard. The look in her eyes was the look a dog gives someone when he bites too hard when playing tug of war. I shrugged it off and told her not to worry about it. Probably a common thing.

"My turn."

I closed my eyes and took a deep breath before taking Shannon's hands. I braced myself for the pain to enter my temples and make my head throb, but it didn't feel like that.

It was worse. So much worse.

The pain pulsed black and red behind my closed eyes. I could feel my fingers tightening on Shannon's, but I couldn't let go. A pounding in my ears felt like my entire head was inside a vice, increasing its pressure on my skull.

I could hear Shannon tell me to let go. I felt her eyes open. I heard her say it was hurting her. I heard her screech for help.

Then blackness enveloped me. I couldn't feel Shannon's squeezed hands in mine. I couldn't feel the smokey room around me or even the floor beneath my feet. Everything was a dark emptiness.

"They don't know." I heard Natalie's voice waft through the foggy unknown of my mind. "She was unreachable for a few minutes before she fell to the ground. They said she was in a comatose state."

"They've never seen this before?" Someone else spoke. Was it Maisy?

"Never. Students have had different reactions, like a simple headache or dehydration, but Nurse McClintock said she's never seen this before from telepathy."

I felt something. A hand on mine. It was a cool, dry hand. Comforting. The thumb stroked the top of my hand. The rhythm was reminiscent of the pulsing that had been in my head.

I sat bolt upright and snapped open my eyes, not wanting to relive that experience again. My heart was racing, and it felt as if I was almost panting. The shocked faces around me looked as equally panicked as I felt.

"Terhese!" Natalie exclaimed and threw her arms around me. "I'm so glad you're okay!"

"You poor thing! Do you need anything? The nurse?" It was Maisy.

"Take it easy." Mark put an arm around me and had me lean back against the pillow he'd propped up behind me.

His touch didn't make me scared anymore; it was just comforting. I was instantly at ease and felt at peace. So different from what I had ever felt with Nathan. Maybe this was what it was supposed to feel like.

"Water," I whispered. Though my head wasn't pounding anymore, I did have a lingering ache. Probably nothing compared to what happened to my partner. "Where's Shannon?"

Maisy went to get the water, and Natalie sat on the edge of the cot I was lying on. I hadn't completed a day of classes, and I was already in the sick wing. Maybe this story would start spreading more than the other stories about me.

"Shannon went down to dinner not long ago." Natalie

186

waved a hand as if shooing a fly. "She was going to bring you up a plate of food if you didn't make it down."

"What happened?" I asked quietly. I didn't really know what I had done, but I knew it was my fault if she was hurt.

Natalie shook her head like a mother would at a silly child. Mark took up my hand with both of his. I felt like I was about to get a lecture.

"It wasn't your fault."

I stared mutely at Natalie. She fidgeted.

"They haven't been able to explain why what happened ... happened." Mark put my worries at bay. "Shannon said it hurt you just for her to try reading your mind. When you tried reading her, you were lost. She said it was like you had left your body and only pain remained. You were unresponsive. She came to the sick wing with you, and I was working as a hall monitor, so I sent some Helpers to go find Natalie and Maisy. I knew they were your closest friends at the Academy."

Whatever fear and pain I had felt before was wiped away by Mark's unceasing thumb strokes on my hand and shoulder. Just hearing his voice made me feel better.

"It was advised that you not continue Telepathy this term," Mark said.

Natalie gave a small eye roll, and she hopped off the cot. "You don't have to listen to them, Rhese. It was probably a one-time thing. You could go talk to the headmaster, I'm sure."

I felt Mark's gaze on me, and I looked into his eyes for the first time since I'd regained consciousness. They looked concerned and caring. I smiled at him and looked at Natalie, who seemed antsy to leave.

"I think I'll look at one of the classes Maisy was talking about," I decided. "I could take Devils and Demons or something fun."

"So much for working hard at the Academy," Natalie said arrogantly, clearly trying to hide her agitation with Mark. "Are you coming to dinner? Shannon and I can bring you food afterwards if not."

A fleeting notion passed through me that getting Mark's permission to go with her was absurd, but I looked up at him with the question on my lips.

"You head down, Natalie," he said, taking control. "We'll meet you there."

I could see on her face that Natalie was not particularly satisfied with the arrangement, but she nodded, gave me a small wave, and left the sick wing.

Mark squeezed my hand gently. "How's your head?" he asked, looking at the sides of my head like horns would appear.

"I'm fine," I assured him and sat up further.

A slight feeling of dizziness passed over me, but I

feigned perfection. Whether he saw through the farce or not, I couldn't tell, but he helped me off the raised cot and handed me my book for Telepathy. He'd tried to carry it for me, but I needed something to hold onto, something to keep my focus off the lack of equilibrium I was feeling.

When we arrived at the Great Hall, it was packed with students. Even though half of them looked like they had finished eating, no one seemed like they were in a rush to go anywhere. They were sitting at the long tables with empty plates in front of them, playing games with dice or cards, laughing at jokes and imitations told by another, and exchanging first day of class stories.

It was a hive of constantly moving and talking students, until one at a time they saw me and fell silent. When would I be able to stay out of the rumor mill? The silence of the Great Hall lasted only a moment. I couldn't tell if everyone was resuming their conversations or starting new ones about me.

Mark tried to usher me to a table where Evan and others were sitting, but I was starving and wanted to fill my plate. I spotted Natalie at a table with Shannon. They both came over to join me in the line for food, though both of them brought up dirty trays to dump into the wash bin.

"Terhese, I am so sorry!" Shannon gushed. "Are you okay?"

I felt my cheeks flush with the heat of

embarrassment. This interaction just made people stare more. "I'm fine, fine. I don't really know what happened, but I hope you're okay."

Natalie grabbed a wooden platter for me and pushed it into my hands.

"Our first day at Academy." Natalie smirked and let out a small laugh. "You always do find a way to make things exciting."

Shannon laughed, and their carefree attitudes made me feel better about the incident. I stepped in front of Natalie to set my platter down on the long table, covered with food again.

It wasn't as decadent a feast as it had been the night before, but it was nothing to complain about. Chunks of savory meats, thick slices of cheese, warm loaves of bread, mashed vegetables that steamed, and bowls of creamy butter. Hot potatoes, rolled in oil and salts, sat next to bubbling pots of soup. I couldn't find a bowl, so I poured a cheesy-looking soup over my roughly opened potato. It was a generous helping and spread around my platter quickly, seeping into the other foods.

"Rhese, that's so gross," Natalie said, looking around to see if anyone noticed. "I don't even know if I still want dessert now."

"It's so *good*." I picked up a piece of chicken with my fingers, swirled it around in the mess on my plate, and ate it with more exaggeration.

"You are so embarrassing sometimes." Natalie grimaced but laughed and walked over to the dessert table. Apparently I hadn't destroyed her sweet tooth too much.

Shannon had been talking to Mark, and they each made a face at my dinner plate. Hers was similar to that of Natalie, but Mark looked more like he wished he'd thought of it.

"You made an interesting soup there." He grinned. "You ready to sit down and eat?"

I looked over to the table his friends were sitting at and felt no inclination to join them. "I'm going to sit with Natalie and Shannon."

"Oh." Mark grabbed my hand and flashed the weak-at-my-knees smile. "If that's really what you want..."

He hadn't eaten yet either, so if I sat with him, I wouldn't have to rush to leave when Natalie did. It looked like Maisy was sitting there too. I didn't really know Shannon, and Natalie was probably sitting with her to be nice. Mark was still holding my hand, waiting for me to go with him. I took a step towards him, and his smile grew, reaching his eyes.

"Okay, I'm ready," Natalie announced, her platter full of desserts. I didn't know whose plate was more comical. "Don't worry, this is for sharing." She smiled.

I picked up my books and cradled them in one arm so I could grab my plate with the other. "Mark, you can come sit with us or we can catch up tomorrow at breakfast?"

The smile on Mark's face changed to confusion but was quickly replaced by a smile again. He leaned in and kissed my cheek. "You girls enjoy the sweets, and I'll find you later."

The three of us walked to the edge of the room and down half the length. Natalie was sitting at the same table as we had this morning. She was a creature of habit.

We sat across from each other, and Shannon sat next to Natalie.

"He's like a puppy dog," Shannon said when we were all settled down and eating. "You have him hooked on you."

"And he has you hooked on him." Natalie was eating a pie daintily. Her etiquette was better than mine on a good day. At this moment, it was a drastic difference as I shoveled food into my mouth using bread, everything dripping with soup. "I can't see how you hooked him, though."

We all laughed, and Natalie handed me a napkin. I couldn't say why I was so attracted to Mark, and I didn't know how it had happened so fast. It felt like he was sitting by me, like the heat of his body was warming me. It was so different than anything I had felt before.

After my messy dinner, I helped Natalie and Shannon finish off the desserts. We had apple crumble, pumpkin pie, brownies, cakes, and tartlets. Natalie said she couldn't decide, so she had taken one of everything. Though I wasn't the biggest fan of sweets, the apple crumble was divine.

"Are you guys done with class for the day?"

"It's way past dark," Shannon said, looking out the window. "Do they have night classes?"

"I have Astronomy." I pulled out my schedule. "In the North Tower. It doesn't have a room number."

"Let me see." Natalie took the schedule from me and looked it over quickly. "I think this is the top of the Tower. There should be only one room."

Chapter 12

With the little I knew about the Academy's layout, I set off to find my night class. It didn't seem like many students had night classes; the Great Hall remained full. Natalie and Shannon were going to go find the library and study rooms. I couldn't imagine there would be a huge rush for that activity tonight.

As I stood in the courtyard, trying to figure out which way was north, I decided I would sign up for a Helper as soon as I had another opportunity. It wouldn't take me too long to learn the castle, but it would be very convenient in the meantime.

The gates out of the courtyard to the mainland faced mostly west. That meant the door to the Great Hall was on the north side and the North Tower would be behind it. From this vantage point, I saw two towers peeking up behind the Great Hall.

"I guess I'll just hope to find someone along the way," I murmured to myself.

The corridors were empty past the Great Hall. Candles every few feet lit the way, but it was still quite eerie. Every step seemed to echo in front and behind me. I found myself looking over my shoulder to see if someone was there.

It didn't long for me to find the entrance to the North Tower, assuming it was the right place from the propped open door and sign that said ASTRONOMY. The steps to the top of the tower left me sweating and panting. I leaned against a wall to catch my breath, straighten my dress, and smooth out my hair before entering the classroom, wondering how high up this classroom was.

When I had regained enough composure, I walked into the classroom and was pleasantly surprised. It was spacious with a high, flat ceiling and two rows of glassless windows. The cool air was refreshing.

Just a few other students were in the room, but I couldn't tell how early I was for the class. Instead of desks, mats were laid out in a large circle on the floor. I took one of the four mats that were left and sat down awkwardly with my dress. It didn't seem possible to get in a comfortable position while keeping my modesty.

"Hey." A girl tapped me on the shoulder. "An older student told me to change for this class." She pinched the thin leggings she was wearing under her dress. "But I'm sure you'll be fine for tonight."

"I wish I had known that before." I groaned. "I'm Terhese."

"Michelle."

"Good evening, class." A tall, slender woman climbed nimbly through one of the windows on the upper row and clambered down a rope ladder. She wore sandals, woolen leggings, and a long-sleeved tunic, an outfit I had seen only on children. "We are missing a few students, but we will do roll call. Please ask me any questions you have about the Academy or this class when I call your name."

The teacher sat down on what used to be a thick pillow in the corner. She grabbed a slate with parchments on it, quill, and ink pot. I was surprised she didn't have a desk.

"I am Official Jill McKinly, but you can call me Official Jill." She looked up and over the class, as though challenging us to question her Official eligibility. "Megan Deaslen?"

"Right here." A small girl with wispy, brown hair and glasses that made her look as mousey as she sounded raised her hand across from me. Though the mats were in a circle, everyone had turned to look at Official Jill.

"Garrett Banley?"

"Here." This man was sitting on my right and definitely looked older than a first year. "Do you have the sign-up list for a Helper? Ms. ... Jill?"

"Official Jill." She looked up from the paper she was using and surveyed Garrett. "Are you a first year, Mr. Banley?"

"Not technically. I attended a half year last year and I—"

"Did you lose your Helper last year, Mr. Banley?"

The room became more silent than I thought possible as he struggled to respond.

"Yes, ma'am," he settled with.

"Students are not allowed to have more than one Helper," Official Jill said as she scribbled something down. "Please talk to me after class, Mr. Banley, and we will see what we can do.

"Lisa Kittles?" No response. We all looked around at each other, daring someone to speak up. "Lisa ... Kittles? Okay. Terhese Neems?"

"Here." I raised my hand. "Official Jill? Could you explain a little more about a Helper? I was under the impression it was going to be an older student or an intern."

Official Jill stood and grabbed a blank piece of parchment. She dipped her quill in her ink a few times, scribbled something, and underlined it with a flourish. "I will go into more detail about Helpers when our stragglers have shown up. If you are interested in a Helper, please write your name and your dormitory room number here." She handed me the sign-up sheet.

I signed my name and searched my schedule handout to see if my dormitory room was on it. It wasn't. Hopefully, they would be able to look it up by my name. I passed the sheet to my left as Official Jill continued roll call. Michelle Palma signed her name and announced her attendance. Alesia Potts sat next to Michelle, with long blond hair that was almost as white as her skin.

"Nathan Ramos?"

My heart stopped, and I looked around the room in a slight panic. He wasn't there. Of course he wasn't there. He was sitting in a locked cell of an Official prison somewhere. I released a breath I didn't know I was holding and looked up at the sound of someone coming through the door.

"Mr. Livas." Official Jill nodded at the newcomer. "Thank you for joining us."

I couldn't believe how many times I'd run into this man.

"I do apologize for my tardiness," Mark said politely and took an open mat. "I hope it will not happen again."

"I hope so as well," she responded, almost jokingly. "Class, Mr. Livas is my teaching assistant for this class.

He's a third year and has applied for an Official Investigator Internship.

"You didn't happen upon any stragglers, did you?" Official Jill asked.

Mark shook his head and sat down on the other side of the circle. I almost felt sad a spot wasn't open next to me, and then I saw him wink at me over his shoulder.

"Then we'll begin! Mr. Livas, can you explain to the class what a Helper is?"

Mark turned around on his mat to face the circle. "A Helper is a type of creature highly trained in the navigation of the castle and grounds." Mark described it as if he'd done so a hundred times. "They are small, so they don't get in the way of you or others, and they have only one student at a time. You can return your Helper when they are no longer needed, but some students will keep the same Helper for their entire first year or their entire stay at the Academy."

"Do you still have a Helper, Mr. Livas?" the mouse-girl, Megan, piped up.

"You can call me Mark." He smiled, instantly sending a jolt of jealousy through me. "I don't have a Helper anymore, but I kept mine for the majority of my first year."

Though everyone sat quietly, it seemed like we were all bursting at the seams with questions and curiosity. "For those of you who signed up, you'll receive your Helper by the morning. Now, let's get started."

I couldn't focus on Astronomy with my imagination running wild about the mysterious Helper. Was it invisible? Was it microscopic? How could it help me? What did it do when I was in class? Would it take notes, too?

I found myself staring off into the distance when a pile of parchment drifted onto my lap. It wasn't an ingredient list, like my Baking class, but it was twenty or more pages of dots and diamonds. This seemed like something children were given to express their creativity by using colors. It seemed Official Jill was closely attached to her childhood.

"We will not be looking at these all in one session, or even in one week." Official Jill flipped through the pages of her own packet. "I do want you to look over each constellation and start looking at the skies. Familiarize yourself with the phases of the moon and major stars."

With that, Official Jill dismissed the class. I was glad I hadn't had more time to daze off, or I would have started to use my constellation maps as the dot-to-dot coloring sheet I had thought it to be.

I gathered all the papers I had collected throughout the day and piled them neatly on top of my books. It was time to get a book bag from the shop. Going to the mixer the night before had created some difficulties today.

It took me by surprise that Mark had left the classroom already. I picked up my stack of belongings and noticed Michelle had left too. I kept a sigh inside and hoped I could figure out how to get back to the Keep stairs, let alone my room.

"That was a surprise."

"Ah!" I shrieked as Mark came out of the shadows on the wall. "What the hells? Don't just pop up like that!" I tried to slow my thumping heart, but I was tired and now the dizzy sensation reappeared, which made me irritated.

Mark's face looked genuinely apologetic. "I'm sorry, I was just trying to stay out of everyone's way as I waited for you." He held his hand out to me with a smile, daring me to grab it.

I did.

The warming rush of butterflies in my stomach wasn't so much a surprise as it had been before, but it felt more powerful, like it would soon suffocate me if I didn't accept it. He kissed the back of my hand warmly and led me down the spiral stairs.

"I'll walk you back to your room," he said. I wanted to ask how he knew where my room was, but I assumed he was the one who'd made sure I arrived back at my room last night.

I let Mark lead me to the bottom of the tower,

through corridors and past the Great Hall, whose doors were still open wide, but the torchers were extinguished. We ascended the great staircase until we came to the landing where it split into several directions, vertically and horizontally. We went up a few levels before going down a long corridor to more stairs. At the top of these, I finally recognized where I was or where I was close to.

"I know you missed homeroom this morning." Mark tried to hide a smile. "So let me give you a couple pointers about this floor.

"This is the first-year dormitories. There are no teachers, classrooms, or upperclassmen. Once you get to second year, you'll move to a tower or a different part of the Keep that houses students of your specialty. These," Mark stopped at a door that had an identical one opposite it, "are the showers. Don't lock yourself out of your room while showering."

I grimaced at the thought of that.

"This floor has two hallways that cross together to form a commons area in the middle, which is this. From here, the layout is the same on all four sides."

I turned in a circle and saw old couches, patterned rugs, and rickety coffee tables. Everything was in the same spot. The only things I could try to use as a marker were the paintings on the wall. Rather, the lack of one on the left wall that we passed to head towards my room. We walked down the seemingly endless hallway of dimly lit doorways. I counted to thirteen.

"I believe this is yours, and this is where I must leave you." Mark leaned close to me, smiled, and kissed me. This wasn't a kiss on the hand or the cheek. It was deep and sensual. I felt his hand on my cheek and the nape of my neck. When he let go, I was breathless, not wanting to open my eyes. "I'll see you at breakfast."

I wanted nothing more but to pull him into my room and keep him by my side forever. He didn't give me that option but instantly turned on his heel and walked down the hallway. I didn't even know what part of the castle his specialty was housed in.

With my head swimming, I fished my key out of my pocket and unlocked my door. Still no roommate. It was lonely, and a bit scary, to sleep in this room. Fortunately, I was tired and worn out from last night and the day's activities. My head hit the pillow just moments after getting undressed and setting the clock for seven bells; papers and books lay toppled on the desk where I'd dropped them. I had so much to do to get organized. I fell asleep making a to-do list in my head.

Chapter 13

I woke feeling rejuvenated. Remnants of my imaginary list of tasks trickled through my mind until they fell onto parchment from the ink on my quill. I added a few extra things I hadn't thought up the night before, like a keychain and fabric to use for blinds.

The bookshop had been quite extensive, but it didn't seem to be a place with household items. What happened if I lost all my hair pins before returning home for winter break? I lost those two-pronged pieces of wood faster than I caught a Pebble on fire.

TAP! TAP! TAP!

I looked around my room cautiously. There didn't seem to be any extra space where someone could be hiding, but the hair on my arms was standing and I knew I could feel the presence of someone. Something. Was someone spying on me? Jensen had warned me...

TAP! TAP! TAP!

The noise came again, more fervently than before. It was probably another student next door or in the hallway. Actually, it was probably Mark! I felt giddy and ran to the door. I was still in my nightgown.

I swung the door open but saw no one. Feeling slightly dejected, my eyes looked down, and I saw a woven box. It looked more like a cage than a box, complete with a twiggy knob on top to pick it up. I carried it into my room, setting it on my desk. Something was moving inside.

"What the...?"

TAP! TAP! TAP!

The noise was coming from the creature inside. It looked like it was jumping up and hitting its head on the top of the cage. Was it safe to let out?

I knelt down before my desk to peer inside the cage. It was only a foot tall, including the handle on top. The glare I was faced with took me aback in more ways than one. The deep, purple eyes stared at me like I was a bug to crush. They took up most of its face, sitting above a small nose and pursed lips. If I had to guess, I would guess it was female. She had a fragile bone structure, long eyelashes, and delicate, pointed ears.

TAP! TAP! TAP!

The creature was getting more insistent and hit the lid to her prison harder. She wasn't jumping though.

Magnificently blue, purple, and green wings spurred her quickly up and down, letting her smash her hands on the roof. I sat back on my heels, mesmerized.

"What are you?"

TAP TAP TAP TAP TAP TAP!

"Okay, okay." I scooted closer on my knees and slowly opened the top. The creature flew out and landed on a book. I had expected her to fly around the room until she found her way out. "Uh, hello there."

"Hello, Terhese," the creature said.

I couldn't respond. This little flying creature had understood me and responded. I sat and stared.

"I am your Helper."

"M-my Helper?" I stammered. "But what are you?" I felt myself turn red.

"I am a fairy," she said, obviously annoyed by my ignorance.

"You're a fairy!" I exclaimed. I'd heard stories, more like rumors, about fairies. They were known to be mischievous and dangerous winged beasts. I had imagined something quite different. Definitely not something so human-like. She didn't have claws or fangs, nor fur or scales. The biggest difference between me and her were the wings ... aside from the size, of course.

"Yes, I'm a fairy. Before you ask any more questions, let me give you the introduction.

"I am your Helper. My name is Lenetta. I can help you with many things throughout your stay at the Academy, including showing you around the castle and grounds, helping you abide by the rules of the Academy when doing classwork and on your free time, sending and retrieving mail, and running small errands if needed. I will not give you answers to homework questions, nor will I attend exams with you. I am not to be locked in any type of box or put anywhere besides the nest I arrived in. If at any time you are no longer needing a Helper, it is your responsibility to return me." Lenetta spoke quickly and in a monotone until she took a breath.

"Do not forget that I need food, water, and sleep. Lastly, do not lose me."

I mentally reviewed the introduction Lenetta had spewed, making sure I hadn't missed anything not commonsensical. If these things had to be mentioned, it was because it had happened before, which was almost laughable, but I held it in.

"Okay, now you can ask questions."

"It seems easy enough." I nodded slowly, still staring at her. "What do you do when I go to class?"

Out of all the questions that I wanted to ask—Where are fairies from? What do you eat? How many are there at the Academy? Do you breathe fire and steal babies? Did you help the Ràej in their tyrannical rule?—I asked that.

Lenetta closed her long-lashed eyes and looked up mischievously. She looked like she could be a dangerous creature as that point. "Whatever I please."

In those first few moments with Lenetta, I could see how Helpers might have been locked in places or *accidentally* lost. If the other fairies were like her, they were a feisty species. At least I didn't have to keep her if I didn't need or want her. She watched me get ready, quietly sitting on my bedpost. If she were a human girl, she would be pretending to clean her nails as she feigned no interest in me.

"Would you like to come to breakfast with me?" I asked awkwardly as I grabbed my books for the day. Lenetta flew from her perch and a little ahead of me but at eye level.

"It is customary for your Helper to accompany you everywhere for the first week," Lenetta responded, as monotone as when she said her introduction.

"Okay." I was excited to show her off. "Should I grab you food or—"

"I'm not your pet rabbit," she remarked and flew to the door, opening it with a wave of her hand. It was apparent that she wouldn't always be monotone and that she had magic. I couldn't help but wonder if she used a tiny Pebble or if she had power like the Ràej. Like me.

I let Lenetta fly as she would. Mostly, she stayed about a foot in front of me and just over my head. When we passed other people, she would fly high and then come back down.

I was alert and watching the air, actively looking for other Helpers. It wasn't until we reached the Great Hall that I saw how many students had Helpers.

They were everywhere. Purple, blue, and green were zipping through the air. They sounded like tinkling bells. Here and there, I saw an orange or red, but they seemed rare. The flash of colored wings above distracted me from everything until Lenetta's form flew into my face.

"Terhese!" she shouted and batted her wings on my cheek. It grabbed my attention so quickly my heart skipped a beat.

"Ah! What?"

"I am going up." Lenetta pointed to the fairy-filled ceiling. "I will come back when you call me. You don't have to shout. Just say my name and I will hear you. Your friends are in line over there."

"How do you know who my friends are?" I looked to find Natalie and Shannon standing in line. When I looked back to Lenetta, she was gone. I gave up on trying to locate her after a few short seconds and jumped in line with my friends.

Natalie gushed about the library as soon as she saw

me. "You wouldn't believe it! Our whole primary school could fit into that place. Unfortunately, most of it is off limits to first years, but you would love it anyway. There were dozens of nooks and crannies to study in."

I did love reading. It had always helped me to excel in my studies and kept me occupied when there was no school. Granted, reading was what led me to try using magic that I was incapable of doing. This led to small explosions, a few fires, and many bizarre incidents. Ironic that it didn't matter how much I studied or practiced Pinching; Ràej could not pinch.

"Terhese! Natalie!" Maisy waved us down as we left the line with laden trays. "Come sit with us."

I could see from Natalie's demeanor that she was torn between walking to the table we had claimed and sitting with a table of new friends. She loved both. The attention won her over though, and a smile spread across her face as she led Shannon and me over to the table.

"Maisy, this is our friend Shannon. Shannon, this is Maisy, Evan, Danielle, Tilly—" as Natalie introduced Shannon to the ever-growing group of people, I stopped listening when I heard Tilly's name. I tried not to glare, but her dismissive glance at me and exaggerated welcome to Shannon irked me. Our brief truce during move-in had expired.

Somehow, Natalie and I were able to sit across from

each other, like we had for the past fifteen years of school. Natalie was sitting next to Maisy, and I practically pushed Shannon into the open seat next to Tilly so I wouldn't have to sit there.

"Did any of you get a Helper?" Maisy leaned into the table on her elbows; her excitement was palpable, and it ran through all of us simultaneously.

It was reassuring that I wasn't the only one with a Helper. I'd known Natalie was going to get one, but it had still made me feel foolish and ignorant to need one. The only thing keeping me from standing out like a sore thumb was my wardrobe. At least my Helper sounded like she was low-key. Everyone had been surprised by the brashness of their Helpers.

"Meola seemed very sweet," Natalie said. I couldn't tell if she was being honest or was just trying to be polite.

"You're lucky!" Maisy exclaimed. "My Helper sounded like she would only help if absolutely needed and she is my last resort. I guess we'll see what happens after the first week." Maisy shrugged.

"What do you mean?" Shannon asked and looked up at the sparkling mass of Helpers.

"They have to accompany us everywhere for the first week. After that, it's assumed we know how to get to our classes and everything else is nonessential," Maisy said matter-of-factly.

"After that," Tilly chimed in, "your Helper becomes a little scatter-brained. If you have a good relationship with your Helper, they will be more likely to keep helping you. If you do not, and you are not nice, then they won't be nice."

"And what does that mean?" Shannon asked nervously, looking up again.

"It means you can have a Helper that will tell you when you're making an explosive or a love potion." Mark sat down next to me. He leaned over and kissed my cheek.

"You're looking great today. How's your Helper?" Mark looked up slightly but didn't show too much interest. I felt his hand lie comfortably on my thigh; the heat warmed my body and filled my cheeks.

I looked up and, surprisingly, saw my Helper. Before I pointed her out to Mark, our eyes connected and I felt it wasn't the time to do so.

"She's great," I blurted out. "I've never seen a fairy. She's beautiful. Such an amazing creature."

Mark nodded and began eating. He didn't seem like he was listening to anyone. I felt like Lenetta was listening to all of us. The conversations bounced around from Helpers to library, Astronomy and Baking to the professors and students. Occasionally, I would look up to see the behaviors of the Helpers, too. It was similar to the students; energetic at the beginning of the meal and calm and collected at the end.

Lenetta appeared at my shoulder again. Her feet were bare, and she stood on my shoulder. I felt the disturbance of the air at my ear more than the weight of her. She spoke into my ear. Her voice was so quiet and gentle I couldn't believe she'd talked so loudly before. It seemed absurd that a being so little would talk at the same volume of a human, but I swear she had.

"It's time to go to class," she said in my ear. I looked up at the ceiling and most of the Helpers were gone. My schedule was tucked into a book. I didn't know how Lenetta knew what class I had or what time it was.

"Thank you," I said quietly.

"What was that?" Mark leaned in and snaked his arm around my back to hold my waist. I wasn't sure what the protocol was with the Helpers. Was I to share everything they said or was it polite to keep those conversation to yourself?

"I have to go to class." I leaned into him and let him kiss my forehead. Every time he touched me, I felt blissful.

"Oh no!" Natalie wiped her mouth and started piling remnants of food onto her tray. "We have Cauldrons, don't we?"

Mark tightened his grip on me a little and pulled my

face to his with his other hand. His lips were soft, and I could feel the sparks fly. Maisy made a cat call, which was followed by some whistles from Evan, then students from close-by tables joined in.

"Go have a great day." Mark smiled.

I laughed with the overflowing giddiness and slight embarrassment from the audience we had. I couldn't complain though. Whatever was happening between us was burning hot and happening fast. He kissed my hand and I walked away with Natalie.

"I can't say I'm not happy for you," Natalie said as soon as we were rushing to class, "but I can't help thinking I'm glad I didn't know about you and my brother before. I might've felt a little sibling protectiveness about this."

I couldn't tell if Natalie was making a joke or not. She seldom joked because she was too naive and trusting to understand one. That made this feel like a slap in the face. More so that I had actually forgotten about Nathan. And Jensen. I wondered where he was.

Our Cauldrons class was in the same corridor as the bookshop. We ended up being early since it wasn't far away. The room was smaller than the many-leveled bookshop. It had one level and was more narrow than other classrooms, but it sloped downwards towards the back to an unlit area.

"What do you think is over there?" I asked Natalie.

"Storage probably."

I nodded but wasn't convinced. It felt like there was draft coming in with a fish-like stench attached to it.

We sat next to each other, claiming one of the eight bar tables that fit only two. A longer table in front was full of odds and ends and an Official with hair that poked out every which way. If I had to guess, I'd say her hair used to be reddish. That was very rare these days. I heard rumors that the trolls used to have different colors of hair, similar to the bright colors girls streaked their hair with for events.

"Morning, class," the woman at the desk croaked. If I hadn't known trolls were extinct, I would've believed her to be one. Even her voice seemed a little inhuman. "Welcome to Cauldrons. You can call me Professor Hadritch. I am proud to say, I am *not* an Official."

This proclamation created an astonished buzz throughout the class. This was the second teacher I had that was not an Official. Every student worked towards being an Official. We had been told all through primary that an Official was what we were supposed to be. Help keep Omneth safe and protect all magics. I wondered what Jensen would think of that.

"We have a lot to cover today." Professor Hadritch started talking as students were still settling in. "I am passing around the rules and procedures you will be quizzed on next class. These are *not* guidelines. These are the laws of my classroom.

"We will be handling dangerous substances. This is *not* your baking class. You get two chances and you're out of my class.

"Let's begin."

The teacher was able to talk about rules, policies, and procedures for the full class period. It was boring and tedious. The pack of papers she gave us was almost as thick as the Astrology packet. We read through the first half; the second half contained all the ingredients we would be using, their uses, side effects, and more. She hadn't been joking when she said they were dangerous. It seemed a little bit of anything could be beautiful, but the wrong dose could be lethal.

Natalie gasped slightly when she heard something truly appalling to her. Whatever a nerfig nut was, it could make your body erupt with pus-oozing boils within hours of consumption. Hadritch said the most dangerous thing about the nerfig was the time it took for someone to realize they had eaten that instead of the common Omneth nut used to make flour. If they didn't take the antidote before the boils reached their insides, they'd die by choking on their own blood.

At the end of class, the chatter was non-stop. Students were excited and nervous about what they would come across during this semester. I had my mind set on getting everything I needed from the bookshop.

"Rhese, you want to go check out the beach for a couple hours?" Natalie was tying her hair into a low braid as she spoke. "Maisy invited us. She'll be waiting in front of the Great Hall."

"Um." That sounded more tempting than the bookshop. Before I responded, Lenetta appeared at my shoulder. I felt, more than heard, her urging me to go to the bookshop. "No, you go. I have so much to get at the bookshop and get organized.

"I'll go next time though," I reassured Natalie after seeing her slightly sunken face. "I have one afternoon class, then you can show me the beach. Give me the grand tour."

"It's a date!" Natalie smiled, waved, and hurried towards the Great Hall.

I turned the other way and was thankful the bookshop had no line today. Lenetta flew a little ahead of me. I didn't know her well enough to understand each expression, but the one she wore seemed almost worried.

"Welcome to the bookshop!" An excited second year stood in front of me. "Do you need help finding anything today?"

"No, thank you," Lenetta said. It was amazing how she could change the volume of her voice so drastically.

"Do you know how to find all these ingredients?" I

217

asked Lenetta, pulling papers from a book I was carrying. I sorely needed a book strap or bag.

"I can help."

The vague answer from my Helper fairy made me feel like I'd be spending more time here than I would've with the second year. I wasn't about to refuse Lenetta though, so I followed her through the maze of the bookshop. Other Helpers were leading their students. Some of them seemed to be being chased by their students.

"This is the supply closet for most of the baking supplies." Lenetta hovered in front of a heavy metal door. I had to use both hands to open it. Inside was a huge temperature difference. Dry and cool. Large bins lined the long wall, each filled with a type of material for baking.

Each container was stone, with a thin stone lid and handwritten label. A hand shovel lay on top of each one. I walked down each wall, reading off the different soils, most of which I recognized from my baking class.

Hooks were pinned into the fourth wall to hold various items for baking: stone mallets, rolling pins, measuring cups, sifters.

"I thought the classroom would be supplied with equipment," I said absentmindedly.

"These are just spares," Lenetta said, flying overhead and perching on a torch post. It seemed she didn't mind the heat or light coming from it. "In case something melts or breaks during class."

Everything at the Academy seemed to hold a little danger. I had been melting things for years. I wondered what they would do if I burned a hole in the floor.

It didn't take long to scoop the needed soils into the hanging canvas bags. The weight of the bags increased quickly. I battled with myself on whether I should take two trips, but I didn't think I would have time to come back again before my next class.

"Don't tell anyone." Lenetta sighed and waved her tiny hand over the pile of bags I was struggling with. They became weightless. I tried not to let my eyes bug out of my head, but I knew she'd used her own magic to do what a Weightless Pebble did.

She flew out the door to the main room. I was still dumbfounded. Higher magic was supposed to have been eliminated by the Ràej, who were also supposed to have been eliminated. Did the Officials know about this? If they did, what else did they lie about?

"Terhese, you coming?"

I rushed out of the storeroom with the bags, closing the door behind me and erasing my stupor. I still needed to complete my list, and I was more appreciative of Lenetta's help than scared.

Lenetta was able to direct me to the appropriate

sections and aisles. It took almost an hour to gather everything I needed. When we arrived back at my room, my arms were full of bags and boxes, haphazardly stacked. Fellow students must have thought I was extremely strong, unless their Helpers had done the same thing. I didn't think so.

"Thank you," I said to Lenetta after I deposited my bundles on my bed. I could see their returned weight pressing into my quilt. She landed demurely on my windowsill.

"We aren't supposed to."

"I won't tell," I vowed to her and told myself that I couldn't tell Natalie either.

"I know."

Lenetta seemed stoic as I bustled around my room, unpacking luggage from home and parcels from the bookshop. It didn't seem like I was going to have a roommate, so I used one wardrobe for my school things and one for clothing and shoes. When everything was put away, I felt like I was the Ràej queen herself. I had more space than I had ever had before. It was time for my last class of the day, so I had to stop my reveling.

Chapter 14

I grabbed my new shoulder bag, filled it with just what I needed for the one class, and left my room, Lenetta by my side. This was the class I had been most excited for since I could remember: Pebble Pinching. Though Jensen had told me I wouldn't be able to pinch, I still wished I could. Who wanted to be a hunted Ràej with some power but unable to use it and unable to do what others could?

It was time to put this thing to the test.

Pebble Pinching was held in a large room behind the Great Hall. I was thankful Lenetta guided me, for I never would have found it by myself. The path had no stairs to traverse, but the corridor was long and winding. I would have turned around at several points if she hadn't told me to keep going. It felt like the path was moving downwards; the temperature suggested it too.

It was by far my largest class. I saw a few familiar faces,

but no one I had made friends with yet. It did look like I was the last student to arrive, so it was no wonder I hadn't seen anyone on the long journey. This room was more of a cavern with bleachers against one wall where the students were sitting. As I went to sit, I saw Maisy waving from a middle row. A small relief to have a friend, especially when the other faces I recognized were Tilly and her posse.

Maisy was sitting right below them, but I really had no other choice. I gritted my teeth and made my way to her, waving hello to the others.

"Are you not beyond excited for this class?" Maisy squeaked with her own excitement.

I was more nervous than anything. "Yes." I tried to replicate her voice with my own.

All the bleachers were filled with chatter. It was electrifying. I even found myself talking to Tilly and her friends. Though this was a first-year class, they said they hadn't had room for it last year.

I assumed the teacher of this class would be an Official. His appearance left no doubt. A hard-eyed, thin-lipped man with high cheek bones and a lack of facial hair, as was the Official way. Official Loren. The simplicity of it just added to the Slate-likeness of him.

"Raise your hand if you have pinched a Pebble before," he said. The unanimous ruffle of arms shooting in the air filled the cavernous room. "That means I am teaching an entire class of delinquents."

All hands dropped and the silence was painful. We all knew it was illegal until we passed a certification exam. That's when our magicprint was recorded. I was just glad I wasn't the only slow-wit to fall for that question.

"Starting now, there will be no unauthorized use of Pebbles until you pass your PPC exam. This includes practicing in your dormitory, an empty classroom, or on the grounds." Official Loren's eyes were black and beady like those of a mischievous rat. "You may receive written permission to practice under a licensed Pebble Pincher. Certified students do not count, but we do have some licensed interns."

I wondered if Nathan had been licensed or certified. I hadn't known there was difference. I realized more and more how ignorant I was about the Official world and the Academy.

Jensen was probably licensed.

"Okay, since everyone has pinched before, leave your stuff on your seat and make a circle around me."

Awkwardly, we did as he said. I stood next to Maisy and a girl named Pamela. As people squeezed in and the circle expanded, Pamela was replaced with Travis. When everyone was finally in a spot surrounding Official Loren, he tapped our shoulders in turn. "One, two, one, two, one, two."

It quickly dawned on me that I wouldn't be with Maisy or Travis, but I hoped I would be with Pamela instead of someone I didn't like. She seemed easy enough to like.

"If you are a one, turn to your left," Official Loren shouted so we could all hear. "This will be your partner today." I turned to my left and saw Maisy. "Okay, teams, spread out in the room. Introduce yourselves, and I will come around with today's activity."

Maisy grabbed me by the arms and pulled me to an open spot. She was smiling from ear to ear.

"How have your classes been? What's your favorite so far? How is Mark?" Maisy's questions came rapid fire, but I filled her in on everything. Everything except Lenetta. She was my secret.

"One and two, names please." Official Loren appeared at my side with a paper.

"I'm one. Terhese Neems." I saw his lip twitch ever so slightly. News of my Telepathy class must have traveled to everyone.

"That makes me two!" Maisy said cheerily. "Maisy Nolene."

"Thank you, ladies. Here is a pouch of Pebbles. There are five for each of you. Do not start until I finish giving instructions." He looked around the room, making sure everyone was obeying. "Welcome to class."

"He was quite charming." Maisy smiled.

I laughed at her. "You think everyone is charming."

"Almost everything has a certain charm if you look hard enough." Maisy's glazed over face charged suddenly. "Except the way you eat."

Her Official etiquette and my farm etiquette, so she had coined, were vastly different. A few groups turned their heads to see what had started our laughter.

"Ah-hem, ladies." Official Loren quieted us and the rest of the room. Before we could pinch, we listened to his half-hour lecture. The whole time I wondered why we couldn't have done this while we had been seated.

It wasn't the most boring lecture of the day, nor of the week. I was actually fascinated by it. Official Loren talked about how Pinching worked physically and magically. He gave us more information about baking than Baking 101 had. Pinching needed correctly made Pebbles that needed to be pinched in the right way, at the right time. Squeezing our thumb and forefinger at the wrong angle could change the effect of the Pebble. It could create a dud, an explosion, or something you just didn't want.

Pebbles made outside controlled areas had a much higher chance for error when Pinching. A Pebble's soil being made with the wrong consistency or a Pebble being underbaked or overbaked could all be contributing factors.

"Keep in mind," Official Loren stood up, "we are not fighters. The Officials protect the peace, and we ensure no division between lesser and higher magics again.

"Pebbles bring us together. They level the playing field in case a higher magic reappears. We will be learning some defensive Pebbles, but most Pebbles you will use are for day-to-day use. I am going to teach you the right way to pinch so you don't blow up your house when you want the floor swept."

This elicited laughter. I couldn't help but think of what he started with. The Officials *protect the peace.* I wished Jensen were there so he could tell me what he thought of that.

When we were allowed to practice, we used a Sound Pebble. These were more for entertaining children and were closer to Play Pebbles. We practiced distance. If we threw too far, the Pebble might not work. Too close, it might react too strongly or smolder in fire, depending on the magic inside.

I was instantly frustrated when my first one bounced around another group's feet, not breaking at all. It didn't look like I was the only one having problems. Travis kept throwing his too hard at the ground, so it exploded at Pamela's feet, catching the edge of her skirt on fire. The teacher regarded this with mild interest.

Maisy was a natural. She said it came from growing up in an Official household.

"My parents were always strict." Maisy twisted the Pebble nimbly over her fingers. "But they also believed in perfection. I've had a tutor since I was four!"

With a little flick of her wrist, she released the Pebble. It landed about a foot in front of me and opened perfectly. The magic was supposed to use the Pebble as an energy source once it was released. The more the Pebble consumed, the more powerful the magic and the less remnants. Maisy's Pebbles left crumbs, and the sound was released at the desired pitch and tone.

When I finally made my Pebble open, it cracked like an egg, letting out a shrill hiss.

"You did it!" Maisy exclaimed.

I winced. "Not really." I thought I'd just thrown it hard enough and enough times that it broke.

"You'll get it, Terhese."

When the class ended, the dungeon smelled more dank than it had when we had first entered. It looked like there had been a rockslide with all the debris. A faint smell of burnt hair lingered in the room, too. I wanted to see who had fringed themselves or their partner, but Maisy was in a rush to get to the beach.

"Did you invite Mark?" Maisy asked, leading me

through another honeycomb of corridors I had yet to go through. I couldn't tell if she knew where she was going or if she was just following people ahead of us.

"Oh, no," I stammered. "I told Natalie I would meet her this afternoon. I don't know when his classes are."

"He'll probably be there. I believe Natalie said Evan was going, so I'm assuming a lot of that group will be there."

I wasn't sure how I felt about the group she was referring to. Even quiet, reserved Natalie seemed to have melded into it.

I could smell the ocean before I could see it. It was low tide, and the smell of fish was strong. We had to walk a decent ways to the water where students were standing. For most of us, this would have been the first time to see the ocean. The unending expanse of water, wave upon wave.

"Terhese! Over here!" Natalie shouted and waved at us. She was sitting on a seaweed-covered rock, higher up on the beach. "You guys got here at the perfect time. Take off your shoes and socks, and let's go feel the water."

Maisy and I found a dry spot on the rock to sit down. Several piles of belongings were scattered over the outcropping of rocks. Here and there, I saw a shelled creature clutching onto a piece of clothing, pulling itself over a fold, and searching for microscopic food. Once I stuffed my socks into my ankle boots, I picked up a creature in a spikey orange shell. Its claw immediately covered its head and disappeared into the shell. All I could see was the smooth bump of its curved pincher. I put it gently on the palm of my hand, watching its legs slowly creep out, lifting the shell on its back and poking its stalked eyes out.

"Ew, what is that?" Maisy asked in disgust.

Natalie was barefoot next to her. "I remember your Aunt Chloe telling us about those."

"Yeah," I whispered, as though it would hear me speak. "She called them hermit crabs. They aren't born with shells, like snails, so they have to find one to live in. As they grow, they find bigger shells."

I lifted the little creature up by the shell, placed it on a strand of kelp, and stepped off the rock and into the sand. It was warm and soft. I dug my toes in, lifted my foot, and let the sand fall between my toes. As I followed Natalie down to the water's edge, the sand became wet, hard, and cooler. With each step, a little indent was left behind, some filling with water or bubbles.

"Is it cold?" I asked when I saw Natalie's face turn from an excited smile to an eyebrow-raised, voiceless shriek.

"Ooh." Natalie grabbed my hand. "It's refreshing. Come in with me."

229

I squeezed Natalie's hand as the cold water washed up my feet. It was refreshing and not as cold after a few seconds. Maisy stepped in next to me.

"Do you guys know how to swim?" she asked, pulling her dress over her head and throwing it on the beach. In just her underclothes, she submerged herself under the water. Maisy had surprised me again. Her Official etiquette didn't always align with her spontaneity.

Natalie dared me with her eyebrows, pulled her dress off, and threw it up on the beach. I didn't know how to swim and my heart was already panicking from seeing Maisy's head disappear beneath the water. She popped up just ten feet away.

"Wait for us!" Natalie waded into the water and closed the distance by making a couple of strong, swift strokes with her arms. "Rhese, come on!"

I looked around to see if anyone would be watching me. Everyone seemed too preoccupied with getting in the water themselves. I undressed quickly and tossed my dress and then hurried into the water until it was up to my waist, looking down at my eerily white feet. When I tried to look farther out, the water was deep and blue, nothing else. The unknown in those depths scared me. I wasn't sure how far out the Devil's Trench was, but I knew it was in the direction I was looking. As I stood in a fear-filled daydream of needle-toothed monsters with long tails and fins, the tide started to come in.

The waves rolled, increasing my apprehension of going to my friends, who were getting farther and farther away. The swells seemed to slowly grow.

It's all in my mind.

It wasn't. After a handful of waves hitting my chest, the next wave rose high and made me turn towards the beach to save my face from the burn of the salt water. The strength of the water pulled my feet out from under me. It was unlike anything I could have imagined. Panic rushed through me. I blindly flung my arms out, hoping to find something I could hold onto. I knew my feet were somewhere behind me, horizontal to the rest of my body, but I didn't know which way was up. The fear was filling my mouth and nose.

Not fear, water!

Overwhelmed, I clenched my fists and closed my mouth. I was not going to be humiliated again at this blasted academy. My only thought was to get out of the water. To fill my lungs with air.

Water rushed over my skin, erupting in hundreds of tiny bubbles. Instead of feeling like I was being pulled down, it felt like I was being propelled. I felt the warm air on my face before I realized I'd broken the surface.

"Terhese, what happened?" Natalie grabbed my arm.

I coughed and blinked. Evan and Mark were

swimming up.

"I think she was stuck in an undertow," Maisy said, treading water to make room for the two guys.

I spit out more water and looked at the beach, nodding in agreement. Though I wasn't positive about what had happened, I didn't really think it was an undertow, whatever that was.

"Terhese, you okay?" Mark was between Natalie and me. I nodded again, not ready to trust my salt-scarred throat with speech.

The absence of ground beneath me was daunting. It felt so alien. I tried to see anything below the water, but I could only see a flash of someone's limbs. Aside from not knowing what was beneath, I was struggling with keeping my head above the water. The water felt refreshing until it splashed in my mouth and the salty taste made me sputter.

I could feel the waves getting big again. They moved our group up and down. I watched them crash as they got closer to the beach.

"The tide's coming in," Evan noted. "You guys wanna head to the beach?"

"Yeah, let's have the waves carry us in," Maisy said, instantly lying on her back and floating.

"I don't know how to do that," I admitted. I seemed to be the only one out of sorts in this endless expanse of water. Though Natalie had grown up where I did, her aunt lived near the North Coast, probably close to where Maisy grew up.

"I'll help you." Mark gave me his broad smile and grabbed one of my hands. Reassurance rushed through me at his touch.

I nodded in response to Natalie's worried brow and Maisy's intrigued one. They turned towards the beach with Evan and rode the waves on their stomachs.

"I don't want to teach you how to swim when we are this far out and the tide is coming in, but I'll keep you afloat." Mark pulled me behind him by the hand and put both my hands on his shoulders. "Hold on here and wrap your legs around me so I can move my legs without kicking you."

I held tight to his muscular torso with my legs and had a brief glimpse of my night in the cabin with Jensen. Before I became too distracted, Mark's feet found solid ground. He lifted one of my hands to his lips and planted a long kiss as he walked a few feet more.

"Okay, can you touch here?" Mark pulled me in front of him.

I was confident the ground was just under me. As I let my feet drift down to the ground, I realized too late that I couldn't touch yet. Mark grabbed my arm to keep the water from going over my head, but another wave came up and washed over both of us. I didn't get lost in this wave, but Mark held me in front of him by the elbows, lifting me with him as the waves came and went. He helped me get to waist-high water and then intertwined his fingers in mine.

"How did you never learn how to swim?" Mark was playfully pushing me out and pulling me in like a human accordion. No longer in danger of drowning, I found the water to be enjoyable. It gave me a feeling of freedom I hadn't experienced before.

"My Aunt Chloe raised me by herself." I shrugged. "We have a lake up the hill, but I spent a lot of time helping her with her tomatoes."

"Tomatoes?" Mark asked. That big smile made me laugh as I told him about Aunt Chloe's tomatoes.

"She has the best recipes for everything."

"How much can you do with a tomato?" Mark pulled me close and kissed my neck, right below my ear.

"Well, there is salsa and sauce. You can make jam, ketchup, or tomato paste, or you can stew them and can them for later."

Every tomato product came with a kiss. I realized my feet weren't touching the ground anymore. Startled, I looked at the beach and noticed it was farther away than it had been a moment ago.

How long had I talked about tomatoes?

"Did we drift out?" I asked, staring out at the horizon

of the ocean, which was getting darker as the sun set in the west.

"Don't worry." He kissed my cheek and pulled me to his back again. "The tide is coming in fast. Let's get to the beach before the ocean claims our clothes."

I was glad he couldn't see my look of mortification as I realized I'd be walking out of the water in my soaking wet underclothes.

He held my hand and led me up the shallow water and onto the wet sands; formations of bubbles showed where waves had previously hit. The air on my skin gave rise to goosebumps, which were soon relieved by the hot and dry sand at the base of the rocks where my clothes were.

"Where did everyone go?" I grabbed my dress but noticed no other piles lying around nor people on the beach.

"Come on." Mark beckoned me with a toss of his head. "I'll show you."

I stuffed my dress into my bag and held my shoes with my fingers, trying to keep everything dry. The sun wouldn't be up for much longer.

It looked like we were going back to the castle, but before we reached the door, Mark turned towards the unruly forest. His feet were bare, but he didn't seem worried about stepping on anything, so I followed. His hand found mine, and I lost any reservation about cutting my foot or being attacked by a woodland creature.

We didn't go far before I felt sand under my feet again. The trees thinned out to reveal a circular opening. A dozen or so students were there already. Natalie and Maisy were standing with Tilly and Danielle. It seemed casual yet secretive. As soon as we entered, Mark leaned down and grabbed something from a clay pot.

It was a Pebble. With a practiced and calculated flick of his wrist, Mark pinched the Pebble so it broke hip high. I saw remnants of the shell explode up and down and then seemingly disintegrate as the magic within consumed it.

"A shield," Mark explained. "Technically, students aren't allowed at the beach without attendants if they are first years. And no matter what year you are, there is to be no Pinching, no fire, and no liquor."

With a flourish of his hand, he pointed out the banned activities. Tilly and her friends were passing around a bottle, something Natalie seemed against trying but Maisy was merely hesitant about. Evan was standing with a couple of guys I hadn't met yet, Pinching Pebbles over a large pile of kindling, igniting a roar of flames.

I followed Mark to the fire, wanting to join Natalie but not wanting to take my hand out of Mark's. The fire was warming and slowly drying my wet underclothes as we stood. The heat was very welcome.

"Hey, Evan." Mark shook his hand and those of the other guys. "Luther, Jared. Either of you have a Dry Pebble on you?"

Jared had a small Pebble in his fingers and, without another word or acknowledgement, he pinched it at me. I flinched as I saw the Pebble implode and felt a hot spray of the magic-fueled sediment cover me.

I almost shouted a rebuke but realized my clothes and hair were perfectly dry. A Dry Pebble.

"Oh, wow," I murmured, still touching parts of my thin underclothes. "Thank you. Uh, I'm Terhese."

"Jared."

"Luther."

I nodded as I pulled my dress out of my bag.

"Nice to meet you both," I said, awkwardly putting on my dress as I tried to do so quickly.

"My apologies. I should have introduced you all." Mark gave a sheepish smile and wrapped his arm around my waist, pulling me close to him. "Terhese is my girlfriend."

I couldn't say anything to this unexpected comment. It seemed fast and abrupt, but I batted my eyes and giggled like a primary school girl. Luther and Jared said some sort of congratulations and asked the respectful questions. I saw a weird question lurking in Evan's eyes and a polite smile. But with Mark's touch on my skin, I wasn't worried.

"Terhese!" Natalie jumped in front of me and hugged me. "I can't believe you two are together! You hadn't told me yet."

Natalie's eyes were glossy and her cheeks were flushed. Maisy bumped into Jared, and she looked the same. I was curious what was in the bottle they had been passing around; they hadn't had much time to drink it.

"Did this just happen?" Maisy asked as if it was the most important question. She opened her mouth and feigned pride. "I'd like to take this moment to say that I was the brilliant matchmaker for this relationship before us."

"Oh, Omneth." I turned into Mark's shoulder, trying to hide my face.

"Anyone have a bottle?" Mark was searching the ground by everyone's feet, looking for the brown, clay bottle. Tilly sauntered up, squeezing between Natalie and Evan.

"I have one." She grabbed the cork with her teeth, pulled it out, spit it into the fire, and took a swig. She dramatically played out the intensity of the drink as she bumped against Evan and giggled in his face, pushing Natalie farther away.

I felt more than saw Mark turn a stony eye on Evan.

"I'll take that."

The smell from the bottle Mark gulped from was not

as bad as I had thought it would be, judging from Tilly's reaction. It smelled sickly sweet, like honey. He put it in my hand. I looked at the other girls and some of the guys who were standing around the fire. We hadn't been there for very long, but it seemed like this liquor was wanted. And potent.

"Go on, Terhese," Tilly goaded. "Don't be a Hillgirl!"

"Fuck off, Tilly." I took a deep swig from the bottle. If she hadn't used such slang against me, I probably would have been able to refuse the liquor. Orientation night and the morning after were still fresh in my mind, and I didn't want to let liquor get the best of me again. All she ever made me want to do when I saw her or heard of her was to beat her. Whether I wanted to straight out hit her or just be superior to her in everything, I wasn't quite sure.

Though the outside of the stone bottle was cool on my hand, the liquid was lukewarm. It had been flavored with honey, but it was gross and burned my throat. I licked my lips and pretended it didn't faze me. This elicited a celebratory whoop from the onlookers. Tilly glared at me and swung her arms around Evan.

"Come on, Evan." She tried grabbing Evan's hand, but he pulled out of her reach.

"I think I'm going to stay here," he walked around to Natalie's other side, "and hang out with Natalie."

I watched Tilly's face go from confusion to anger. She obviously didn't experience rejection very often. Instead of grabbing Evan, she grabbed Danielle and stomped off to the rest of their posse at another fire. Natalie had the opposite reaction; she was flushed with excited embarrassment.

Mark gave me a little squeeze, as if it was a victory for him as well. I settled back against his chest, letting him hold me with one arm and pass the bottle to me as it was passed around our little circle. It was nice to see Natalie as happy as she was, talking animatedly and laughing with Evan. I liked Maisy, but I was glad he'd chosen Natalie.

Chapter 15

The first two months of school continued the same as the first week. We all ate together, I walked with at least one of my friends to class, and we went to the beach in any free time we had. I couldn't tell you which couple became closer faster—Mark and me or Natalie and Evan—but Maisy was our solid, dependable fifth wheel. If Natalie was somewhere with Evan, I would have Maisy to hang out with, and if I was with Mark, Natalie would have Maisy.

I had never felt so close to anyone in my life before I met Mark. He was dependable and would even show up where I wasn't expecting him. Natalie had thought it was odd I'd fallen for a guy so quickly and so passionately, but when she fell for Evan, it all made sense to her. I knew she still felt a little weird about her brother and me, but it made me feel more confident about the decision I had made about not telling her about us before.

Maisy was thrilled that we were both dating Official men. She would tell us about how our futures would change if we were married to an Official and how our status would change just by dating someone from the Official city. Though the Academy had plenty of eligible men, it seemed Maisy was not interested in dating. Her joy throughout the day was to live vicariously through us and study as much as she could.

The only one who didn't seem pleased about the dating arrangements, mine specifically, was Lenetta. I'm not sure if it was an Academy rule or personal preference, but Lenetta never joined me at the beach. The first time, she had vanished by the time I reached the entrance to the beach. After that, I asked her what happened.

"I had other things to attend to." Lenetta flew to her nest and closed the little door. I had hung it up in the corner of the room by the window, not knowing whether or not she liked the sun.

It wasn't just the beach. If Mark walked me from class to class or to the Great Hall or anywhere at all, I would feel Lenetta's disappearance. It started with her anger, like a cloud emanating from her tiny body. After a few minutes, there would be nothing. The first week or two, I looked around and called her name to no response. I quickly realized she was disappearing when Mark was there. If it wasn't for that feeling of anger, I would have thought she left because she knew I was safe with him.

The security I felt with him trumped anything else.

"Can you believe it's already midterms?" Natalie twined her arm through mine as we walked through the Commons after Healing towards the Great Hall for lunch. Lenetta was sitting comfortably in a little chair I had made and connected to the opening of my shoulder bag.

"It came so fast!" I exclaimed. Though I'd missed my first Healing class, I had caught on quickly and was excelling at it. Natalie had switched her classes around so she could take Healing at the same time as me. We had just practiced the art of healing with water. After a week of lectures about the different types and temperatures of water and when to use each one, it was great to be able to try it.

"I don't want to go first," Natalie had complained.

"That's okay, I'll go first." I pulled up my sleeve and grabbed the blade shaking in Natalie's hand.

"No!" Natalie slashed her hand with the little blade, leaving a thin line of new blood.

"That was a quick change of mind." I laughed.

"I don't like seeing other people hurt." Natalie smiled, shrugging at her action. "Okay, heal me please."

I put Natalie's hand in my palm and pretended to look at the severity of the wound. We had just sharpened the blade, so I knew it was a clean cut. The blade was very thin, so I knew it wasn't going to be a deep wound. It shouldn't be much wider than a paper cut.

Five bottles of water were lined up on the table next to us. Each one was labelled with its contents and set out alphabetically: cave, elven, glacier, hollow, spring. I grabbed the spring water, pulled the cork out, and poured a drop into Natalie's palm. Still holding her hand in mine, I laid my other hand over hers and closed my eyes.

I could feel where our skin touched and the space between my top hand and hers. I felt the wound. The depth, the size, and the pain. It was more of an irritating itch than pain. The skin wanted to have its bonds reconnected. I felt the water, refreshing but not cold. With a slight urge, I willed the water to move along the length of the wound. I willed it to help the skin grow and mend. I never knew if the water was doing as it should or if I was using my own magic, but I excelled in this class.

"I don't understand." Natalie moved her hand up and down, looking at it as though she would see through an illusion. "There isn't even a line. Like it never happened."

"Well, if it were a bigger wound, the healing process would take longer and there would be larger chance of scarring," I recited from the lecture. It was nice to be able to finally do something right.

244

"I have a Healing Internship, and I can't heal as well as this," Natalie whined. It was true. The one thing I could do, I could do better than most students. I wished I could ask someone if that was a Ràej trait.

"Natalie, you are a great healer!" I reassured her. "You're just not that great at water healing."

We both laughed. Natalie was unable to heal my wound. She hadn't watched which water I'd chosen, and I had to stop her from using the wrong one. The glacier water she'd originally picked was one that would never boil and was always cold. That water was best used for high fevers, festering wounds, or causing frostbite if misused.

But even after Natalie had selected the correct water, she was unable to will the water to heal my hairline wound. When she had given up and started cleaning up our workstation, I waved my hand over my palm and healed myself. It was more of an experiment, but I was secretly proud I could do it so easily.

Natalie skipped with glee as we walked across the Commons. "Just a couple months ago, we were living in the Hills and now we're at the Academy and we're dating Official men! This is all my dreams come true."

I smiled. Coming from the Hills used to be something I would cringe at. If someone called me a Hillgirl, or anything relating to that, I would fume. Now I felt proud to be away from the Hills. It made me feel confident and strong.

"I heard the study rooms at the library are going to get booked fast," I said, knowing Lenetta would remind me about this again later today. "Do you want to go put our names on the list after lunch?"

"Evan invited me to go to the study rooms in his tower." Natalie's step faltered, and she gave me with a worried look. "Please don't be angry."

"Oh, no, of course not," I assured her and started us walking again. "That will be fun. And romantic! You guys will be locked up in the room all night for hours and hours."

This made us erupt into giggles and more raucous jokes as we walked into the Great Hall for lunch.

"Hey ladies." Mark wound his arm around me and kissed me cheek. "What are we laughing about today?"

Lenetta left her chair and buzzed enough times around Mark's head to make him give an irritated glance before she flew up to the ceiling with the other Helpers. The number of Helpers had decreased dramatically since the first week, but I had connected with Lenetta and didn't want to lose her. When I told her it was up to her and that she could leave me at any time, I thought she wouldn't return after dinner, but she did.

"Just girl stuff." Natalie smiled and walked over to

where Evan was standing in line. I turned back to Mark and saw a weird expression cross his face.

"You okay?" I asked, trying to catch his eyes.

"Yeah, yeah." He looked down at me and kissed me. "I'm fine. Let's get in line." I let him lead me over to Natalie and Evan.

I was never left wanting when I went through the buffet line at the Academy. Fresh vegetables were always available, along with an array of meats, steaming soups, and warm breads with crocks of soft butter. I did tire of the dessert table, but Natalie and Maisy never did. Today, I fancied a simple, tomato-base soup with sourdough.

"Terhese, you have Astronomy tonight?" Maisy asked.

My mouth was full of bread, so I nodded.

"I had it last night, and you are going to love it! You go out on the mainland and look at the stars from a different spot to see if you can tell the direction and constellations." Maisy picked up her sandwich, lifting her little finger on each side as she did so.

"That sounds more fun than looking at the same sky and charts for two hours." I took a sip of my coffee, not needing the caffeine at this time of day but enjoying the warmth it gave me.

"Make sure you dress warmly," Mark advised. "It looks like it will be a chilly night, and it's a bit of a walk to where we go."

"Oh right! You're the teacher's aide for that class, aren't you?" Maisy asked.

Mark nodded and smiled. "Yes, ma'am, I am. It's the best class to be an aide for."

"Why do you say that?" I asked.

"It's just easier than other classes." Mark folded his arms on the table as he spoke. "There are very few papers to grade. You get to be outside the majority of the time. And there's nothing to clean up."

"What would be the worst class to be an aide for?" Natalie asked.

"I think baking would be," Maisy said. "I would hate to have to clean up that mess."

"Ask Evan." Mark tossed a crumb from my bread at Evan. He caught it and tossed it at Natalie.

"Pinching, definitely."

"Really?" I asked. I had thought being the aide for Pinching would have been the best. You would learn so much, and it looked like fun.

"I was an aide for Pinching last year," Evan explained. "Aside from the piles of debris you have to clean up after each class, you are constantly in the line of fire of some first year's wayward Pebble."

"How many times were you caught on fire?" Natalie teased.

"Too many to count." Evan shook his head and laughed.

I enjoyed my coffee and listened to the banter. Though we girls were all first years, we had almost as many stories as the guys did about Pinching gone wrong. It was quite comical, watching everyone tell their story.

"That was the first time I thought Terhese would make me explode." Maisy laughed, bringing me back into the conversation.

That had been in our second week of Pinching class. We were supposed to be Pinching Light Pebbles, but mine had turned into dozens of tiny little fires that popped and sizzled across the floor, mostly around Maisy's feet. After that, she had stopped standing next to me or behind me when I pinched.

"You'll get the hang of it." Mark kissed my forehead after joining in on the laughter. My Pinching failures disappeared with his kiss.

"Terhese." Lenetta landed softly on my shoulder, whispering into my ear. "It's time to get to class."

I hadn't realized how long we'd been sitting down. Everyone had finished their meals, and their glasses were empty as well. I looked over to see that Natalie was getting ready to stand. She looked up at me and nodded.

"I'll see you in Astronomy." Mark kissed my hand. I said bye to everyone else, leaving my tray with Mark.

"Let's go." Natalie kissed Evan's cheek and joined me, walking down the aisle in the Great Hall.

"You two look like you're going strong." I bumped her shoulder with mine as we walked to Baking. I saw her cheeks turn color.

"Yes," she said slowly. "I'm very happy with him."

"That's great, Nat!" I said, truly happy to see her first relationship going so well.

"He asked me to go to the Fall Formal." Her smile reached her eyes, and I thought I would have to keep her from floating away.

"I'm so happy for you."

"Did Mark ask you?" Natalie looked at me sideways from under her bangs.

I hadn't even known about the Fall Formal.

"He hasn't, but I'm sure he will." I nodded, not knowing if I was reassuring myself or her.

"Of course, he will." Natalie gave me the famous Aunt Chloe chin tuck and smile.

As we left the Great Hall, I felt Lenetta's energy switch from tense to calm. Now that most of the other Helpers were gone, she spent more time with me. I could barely feel her weight, so she split her time between sitting on my shoulder and on her holder in my bag. Mark asked me how I wasn't annoyed with having a little creature whisper in my ear and listen to everything I said.

I rather enjoyed having her there. She was kind of like having a roommate. When I was done with classes, I could ask her questions or discuss something interesting about what I'd learned. She skirted over some things, though. I couldn't tell anyone I was Ràej, but it seemed like she knew more about the Ràej Kingdom and the Ràej War than she let on.

We filed into Baking class, and into the back room where we set our things. The logic of it all had come easily. Once I learned the properties of the different soils, it was simple to know which ones to use for which kinds of magic. No one would ever give me a straight answer on how magic was put into the Pebbles though.

"That will be taught at the internship level," Official Kane would say, "if you are so lucky to get a Baking Internship."

"Where does the magic come from though?"

"You won't have to worry about that in this class," Official Kane would assure us. "You will only be introduced to that during an internship. Magic is very dangerous and highly regulated."

It irritated me that no one would tell me where this magic was coming from. Mark said we were gifted magic from other lands and some allies the Officials had made. He'd applied for an Investigator Internship though, so he said he might never know how it was really done. Like everyone else, he said magic was dangerous and it was highly regulated.

Baking class was not challenging or fun, but it was relaxing for me. I would look at the day's list, grab my materials, and start kneading. Each soil had its own properties, so some of them were easy to knead and some took a lot of muscle, even when using the extra-large rolling pins. When baking at home, we used water and oil to mix with our dry ingredients. In baking class, we used a substance that bound the soil together until pinched. We all called it goo. It was a milky green color with a stickiness that cemented when heated. I would later find out that this came from a giant slug.

"This is my least favorite class," Natalie grumbled, trying to slide the goo from one finger to another but ending up with her fingers splayed in front of her, partially stuck to each other.

"I find it calming." I finished kneading my ball and set it in the tray in front of me. Once the tray was filled, I would bring it to Official Kane who would grade it before it was sent to Baking 201. We made the soils and prepped them for the next step in that class.

"You find everything calming." Natalie now had her hands stuck to each other in an odd way. "I have to study for hours to memorize my text and notes, but you recall it instantly. I'm so jealous of your brain right now."

"Well, now you can be thankful for my brain, too." I tried to stifle my laugh as I dunked the corner of my apron in a clay pot, bringing it out wet and purple. I rubbed it vigorously between her hands to get them apart and passed her the little pot. "Here you go."

"Ugh, you're right." She laughed. "I forgot about the solvent."

I knew Natalie didn't like having a difficult time succeeding at the Academy, but I was fortunate I wasn't having as hard a time. The only reason I was doing well in my classes was because the majority of them were research based. As long as I followed the instructions, I was able to fly under the radar.

"Okay class." Official Kane clapped her well-manicured hands together to get everyone's attention. "Midterms are in one week. We will meet in the library for a study hall next class. There will be a pop quiz we will use for a study guide. Focus on your soils, their characteristics, and the characteristics of each component. Do not worry about temperatures or anything you have heard about Baking 201. See you then."

"I enjoy the library," Natalie said, packing up her supplies. "I have to run to the bookstore before my next class, but I'll see you at dinner."

Natalie was out the door before I had finished folding my apron and putting it in my bag. I tried to keep the purple solvent-saturated part of the apron on the outside of my bag so it didn't stain anything.

"Here." Lenetta leaned down from her seat in my bag and touched the spot. I watched the stain dissolve, leaving my apron white again.

"Thank you, Lennie," I said, wishing for the millionth time she were big enough to be petted or hugged for the appreciation I felt towards her. "Do you need anything before our next class?"

It was rare Lenetta took me up on my offer to get her something or go somewhere. It was usually taking her to a part of the castle, but I never understood why. After two months of having her with me almost all the time, I still didn't know what she ate. It was a pleasant surprise when I saw a smile flicker on her face the first time I called her Lennie.

"You ready?" Shannon startled me.

"Oh, yes." I entered the hallway. "Where did you come from?"

"I ran into Natalie a couple seconds ago, and she said you were still coming out."

Shannon had felt so bad about what had happened to me during our Telepathy class that she had dropped it and enrolled in Devils and Demons with me.

"Are you going to the beach today?" Shannon asked as we walked to class. The corridors were swarming with students rushing to get to their next classes and to their study hours. It seemed midterms was a busy time for everyone.

"I'm not sure." I tossed my head back and forth like I did with the decision. "I have Astronomy after dinner."

"Well, if you guys want to come down for a little bit after class, I'm sure the fire will still be going," Shannon offered.

The fire was the majority of the problem. As long as the fire was going, the alcohol was passed around and we would stay up until the early hours of the morning. This made for a long next day where I was always tired and groggy. The fire stopped when the Fire Pebbles ran out.

As soon as we took our seats, the thought of the beach was no longer an option. We each had a thick packet of papers waiting for us.

"Pop quiz everyone!" Official Wormill announced. "We are going to spend today's and next session in the library, so don't settle in.

"The first page of your packet is the actual pop quiz. Fill that out and hand it to me. The rest of the packet you are going to complete with a partner, just one, thank you. This packet needs to be completed by the end of next class. You can begin."

Shannon and I had a silent agreement that we would work together on the packet. I grabbed my quill and ink and looked over the pop quiz. It was true and false. Some of the questions were about general, anti-Ràej knowledge:

The Ràej wiped out thousands of lesser magic beings.
The Ràej stole their power from the wood nymphs.
The Ràej enslaved trolls to trample villages.

Then there were the magical creature questions:

The blood of a unicorn used to provide more powerful healing than any water.
Trolls had acidic saliva.
Spirits used to live in the south of Omneth.

I had no idea about some of the questions, so I guessed. The quiz had fifty questions in total and contained more creatures I hadn't heard about than ones I knew. The majority of our first quarter in this class had consisted of learning how the Ràej were tyrants. The teacher called the Ràej the devils.

After I handed in my paper, I waited for Official Wormill to usher us out the door and lead us to the library. Though I knew vaguely where the library was, I had never been inside. The ceilings were low, illuminated with a golden glow from the torches on the wall.

Chapter 16

"You are going to love this place, Terhese," Shannon whispered as we walked through the maze that was the library. I had heard this was a place students could get lost in easily, especially without a Helper. Most of the students chose to stay closer to the entrance so they didn't get lost. I didn't think I would mind.

"Okay, class." Official Wormill halted us before the corridor opened into a small cavern of shelved books and study tables. "Our librarian, Ms. Primrose, is hard of sight, but she has amazing ears. Please abide by the quiet rule while in the library or she may escort you out.

"No more than two people to a table. You have many resources at your hand to complete this packet. At your table, you will find a list of books that may help you. You can utilize Ms. Primrose, your Helper, the librarian Helpers, or me if you need further direction in finding what you are looking for. Keep in mind," Official

Wormill paused and looked at each of us, "the library is a honeycomb. Today is not the day to get lost in it. If you do not know your way around, please ask for help."

Shannon and I sat at a table and took what we needed from our book bags. I was pretty excited about this assignment.

"How did you do on the pop quiz?" Shannon asked.

"Oh, Omneth." I grimaced. "I had no clue about most of them. Growing up in the Hills, we didn't learn much about any of this."

"Me either." Shannon shook her head in agreement.

"I always assumed you were from the Official city," I confessed, feeling a new kind of bond with her.

"Nope." Shannon smacked her lips. "I'm from a tiny coast town half a day's ride north of the Official city."

"You came from the coast?" That piqued my interest. "Did you learn to swim?"

Shannon had learned to swim. She said their house was less than fifty yards from the beach, so she went almost every day. The beach at the Academy wasn't anything special or exciting to her, and she hadn't been to see it yet.

"The beach here is the first time I've ever seen the ocean," I said, thinking of the waves and the sun glinting off the water as it rose to its zenith. "I can't get enough of it. I go whenever I get the chance."

"I would be the same if I went to see your hometown," Shannon said, leafing through the pages of the packet. "I love the mountains, but I've only ever seen them once. I'm glad to get away. Our lives were made from the ocean, so my childhood and bringing up had a lot to do with making and mending nets, gutting fish, cleaning fish, and cooking fish."

I wrinkled my nose, thinking of the stinky, dead fish I had found on the beach at low tide one morning. The flies were buzzing around it until two seagulls fought over it.

"I can see how this is a good break for you." I nodded. "I grew up with my Aunt Chloe. She's a tomato farmer. If I never have to transfer another tomato from boiling water to an ice bath again, it would be too soon."

Our hometown chatter continued as we looked at the different creatures in our packet. I didn't know what most of them were, and those I recognized I had thought were mythical, something from a fable for children.

"I guess, let's just start at the beginning?" I ventured. "I thought it would be easier to do the ones we knew first, but I'm not seeing many of those."

Shannon agreed, so we went back to the first page. Each creature was accompanied by five items: habitat, diet, physical characteristics, personality traits, and magic. The first on the list was an Aeon Bill.

"An Aeon Bill," I read. "How in Omneth are we supposed to find information about this?"

"Don't forget you have your course text," Lenetta said, walking across the table near the top of my paper.

"Of course," Shannon said, rolling her eyes at herself. "*Who Walked Amongst Us* probably has an index of most of these creatures."

Sometimes I thought our professors were seeing how many times they could trick us rather than teach us. Bringing us to the library made all of us assume we needed to use the books from the shelves. It looked like Shannon and I were the only ones who didn't immediately venture into the catacombs of dusty books. This was the hundredth time I was thankful for Lenetta's guidance.

"Here it is." Shannon had her finger on the index page. "The Aeon Bill is on page one twenty-eight." I flipped to the page she said and quickly read through the description of the Aeon Bill. It was the largest known avian creature in Omneth and was thought to be the only non-humanoid with telepathic powers. The lesser magics could only use telepathy through magical herbs or stones, but the Aeon Bills used it as their only way of communication. It said the Ràej got their telepathic abilities from drinking the yolk of an Aeon Bill egg.

"The Ràej Kingdom viewed the Aeon Bill egg as a delicacy. They would serve it at feasts to all the Blood.

When the war started, they slaughtered the Aeon Bills and took any eggs they found to prevent anyone else from using them and getting telepathic powers. The Aeon Bill is now extinct," Shannon read. "They were atrocious."

I flipped the page to find a hand-drawn sketch of the Aeon Bill, which made it all more horrifying. The Aeon Bill was sitting on its canine-like haunches. The tail was long and sleek, wrapped around the front of its body. Its eyes were large and round, sitting above a large flat bill the size of its whole face, if not bigger. From the top of its head, down its chest and to the tip of its wing were dark feathers. It was such a beautiful creature. And my people killed it. Could that really be true?

"Terhese, you okay?" Shannon tapped her hands on the page I was staring at.

"Oh." I snapped out of my Ràej thoughts. "Yeah, yeah. I was just thinking of, uh, how cruel they were."

"Yeah, horrible what they used to do." Shannon shook her head and started writing down information in her packet. "It says they used to live by the ocean up north. They would fly out to an island for mating season and lay their eggs high on the beach so the water wouldn't get them. This is when the Ràej would steal them. It sounds like the same place I grew up," she mused.

"Wow." I thought of what the beach would look like covered in Aeon Bill eggs. "I wonder what creatures used to be in my hometown."

Not all the information we needed was in our *What Walked Amongst Us* text, but we retrieved enough information to know where to look for the answers. Some of the secondary texts we used were location specific, and we would find the chapter on the creature we knew lived there. Other books were history books about a certain part of the Great War because a creature was integral to it, like the mermaids.

When the Slates heard about the tyrannical rule of the Ràej over Omneth, they were thwarted by the enslaved mermaids at all access points across the ocean. Over a period of a few years, the Slates were able to rescue the mermaids from the Ràej and deliver them to another part of the ocean, to safety. This is when the Slates were able to set foot on Omneth and bring the war to the Ràej.

"The more I learn about the Ràej," Shannon shook her head grimly, "the more thankful I am to the Slates for overthrowing them. They were so evil."

I didn't know how to respond. Everything we were reading was treacherous, but I couldn't bring myself to believe anything written in our textbooks anymore. The library contained thousands of books though. They couldn't have changed all of these books to reflect a false history. The Great War was barely twenty years ago.

I decided to acknowledge that I'd heard her. "Yeah."

At the end of class, we had found information on all the creatures in our packet, but we had only completed the questions for half of them. I knew we had all of next class to spend in the library, but I wanted an excuse to come back on my own and look through the books on Ràej history. Natalie was right; I could spend my days wandering this library.

"All that research made me hungry." Shannon stood, stretching her arms up and out. "You ready for dinner?"

"I'm famished as well." I smiled. My Silver days had two classes between lunch and dinner. Though neither of those classes were too strenuous, they still made for a long day.

Classes on White days were longer and more tiring. Cauldrons was an interactive class that involved chopping, grinding, muddling, stirring, lifting, draining, and all sorts of activity for our arms. Pinching made me sweat from sheer effort. When done correctly, it would drain a little magic and energy, but I was still incapable of doing it right. I wondered how many students and professors thought I was a true slate.

It seemed like everyone had been released from class at the same time today. The line for food was out the Great Hall door. We searched for anyone we knew, hoping to cut in line.

"Do you want to grab a seat first?" I offered. "I would

rather wait at the table until the line goes down."

Shannon agreed, and we squeezed past the line of people blocking the way. More people were there than on our first night. I tried screening the crowd for Natalie or Mark or Maisy or even Tilly, but the swarming mass kept moving and my vision kept getting blocked.

"Well," Shannon said slowly, looking around, "this is new."

I was an average height girl, but the number of people in the Great Hall made me feel like I was going to be trampled. The walls were closing in, and I started to panic. It felt like that first day at the ocean. I had no control over what was happening. I couldn't get free. I couldn't move. I couldn't breathe. I needed to calm down, but I couldn't.

Something stirred inside me. Something warm, turning hot, building within. I closed my eyes and saw the power that was growing.

Calm down.

Lenetta's voice made it through my panic. I had asked her before if she was telepathic, and she had no idea what I was talking about. It was the only logical explanation as to how I could hear her tiny little voice when I couldn't even see her. According to her, and the *What Walked Amongst Us* text, fairies no longer had any powers. At this moment, I no longer believed any of that.

Can you hear me? I asked her, my eyes still shut and

talking in my mind only. That was what they were trying to teach us that first day in Telepathy. I focused on where Lenetta stood. Her tiny feet on my shoulder, her hand holding on to the side of my ear. *Lenetta, can you hear me?*

If nothing else, my possible delusion of her being telepathic was calming me down. I took a deep breath in and a slow breath out, and then I focused on the power I had felt and tried to push it with my words. *Lenetta? Can you hear me?*

Yes. Stop now. You must calm down and quench your power immediately. I'll explain later.

I opened my eyes and felt Shannon squeezing my arm.

"Terhese, are you okay?" She was staring at me, worriedly. "You look like you may pass out like you did in Telepathy class."

I blinked my eyes a few times and smiled. "I'm fine. I just got a little claustrophobic with all these people in here."

"I still can't— Oh!" Shannon jumped up with her hand in the air. "There! I see Maisy and Natalie."

Relief. I followed Shannon, pulling my bag close behind me to get by. I felt Lenetta at my ear, so I was able to squeeze my bag more than I would be able to normally. When we got to the crowded table, the familiar feel of

Mark's hand on my wrist made all my worry evaporate. As soon as I felt him, Lenetta flew to a chandelier.

"I was afraid you wouldn't find us." He pulled me in and kissed me, like he'd been waiting to do so for years rather than minutes. I had to push him away to get air again.

"Yeah," I said, still distracted by the commotion. "What's going on tonight?"

Mark looked a little hurt that I had stopped the kiss, but he settled on kissing my forehead and pulling me to his chest. That made me feel claustrophobic again, then a little irritated and angry that he wouldn't release me.

"You have nothing to worry about," he said as if he were tending to a child's bruised knee. "I heard through the grapevine that a group of Ràej supporters were captured. They are going to announce the good news."

I wriggled out of Mark's embrace and searched for an open seat at our table. Natalie was sitting between Mark and Evan, but they didn't have any food or drink yet. I climbed where Mark had been sitting and sat on top of the table.

"Are you seriously going to sit on the table right now?" Mark whispered into my ear. I wasn't sure if his displeasure came from me rejecting his touch or the fact that I was throwing out all etiquette.

"Yes."

"You know Terhese by now." Natalie climbed up next to me. "She'll never conform to society."

I smiled with Natalie, enjoying having this camaraderie.

"As she wishes then." Mark smiled back. It wasn't his broad smile, but the smile that appeared when it looked like he had his own secret joke. He sat down on the bench with his back to me, leaning up against one of my legs. Like second nature, my hand gravitated towards his waiting on his shoulder to take mine.

More people than I had ever seen at the Academy were trying to file in. As I observed people individually, I noticed a majority of them weren't students. A lot of people wore Official attire, some of which were interns, but most seemed to be older. Similar to the first night, a head table was set up at the far back of the Great Hall. The magistrate made a motion with his hands, followed by the other Officials at that table.

"Everyone settle down," I barely heard him say. The room was quite loud, but Officials were passing the message throughout the room.

Mark had said he'd heard there was news and not to be worried. Without that reassurance, I would have assumed something dreadful had happened. It seemed these announcements were heavily viewed and the Academy was the best place for it.

"If you cannot hear me," the magistrate said loudly, "then tell your comrades to be quiet so that you can."

Light laughter carried through the hall. Surprisingly, it worked. Starting at the front and moving like a wave, the Great Hall was silenced, as was the line of students filling up the doorways.

"I will try to make this quick," he continued, standing at the front of the head table, facing the crowd before him. "I know you all have important schedules ahead of you. My first announcement is about the Fall Formal."

A polite clap came from the Officials in the Great Hall, then some excited whoops and hollers from the young women.

"Official Kane," the magistrate introduced her with a low sweep of his arm, "would you take this one, please?"

"Of course, Magistrate." Official Kane slid from her spot at the table and appeared at his side as if she had floated there. "Fall Formal is a tradition at the Sandstone Academy. Though some of you may not believe this, our academy is the most liberal academy in Omneth."

I saw Tilly and Danielle raise their hands in the air and give another whoop. This was met with some derisive remarks and glares from other students and Officials. I felt the division between Official students and non-Official students quite clearly, but I was glad I wasn't as boisterous as some.

"I am not saying this to give you any allowances," Official Kane said sharply, looking around the room and pausing on a student here and there. "I am reminding you that this is a privilege. Homeroom will be an Official etiquette training for all first years, but any year is welcome to join."

As Official Kane glided back to her seat, back straight, head held high, some students issued small groans.

"Thank you, Official Kane." The magistrate led a small round of applause. "Now, for my other announcement. A camp of Ràej supporters was found and captured!"

The Great Hall erupted into applause and cheering until the magistrate waved it down with his hands again.

"This was a huge triumph for the Officials, the Academy, and all of Omneth! I have a special congratulations to the intern that helped in this campaign."

A curious chatter ran like buzzing bees from table to table. Everyone wanted to know who it was.

"Please give your applause, and your appreciation, to Jensen Dontane." The magistrate opened his arms wide. Mark tensed at my legs and his hand tightened briefly on mine. When I looked back up at the head table, I saw him.

Jensen. He walked up to the head table and received a big handshake from the magistrate and the other Officials who had been sitting at the table. One by one, they extended their gratitude.

"We are giving Mr. Dontane this badge for his honor and patriotism." The magistrate put a red ribbon with a gold medallion around Jensen's neck. "He is also receiving a job offer to work as an Official Investigator as soon as he completes his internship."

The applause and cheering that followed was one that the magistrate could not dampen. It went on for a few minutes before he was able to speak again.

"Students, please make a path so non-students can leave the Great Hall."

The students backed against the walls and the Officials left in an orderly fashion. I tried watching Jensen to see where he would go, but I lost him in the throng of people. It looked like he was going to be celebrated by each student.

"I'm going to go find Jensen and tell him congratulations." I stood up, but Mark held my hand and pressed his lips to the back of it.

"He'll find us if he wants to," Mark said. "If you try to find him in this mass, he'll probably be sitting right here by the time you give up on looking. And you'll miss out on food."

I squeezed in next to Mark on the bench. The rhythmic stroke of his thumb on my hand was comforting, but only lasted until I saw Tilly and Danielle sit down, saying how great it was to see Jensen again. Jealousy and anger instantly coursed through me.

"You okay?" Mark whispered into my ear, kissing my temple and easing my hurt.

"Yeah, I'm just wanting food," I said, though I didn't think I was going to get any of that either before I needed to leave for class. My anger was making me feel almost itchy when the dinner hour was over and I couldn't see Jensen anywhere.

Eat.

Lenetta dropped a bread roll in front of me and flew back up to her perch. I wanted to thank her but heeded her warning about not responding at this time. Instead, I devoured the roll by pulling it apart and eating the warm, fluffy insides first. I usually enjoyed eating the crusty rind with any type of soup, bisque, or chili, but I had to do without tonight.

"Okay, that will have to hold me over for now." I dusted my hands off over the table. Mark looked confused. "Astronomy."

"Right, right." Mark nodded. "Let's get going."

I had wanted to go by myself and accidentally run into Jensen while I did so. I thought it might be awkward if I did while Mark was with me. I swung my bag on my shoulder and walked towards the exit.

Mark's touch usually calmed me down instantly, but when he took my hand this time, my irritation grew. He gently squeezed my hand and rubbed his thumb back and forth over my skin. Back and forth. Back and forth. I recognized the feelings of unease dissipate like the cool fog when the sun hits.

"You ready for class?" Mark lifted my hand to his lips.

I felt the butterflies in my stomach and realized I wasn't ready.

"Oh, no!" I laughed at myself, hiding it with a hand. "I need to go to my room and get pants and boots."

Mark nodded and went with me to my room to get a change of clothes. He'd been in my room a couple of times but never for long. I made him wait outside while I changed, though he had tried to come in.

Don't give in, Lenetta said when the door had shut, keeping him in the hallway.

"What do you mean?" I asked, pulling on a pair of thick leggings, trying not to fall over as I hopped on one leg and then the next.

"You say something?" Mark called in.

"No, no," I hollered back. I grabbed a handful of hair pins and rushed out the door.

Don't give in to him, she said as I left.

"You ready?" Mark gave me a quick look up and down and grabbed my hand in his. As we walked, I realized I hadn't grabbed any sort of coat but decided I would be fine.

Chapter 17

Astronomy class was as Maisy described. We walked across the stone causeway and makeshift bridge to the mainland. The boards looked like they should have been replaced years ago, if not decades. Once on the mainland, we traveled a mile west into the woods to a small hill. It had no trees, bushes, or even flowers on it, just lush grass. Official Jill had brought blankets for us from the classroom that we spread out on the grass and lay upon, staring up at the night sky.

"Next week will be your midterm." Official Jill walked between our rows of blankets, our faces white beneath the starlight. "Tonight, I want you to study where the major constellations are. For your midterm, you will be in the classroom and drawing the major constellations.

"This is not a group activity. If you need help, raise your hand, and Mr. Livas or I will come around."

The silence that followed was almost eerie. For a few

minutes, I didn't hear any noise at all. After a few moments of concentration, sounds of the night started to come alive. A bug was off to my right, something with pincers. I could hear it walking through the grass with its tiny, clawed legs and munch its green food.

At least two birds were swooping over us and around us and back to a tree. While one was flying, the other would be cooing. I couldn't tell if it was a romantic sound or forlorn. Every few moments, I heard something in the woods, snapping twigs and brushing through foliage. Its pace changed from slow to fast, like it was hunting something.

I heard my classmates inhale with me when a blood-chilling howl came from the woods and echoed around the meadow. I moved my head slowly to where the noise had come from. No more snapping twigs, no more cooing or swooping of night birds. I couldn't even hear the bug enjoying its twilight dinner anymore.

"Stay quiet," Official Jill whispered. I wasn't sure exactly where she was, but it didn't seem like she was moving. "Mr. Livas, you are going to take lead. We will meet in the Great Hall. Stand up slowly. *No* talking. Follow Mr. Livas, and I will bring up the rear. Do not leave the Great Hall until I let you."

I could feel the tension and fear of the group but couldn't tell what I felt myself. The howl had been a fearful one; it had sounded close, but I was drawn to it.

"Follow right behind me." Mark hauled me up, grabbed my blanket, and pushed it into my arms. He grabbed my hand and beckoned each student in turn to follow the line. "Quick and quiet, everyone."

Mark's voice was firm and steady. I could sense an undertone of something I hadn't heard from him before. Was it fear?

At the top of the tree-less hill, we were easy to see from below. I saw the castle to the east and looked up to see what constellations I could see from here. The constellations I'd learned as a child weren't ones I could easily find anymore. Most of the ones we had learned in Astronomy were named after common things, like the Wheel. That constellation had five stars. One was in the middle, then four surrounding it at equal intervals. The middle star was supposed to be due north. I found the Wheel and saw that the castle was east from where we were.

We had come up the hill on the side where the howl came from. Instead of going down the same way, Mark led us to the opposite side of the hill. We had no trail to follow. I didn't even see an animal trail. This side was steeper than the other, making it harder to keep my hand in Mark's. He would be a foot or more down and in front me, trying not to let go.

I stumbled here and there, catching my balance at the last moment, before my foot finally slipped from under me and I fell hard on my backside. The girl behind me lessened the blow, but she fell down beside me. I wanted to laugh. It was Michelle.

"Girls, let's go," Mark ordered. His voice was quiet but still stern. "Get up, get up."

"What's the hold up?" The line had been moving quickly, and Official Jill had passed our small line to see. "Mark, keep going. I'll follow with these girls."

I could tell Mark was not pleased by this idea. His face darkened for a second, but he agreed silently and took lead of the line again. Michelle and I stood up and waited for the end of the line. Official Jill's eyes were as piercing as ever. Her eyes looked up the hill, down and up each side, and surveyed the dark forest the rest of the class had just entered.

"Ouch!" I took a step and fell again. This time I hadn't stumbled, but the pain in my left ankle when I stepped down made me drop faster than I had a few moments ago.

"Shh, shh." Official Jill was crouching by me, one hand on my shoulder and one on my knee. "What happened? Are you okay?"

"My ankle." I lifted my left leg an inch, leaning on both my hands and my other haunch, trying not to roll down the hill. Michelle sat down next to me and reached to touch my ankle. It throbbed at her touch. I gritted my teeth to stop from crying out again.

"Let me see." Official Jill sat in front of me and touched my ankle gingerly. "I don't think it's broken, but you may have sprained it. Hold on a second."

Official Jill started digging into her pockets. She had a couple of small Pebbles, but nothing she was looking for. Almost anxiously, she looked around the hill.

"Here's a lesson, ladies," she whispered. "Always be prepared. Who would have thought I needed to have an Emergency Mending Pebble for Astronomy class?

"We need to get to the castle as fast as possible. I have a Numbing Pebble, but it is different than what you are used to."

"What does that mean?"

"This is not a Pebble for localized treatment." Official Jill rolled a small Pebble around on her palm. "It is systemic. In order to use this, you have to chew and swallow it."

"What!" I was disgusted and unable to keep my voice down. I ducked my head a little and hurried my questions in a lower voice. "How do I chew a Pebble? Won't I break my teeth or choke? Are you sure that's all you have in those pockets?"

"You'll be fine." Official Jill grabbed my hand and

pushed the Pebble into it. I slowly put it into my mouth at her urging. "This is not hard like a normal Pebble. Once you bite it, it will turn to a gummy texture. Keeping chewing it until it is no longer grainy, then swallow it. You must be quick, Terhese. We really need to go."

Michelle looked over her shoulder. The wind had started blowing, making it harder to decipher noises in the forest. I bit the Numbing Pebble with my molars and was surprised at how easy it was to break in half. My mouth filled with a bitter taste that I wanted to spit out. I'd underestimated the grainy feel. It felt exactly like what I had imagined clay would, except it was almost hot.

"Okay, ladies." Official Jill stood, lifting me with her. Michelle stood also, putting her arm behind me. "We are going straight down and then will walk slightly to the right until we hit the ridge, then we will take that south to the castle."

The Numbing Pebble had worked almost instantly. I thought Official Jill had put me to my feet too soon, but I could barely feel anything at all. We were down the hill in a few minutes and we all felt better once in the cover of the forest. Our voices would no longer echo.

"How do you feel, Terhese?" Official Jill had me sit on a tree stump to assess me.

"I feel fine," I said, moving my ankle.

"Woah, woah, woah." She stopped me. "Just because

you can't feel it now, doesn't mean you aren't hurting it by moving it and using it. We will go slower now that we are in the forest."

The three of us walked through the dark forest. Thousands of stars had been out tonight, but they never seemed to give as much light as the moon did. We weren't walking in a line like we had with the rest of the class, but arm in arm. Our pace was slow as we stepped over fallen trees, dipped under low-hanging branches, and pulled our clothing off reaching bushes. Official Jill on one side and Michelle on the other helped me keep weight off the left foot.

"Official Jill?" Michelle still spoke in her hushed voice. "Was that a wolf?"

Silence held for a few moments. Official Jill was searching the forest behind, around, and even above us.

"Of sorts," she finally responded. After another minute, she gave us a sidelong look. "It was a Moon Wolf."

"Are they much different than a normal wolf?"

"Well, they are much larger than a normal wolf, and they have an incredible blood lust."

"Wait." I paused, thinking back to the packet I had been filling out with Shannon earlier. "Is that the same thing as the Ràej Wolf?"

Official Jill took a moment to pause again. I

wondered if she was deciding on whether to tell us or what to tell us.

"Where did you learn about the Ràej Wolf? she asked.

"Technically, *What Walked Amongst Us*." I shrugged one shoulder. "We were trying to find information on the Moon Wolf, but I saw more references to the Ràej Wolf, and it seemed they had many similarities."

I watched Official Jill nod.

"Yes, they are the same." She looked up ahead, a noise catching her attention. "The Officials call it the Moon Wolf, or the Luna Wolf. It was named so because they are born on a full moon. They say their blood lust is greatest when there is no moon." Official Jill lifted one hand towards the sky and looked up.

"Historically, the people of Omneth called it the Ràej Wolf. It is said the Ràej were able to domesticate these creatures and some were even able to communicate telepathically with them. The wolf has healing powers given to it by the moon, which is why we believe they are so much larger.

"Who knows if those rumors are true." Official Jill shrugged. "We do know that one of them is large enough to kill and eat a small herd of deer."

Michelle and I both stopped walking to stare at our

teacher in astonishment. It was one thing to hear about the size of a beast, but to hear what that size could do was astonishing. This was a creature I wasn't sure I would ever want to run into, even if I were Ràej.

"If these creatures are so dangerous, and especially so on nights like tonight, then why did we come out tonight?" I asked.

Official Jill chuckled. "It doesn't sound like the best of plans," she agreed. "We haven't seen a Ràej Wolf in at least a decade. Not on this side Omneth, at least. They became angered and even more hostile when their Ràej counterparts were killed. So—"

"They were eliminated, too," I finished. It was the Official way. Eliminate the threat.

"Yes. By bounty hunters."

We walked on in silence until we could see the ocean. The stars filled the sky, reaching down to the dark waters.

"Wow," Michelle said, breathlessly, a few feet behind me.

"Yeah." I nodded, feeling a smile spread across my face.

"No, no, no." Michelle had stopped walking. "Wow to that."

I looked back at Michelle, and she was pointing past me, towards the forest ahead of us. There it was. The most magnificent creature I had ever seen. It was hard to tell exactly what color it was, but it looked like it was made from silver with shades of grey and black. Icy blue eyes were above the long, snarling snout. The latter looked as long as my arm from wrist to shoulder.

"Okay." Official Jill had each of us by the wrist, trying to assess the situation. I felt her pulse through her sweaty palm and noticed her ragged breathing.

The bridge was ahead of us on the left, almost directly across from the Ràej Wolf. If it had been high tide, we could easily jump into the water and swim to the island. It was low tide, though, and it was at least fifty feet from the mainland down to the surface of the water, but it was only inches deep at this time.

"We are going to run to the bridge and climb down to the bottom. We can't run to the lowest point; it will definitely catch us. As soon as you get there, start climbing. There is a secret tunnel we can go through once we get to the island."

STOP!

I didn't move. Lenetta was nowhere in sight, but I knew it had to be her.

Lennie?

Yes. Do not climb down. The wolf can jump farther and run faster. It will be on you before you reach the bottom.

What do we do?

"Terhese, let's go!" Official Jill pulled me and Michelle with her towards the end of the mainland and to the bridge. We kept our eyes on the wolf as we sidestepped to the path. It watched us.

No! Lenetta shouted. I felt her energy go through me like a static shock.

It took just one bounding leap for the wolf to close the distance between us. We had taken our first steps onto the wooden planks. Official Jill and Michelle were pulling me with them. The Numbing Pebble made it almost impossible to feel anything beneath my feet; I couldn't feel their hands on my arms.

One step at a time, we backed down the bridge. The wolf took a step for every ten we took, so we didn't get any farther from it.

"Uh, Official Jill?" Michelle laughed nervously. "Aren't we supposed to be climbing down now?"

"I was thinking about that." Official Jill licked her lips, panting from exertion. "Let's try to get as far as we can. If we get further down, we will be able to jump and run to the door. If we get really far, we should be able to get help from the Academy. The rest of the class should be in the Great Hall, and Mark would have sounded the alarm by now. We just need to get further."

"So, which way do we jump if we need to?" Michelle

asked.

"Jump off the north side and run, following the island. It's about a quarter of the way around. There is a narrow ledge that juts out. It is about ten feet long, and at the end of it, there is a door. It blends in with the stone, but it is there." Official Jill took a deep breath.

We passed the lowest point and walked up towards the island, still stepping backwards. I felt the soft thud of earth beneath my feet and my heart was filled with hope, almost giddiness; we had reached solid ground. The wolf was still walking slowly towards us, with us.

Jump!

Taking the people flanking me unawares, I jumped off the causeway, pulling them down with my dead weight. We missed the wolf's attack by a hair. Without realizing who had told me to jump at the time, I hadn't thought to look at how high we were jumping from. I looked up from my back and judged it to be less than ten feet. The Ràej Wolf was looking down with its head tilted. Official Jill and Michelle hauled me to my numbed feet, and we ran towards the hidden door.

Like Lenetta warned, the wolf had no difficulty getting down to where we were. It was like a cat playing with a mouse before it gives the killing blow. We ran through a few inches of water, which slowed us down immensely. I was glad the water wasn't higher, but I couldn't see how we were going to get away from this wolf. The water was barely to the top of its paw.

What do I do?

I asked Lenetta, looking back at the wolf. As I spoke to Lenetta, the wolf tilted its head to the side again, like a puppy does when it's curious. Can it hear me?

The wolf took a small leap towards us, making us scream and run faster. The farther we got from the beach, the closer the wolf got to us. I really did think it was playing with us. We were all panting, my sides were burning, and I was wondering if Official Jill was sure about this hidden entrance.

"I'm going to pinch a Lightning Pebble when we get to the door." Official Jill panted. "That should give us enough time to get inside and barricade the door."

"Lightning? Won't that electrocute like ... everything? Including us?" Michelle had stopped walking.

"Don't worry." Official Jill shook her head, grabbing the Pebble as she spoke. "This Pebble only affects what it hits."

I looked over at Michelle. She nodded. I silently agreed to the plan.

Terhese!

"Now!" Official Jill shouted. She pinched a Pebble at the feet of the wolf and then ran ahead of us and jumped onto the ledge. Michelle and I followed her, both of them helping me up on the ledge. We had made it! As promised, a door had been cut into the sandstone of the island. Official Jill tugged on a short strand of rope that I had mistaken for dried kelp. Michelle tugged on it, too, one foot on the wall for leverage.

Terhese!

I turned to look at the wolf and saw that the Lightning Pebble had sent electricity through the wiry fur. It seemed the wolf was absorbing the electric current. I could see it sparking between each hair and glowing on the saliva in its mouth. It bent its head down, back foot planted, ready to pounce. As I heard the door squeak open, I watched the wolf push itself off its back foot and spring towards us.

Terhese!

I threw my hands up in fear and pushed the weight of my adrenaline off and into the air. My body was thrown back into Official Jill and Michelle, making us all fall through the door they had just opened. Official Jill scrambled to her feet and pulled the door shut with a dangling rope. I didn't see a lock, but I didn't think a wolf would be able to pry the door open.

Our ragged breathing was all I could hear. We were in the dark, in the bottom of the castle. The only thing I knew was that beneath the floor of the Great Hall was the kitchen. A huge dungeon was rumored to be below, but no one had ever seen it. I was about to find out.

"We can't go back that way." Official Jill had stabilized her breathing and sounded closer to normal now. I couldn't see her, but I heard her wipe her hands off on her pants. "Let me see if I have a Light Pebble."

I was straining to hear something on the other side of the door. It sounded like the wolf was out there, much farther away than it had been a moment ago. No one asked what had just happened. Again, it was something I wasn't positive about, but the exhaustion I felt made me believe I had used my power again.

"Okay, ladies." Official Jill hesitated. "I can't see the symbols on these, but this feels like a Light Pebble. If it is not a Light Pebble then ... well, then it is something else entirely."

"What does that mean?" Michelle asked. I imagined her head snapping around to look at our professor.

"If it's a Light Pebble, we will have a little ball of light to hold." Official Jill was fingering the Pebble. "If it is not a Light Pebble, then it could be an Earthquake Pebble."

"What!" I shrieked, not worrying about my volume or etiquette anymore. "Why on Omneth would you be carrying that around?"

"Ms. Neems," she scolded.

"I apologize for that outburst," I said, trying to hold my rolling eyes still, "but that doesn't seem like a practical, nor legal, Pebble to have on school grounds."

As she had throughout the forest, Official Jill took a moment before speaking again. "Our only other option is to sleep in here for the night," Official Jill offered.

Michelle and I both opposed that idea.

"Okay. We will stand here, near the door, and I will throw it to the other side of the room. If it is an Earthquake Pebble, then we will go back through this door and run towards the beach. With any luck, the Ràej Wolf will run when it feels the earthquake. With better luck, this is a Light Pebble and we will see an orb of light."

Official Jill stood in front of us, took a deep breath, and threw the Pebble as far as she could after she pinched it. I couldn't see anything, but I still closed my eyes and held my breath.

"Nothing happened," Michelle said.

"That's good!" Official Jill exclaimed. "Follow me this way. The light starts small, then will grow to the size of an apple."

The orb of light looked like a little star. As we walked towards it, I was able to see the lines of the walls, the low ceiling, and the stone floor. By the time we reached it, the whole room was illuminated with light. It wasn't a dungeon, but I didn't know what it was. The walls and ceiling were of stone. Sand was strewn across the floor in different sized piles.

"Where are we?" I asked, following Official Jill

through another heavy door and down a small corridor.

"We are under the castle," Official Jill answered. "In case of danger, there are escape routes. There are dozens of underground pathways down here and plenty of booby traps. Do not use these pathways unless it is an emergency and you are led by an Official."

I gave my acknowledgement in the form of silence. We passed through narrow corridors that took sharp turns and seemed to double back on themselves. I didn't see any doorways or alternative exits, but I tried to remember any unique signs I could, just in case I ever wanted to explore. After a few minutes, we walked up an old wooden set of stairs that creaked and swayed with every step. It had a frayed rope to use as a handrail.

We went through an iron gate that used to have a lock the size of my head or larger. It lay broken on the ground. In primary, we had learned this castle was one of the first battlegrounds of the Ràej War, but the Final Battle had been at a different castle.

Again, the next corridor had no doors or other rooms. The ceilings were even lower with only enough room for us to walk one at a time. When the narrow corridor opened into a large room, I inhaled deeply and then almost retched.

"Oh, dear Omneth," I muttered. "What is that?"

"Some of the rumors about this castle are true,"

Official Jill said, circling the orb of light away from her so we could see the room we were in. The walls were lined with iron bars. "These are the dungeons."

The smell clinging to my nostrils was that of decay and rot. I couldn't imagine any flesh would be left, but the smell of soiled clothing and unwashed bodies was still strong.

"Something smells burnt." Michelle was holding her hand over her nose, walking delicately as though we were walking through one of the cells.

"There was a large fire in here," Official Jill said. She was continuing straight with some urgency. "Many prisoners were burned alive. The Ràej didn't want the Slates to rescue anyone."

Michelle made a noise of disgust, but I couldn't believe it. The more I heard about the Ràej, the more confused I became, and the more I wasn't sure if I wanted to be one. I needed to see Jensen to get more answers.

"Remember." Official Jill stopped and looked at us. "You do not come down here and you don't tell anyone about this area. Just say you were led through a back door."

We both nodded. Official Jill continued to lead us into a maze, which was more similar to the rest of the castle. We went through doors and rooms, down a few steps, and then over and up more steps. I was sweating and more out of breath than I was when running from the Ràej Wolf. Official Jill pushed up on a trap door. We climbed through and found ourselves on cobblestones out in the far corner of the courtyard. Official Jill shut the huge door with a thud. It fit snugly where it landed and blended in perfectly, having had the same stones stuck to the top of it.

"Let's go." She took off at a brisk walk.

We followed her through the outer bailey, into the courtyard and finally to the Great Hall. She had told everyone to wait at the Great Hall, but it looked like our little class had gathered onlookers.

Chapter 18

"You're okay!" Mark wrapped me into his arms and squeezed me. The Numbing Pebble was still active, and I could barely feel him. I didn't know he was holding my hand until I looked down and noticed it.

The magistrate was standing in the entrance of the Great Hall with a few of the other Officials. They all looked concerned.

"Officials, please wait for me at the head table," the magistrate instructed. "Students, please disperse. Continue to the library, study halls, your room, or what have you. Do *not* cross the causeway until further notice. And," he paused, looking from one Official to another, then to the students as a whole, "it would be wise to stay away from the beach tonight."

It didn't seem like anyone wanted to go anywhere. The magistrate and Officials closed the Great Halls doors, so we all stood out in the hall, Michelle giving a detailed account of what had happened.

"How did you all get back to the castle?" someone asked.

"It was—" Michelle started excitedly but stopped when I shook my head. "It was just a backdoor that Official Jill led us through."

"Terhese," Mark said sharply. I almost jumped.

"What?" I was wide-eyed and completely taken aback by his manner.

"Come here." Mark walked away from the crowd with me in tow. He'd probably been trying to subtly lead me away from the other students, but I couldn't feel it. I followed him a ways down the hall before I stopped.

"Wait, where are we going?"

"The beach," he said moodily. I could almost feel it emanating off him.

"The magistrate just told us not to," I argued. I could see his irritation was turning to aggravation, but that just made my anger spark, too.

"No, he said he wouldn't advise it."

"I think I just want to go to my room tonight." I made to turn, but he stepped in front of me, lifting my hand to his lips. He was trying to entice me to go with him.

"Come on, Terhese." His voice was sweet, but his eyes looked almost menacing. I shook my head. "It'll make you feel better. You can relax by the fire and look at the stars. You love that. Why don't you want to go?"

"Mark, that is a stupid question!" I snapped. "Why would I want to go to the beach right now? I was just chased by a Ràej Wolf and—"

"A Ràej Wolf?" Mark interrupted, raising his eyebrows and quirking his lip in surprise. Or maybe curiosity.

"A Moon Wolf, Lunar Wolf, whatever giant-ass wolf that chased us off the causeway," I muttered angrily. "I sprained my ankle, and I can't feel shit because Official Jill used an apparently super powerful Numbing Pebble!"

Mark looked at me for a moment, as if he was waiting for more, and then he gave me his award-winning, broad smile.

"I see," he said softly, giving me a long, comforting hug. It would have been more romantic if I could feel it, but I understood the gesture. "Come here."

I let Mark tip my chin up, and he planted a deep kiss on me. If I could have felt my knees, they would have been quivering. It was the most passionate kiss we had ever shared. His lips were soft, and I felt the tip of his tongue.

"I'll take you to your room before I go to the beach."

"No, no," I said, eyes still closed. "I'll go. I don't want to be alone in my room."

"Okay."

Hand in hand, I walked down to the beach with Mark. We entered the forest and found the protected circle. Mark reminded me that the wolf would have to swim around the island on either side to reach this spot. We were safe. When we entered the shielded area, five fires were already going with more people than I had ever seen there before.

"What's going on?" I laughed nervously.

Mark rubbed my hand with his thumb, a quiet reassurance that I wouldn't be left alone. "Uh, I'm not sure." His head was held higher than normal, trying to look over others. "You stay here."

I looked at the nearest group of people and didn't recognize any of them. I was alone.

Instead of waiting at the edge by myself with people staring at me, I walked from fire to fire to see where my friends were. Michelle was the only one who had a late class with me, so I assumed Natalie or Maisy would be here. Shannon didn't like to frequent these, so I didn't even try looking for her brown curls.

When I had almost made a complete circle, I heard someone shouting my name. Then I heard several people shouting my name. It turned into a chant.

"Te-Rhese! Te-Rhese!"

I was not an attention-seeker. What in Omneth was happening?

"Here she is!" Michelle announced, grabbing my hand and pulling it into the air. She shoved an overflowing cup into my hand that sloshed a sticky, purple liquid. "She saved my life and Official Jill's life from the Ràej Wolf!"

If I had seen myself at that moment, I would have seen my mouth hanging open and my eyes go through several stages of comprehension.

"Uh, ha ha," I managed, followed by cheering, and then I whispered into Michelle's ear, "What are you talking about?"

"Terhese here is being modest." Michelle smiled. "Right when Official Jill opened the door and we were trying to run inside, you pinched a Pebble and blasted it away!"

The chanting and the cheering continued. People I had never met came up to cheer me with their cups or bottles.

"No, no." I shook my head at Michelle. "Official Jill pinched the Lightning Pebble, remember?"

"Yes, but it didn't do anything!" Michelle emphasized for the audience. "The Ràej Wolf was not hurt by the lightning. It pissed it off, though! Terhese pinched something and the wolf was pushed back by at least a hundred yards. It was incredible!"

"No wonder you're tired," Mark said coolly. He was holding two cups, but when he saw I had one already, he drank one cup and threw it over his shoulder. I heard someone say *ouch* and call him a jerk, but he didn't seem fazed.

Natalie and Evan found us. Everyone was impressed with what I had done. I couldn't tell if Mark was jealous of the attention I was getting or if he was angry I didn't tell him. I couldn't tell him what I really did, and I didn't know how to lie about Pinching, so I didn't say anything. He kept a tight hold of my hand though. The Numbing Pebble was wearing off.

"Does anyone have food?" Natalie asked, looking around the fire at those gathered. No one seemed to have any. "Terhese, you really need to replenish the energy you use while inching."

"You're such an Aunt Chloe," I joked. She knew this was more a term of endearment than anything.

"Terhese, I'm kind of tired. Do you want to head back soon?" Mark said dully, but not quiet enough for no one else to hear.

"Man, why would you leave?" Evan shouted with his arms thrown up in the air. "We have the fires going, the liquor is flowing, and the guest of honor hasn't shown his face yet."

I couldn't see Mark's face, but I could tell it darkened at that moment by the way his body tensed. Before the little assembly in the Great Hall earlier, I hadn't known that Mark even knew Jensen. By the way he tensed up at the mention of him, I assumed he did. It was almost the same reaction Nathan had towards Jensen.

"I don't want to go yet." I looked up at him, but he looked away. "I'll go if you want to, though."

I felt saddened as I said it.

"Ah!" I shrieked as I was lifted into the air, sadness gone. I turned around quickly when my feet touched the ground.

"Glad to see that Numbing Pebble didn't numb your fear of heights." Jensen gently pushed my shoulder.

"Jensen!" I almost jumped into his arms in my excitement. We exchanged a hug and then an awkward moment as I remembered Mark was standing next to me. I was glad the fire had already colored my cheeks.

"Jensen, this is ... a ..."

"I'm Mark Livas." He gave Jensen a firm handshake and gave me a glare I hadn't seen before. "Her boyfriend."

"Woah." Jensen nodded, smiling at me, and looked back at Mark. "Good luck with her, man. She's a wild one."

Mark shook his head and scoffed. They might not have officially met before, but it seemed they knew of each other. He pulled me close to him and returned Jensen's smile, but it was colder than Jensen's had been.

"This pretty lady?" He grabbed my chin and kissed me, hard and quick. "She's as tame as tepid milk."

Jensen clicked his tongue, a clear sign of his annoyance. "I'm going to go get a refill."

I watched Jensen walk over to a table set up with bottles and cups. Tilly and Danielle followed him like groupies. Michelle joined them shortly, realizing the bottle we had been passing around was empty.

"It seems the group is moving to the other fire," Natalie said, looking over at me. Mark's grip tightened on me, but Evan was already letting Natalie lead him away. "Let's go."

"There's something about him," Mark whispered into my ear as we followed Natalie and Evan to where everyone was gathering, to where Jensen was the center of attention. "I don't think you should talk to him."

"I've known him for years," I assured him. "He's fine."

"Let me clarify what I mean." Mark cleared his throat. "You are not to talk to him because I don't trust him."

It was hard for me to comprehend what I was feeling. At first, I was infuriated by him trying to tell me what to do. Not five minutes ago, he'd compared me to warm milk. That also made me want to shrug off his touch and claim my spot as queen of Jensen's groupies. His hand holding mine made me feel guilty about how I thought I felt. Instead of making a scene, I nodded silently and tried to enjoy being guided through the crowd by an attractive upperclassman who had applied for an Investigator Internship.

When we reached the ever-growing group in front of Jensen, and the table that was always set up for food and drink, I could barely feel the effects of the Numbing Pebble. I felt Mark's cool, dry hand against my hot one. Though it had been a cooler evening, I felt like I had a fever. The fires all around were intensifying the heat I was already feeling.

I stood on my good foot between Mark and Michelle. It didn't hurt yet, but I could feel my limbs tingle as they woke up. Natalie was talking to Jensen while Tilly stood close by, trying to get a word in edgewise. I was not positive if she'd had a relationship with Jensen or not, but I knew Natalie and Jensen's friendship would have predated anything they might have had. Just like mine.

"It's him," I heard a girl giggle from behind me. "Let's get closer."

Jensen had become a house brand name. When the magistrate had announced his name as being the intern to help find and capture the camp of Ràej supporters, he instantly became the most attractive man at the Academy, and maybe throughout the Officials. I had been

301

awestruck. He was Ràej. Why would he help the Officials take Ràej supporters captive? Had his uncle been captured? The last time I saw him, he was leaving to go help his uncle.

Then my imagination went from here to there and I had to wonder what happened. Did Jensen get hurt? Did he need anything? Was he okay? Of course, these were the same questions every girl at the Academy was brushing their chest against his shoulder to ask.

"Excuse us." A group of girls shoved between Mark and me. I lost my balance on the one foot and fell hard on the sprained ankle. It gave way, making me fall to the ground in embarrassing agony.

"My ankle," I muttered over and over, slightly above a whisper. As I held my leg close, wanting to touch the throbbing appendage, I rocked back and forth on the ground.

"Are you okay?" The girl whose push had resulted in my fall was looking down at me. She turned to Mark, arms folded. "I barely touched her."

Michelle was crouched over me, Natalie had hiked her dress up a little so she could kneel without snagging the fabric, and Jensen had practically slid to his knees by my head when I fell. He was holding my hand and talking loudly and quickly to the bystanders. It looked like he was talking mostly to Michelle.

For a few moments, all I heard was the throbbing of my ankle. It felt so much worse than it had when it first happened. Someone snapped their fingers in front of my face.

"Terhese! Rhese!" Jensen was squeezing my hand and waving his hand in front of me. I could see Mark standing behind him, that unpleasant look on his face again. These two would never get along.

"Yeah," I breathed out. I let Jensen help me into a seated position, everyone being careful of my ankle.

"Michelle said you had a Numbing Pebble," Jensen said, straight to the point. I nodded. "Did you pinch it or did Official Jill pinch it?"

I was getting irritated with the pain and the heat, and I gave him my best dead-eye response. Then I remembered that only he knew I could never pinch a Pebble and this was his way of keeping up the charade.

"Official Jill."

"Okay." Jensen nodded and waved Mark down. "You applied for an Investigator Internship, right?"

"Yes, sir," Mark said. I couldn't tell if it was with arrogance or pride, but I saw him straighten and smile. The crowd loved that.

"Congratulations." Jensen shook his hand. If these two had a charm battle, I couldn't tell which would win. "Something you don't learn at the Academy is that there are side effects to Pebbles. If Terhese had pinched this on herself, the numbing would have been on just the injured area. That would wear off gradually, and she would have returned to the state she had been in before.

"A Numbing Pebble is a Fighting Pebble, not a Healing Pebble. When used on someone else, it numbs everything for a period of time. You are still able to use every part of your body, but you don't feel it. All of your senses are numbed. When the numbing fades away, you will feel everything you had done in that time period, and it compiles itself. You are then plagued with fatigue and fever, and the pain from any injury is felt more so."

I watched Mark's face go from forced politeness as he had to look at Jensen and listen to him talk to a type of fascination. His tight-lipped smile played across his face. I could see the piqued interest in eyes. People around us were making comments as well, trying to ask questions or saying what they heard from a relative who worked at the Officials.

"That is all very interesting, and I have many questions, too," I said through clenched teeth. "But would you *please* do something to fix it?"

I heard a snicker here and there, mostly from where Tilly and her group were standing. People were turning around and leaving the spectacle I had made once they realized Jensen was no longer going to be sharing his stories.

"Well?" Mark goaded. "Does the Great Mr. Jensen have a hidden Cure Pebble up his sleeve?"

I looked at Natalie in question, but she shook her head with a slight rolling of the eye. There was no such thing as a Cure Pebble. Jensen looked at me with a kind of sadness.

"No," he finally said, looking back at Mark. "There is no Cure Pebble or an antidote to this Pebble's side effects. She needs to drink fluids and stay cool while she has a fever. For her injury, she needs to do what she should have done in the beginning."

Jensen's eyes bored into Mark at this point. "She needs to rest her ankle and ice it. She never should have been walking on it."

"She was running for her life." Mark stood, putting his hand on the back of Jensen's neck. "I hope you understand that she saved people by doing what she did."

It looked like Jensen was trying to stifle a laugh. He shook his head a little and stood next to Mark, shrugging off his hand.

"If you don't want to carry her to her room, I don't mind leaving this party early." Jensen's eyes had narrowed. It was another look I had never seen, but it was equally matched by Mark's. If I hadn't known there was a fire behind Jensen, I would have thought sparks were flying off him.

"Terhese, let me help you stand." Mark lifted me to my feet, one arm around me to keep me from leaning on the injured foot. He was holding both my hands. "Do you want to stay here with me and your friends, or do you want to go to bed?"

My ankle hurt, and I was dizzy and sweaty. I felt his cool hands holding me up. "I want to stay with you."

As the words left my mouth, I was surprised by them. Natalie looked at me worriedly, and she exchanged a glance with Michelle. "Rhese, I think you need to go rest."

Since childhood, Natalie had always been the voice of reason. When we were about to do something dangerous or just plain dumb, she would be my conscience. I didn't always obey, but I always heard what she said and I would remember it later on. The majority of the time, she would be correct, and I would get hurt or in trouble if I didn't listen to her.

"You're probably right." I grinned, thinking myself foolish for wanting to stay at the beach when I could barely stand up.

"You sure?" Mark stood in front of me, holding my hands and letting me fall into his eyes. "You could sit over here, put your foot up, and then I'll take you back in an hour or so."

His expression made me feel like I would be in

trouble if I didn't stay with him. Then he flashed me that smile that I loved so much and kissed me. "Whatever you want, Terhese."

Of course, I wanted to stay with the man that made me swoon.

"I'm going to head back to the Academy," Jensen said, touching my shoulder and breaking me out of my trance. "It was great seeing you, Rhese. I hope you feel better soon."

"Wait." I took my hands out of Mark's and turned to Jensen. "We'll go back with you. I want to ice this and go to bed."

Natalie nodded. "I'll go with you, too."

"Terhese, I want you to be very careful." Mark kissed my forehead.

"You're not coming with me?"

"I'm going to stay down here for a bit longer." Mark raised his head towards Evan, who returned a short nod. He was staying as well. "I'll check in on you before I go to my room."

"Okay." I let Natalie take me by an arm and try to help me hobble away.

"Don't let my clumsy girl get into any more trouble, Mr. Dontane." Mark's eyes glinted with the fire and drink.

Jensen merely tilted his head to him and walked slightly ahead of us.

As soon as we left the shielded enclosure of the beach party, Jensen turned around and scooped me up in his arms. We didn't talk as we made our way into the castle. It took us no time with Jensen carrying me.

"Natalie, could you do me a favor?" Jensen asked.

"Sure."

"Will you run to the kitchens and get us some Freeze Pebbles?"

"Of course!" Natalie turned on her heel and headed to the kitchens.

I tried climbing out of Jensen's arms, but he insisted on carrying me to my room. Lenetta appeared at the top of the stairwell that led to my room. She always disappeared when I was with Mark, so I was quite surprised to see her there. Apparently it wasn't just a male thing.

"Oh." Jensen took a step back when he saw her. "Is this your Helper?"

"Yeah," I said proudly. "This is ... uh..."

"Lenetta," she spoke for me after I hesitated. I hadn't introduced her to anyone before, so I wasn't sure what the etiquette was surrounding Helpers. Or fairies.

"A pleasure to meet you." Jensen smiled.

I directed him to my room, Lenetta hovering slightly above my head. Though she didn't disappear, she stayed silent.

"Right here." I pointed to the door. "Ugh, I have no idea where my key is. I think I left my bag at the beach."

Jensen looked around and jiggled the handle, and the door opened. "We're in luck. You didn't lock it."

Thankful as I was, that had never happened before. I always locked my door. It was more for Lenetta's safety than anything else. I was always worried someone would want to steal her from me if they saw her. She had her own little door above mine, so I was able to keep her safe without her being a prisoner.

Jensen set me down on the bed. He grabbed a pillow and put it under my left leg, elevating it.

"You don't have a roommate?" he mused, looking around at my somewhat messy room. I made a noise but didn't want to talk anymore. My ankle was throbbing, and I felt like I would vomit or pass out soon. Sweat was seeping through my clothes, and I could barely keep my eyes open.

"I have Lenetta." I smiled through closed eyes.

"She seems to be the best roommate you could have wished for," Jensen said as he covered me with a blanket. "Do you think you'll see Mark again tonight?"

"He said he would come by later." I shrugged. "I hope he brings my bag with him."

"So," Jensen hesitated, "you two are dating?"

My guilty conscience hit me like a lightning bolt. The

last time he'd seen me, we had been taking each other's clothes off on a cot in his uncle's cabin. Not two months later, I was dating another man. I pushed myself up to a sitting position and felt like a fog was clearing.

"I don't know how it happened," I started. "I don't even know when it happened, really. It happened so fast."

"It seems like he's treating you good," he said, though it sounded like a question.

"Yeah, yeah, he is." I nodded. "I think we're going to the Fall Formal together." I couldn't look at him. I was scared to see his face. Scared that I'd disappointed him.

"That's good," he said absently. After a moment of silence, I had to look up, and I saw him staring intently at me.

"What?"

"Do you remember the last time you saw me?" Jensen didn't seem displeased or upset in any way like I thought he would be.

I wondered why he wasn't at least jealous. I nodded, not knowing what details he was looking for.

"Do you remember what we talked about? What Uncle Kevitt said?"

"Of course I do," I said. "I haven't been able to stop thinking about it. Everything I learn at the Academy has me confused. I've been dying for you to come back."

"I could tell," he said shortly.

"What is *that* supposed to mean?" I snapped, knowing exactly what it meant, but I wanted to hear him say it.

"Nothing," he said quickly. "Do you want me to get rid of the Numbing Pebble side effects?"

"What?" I looked up at him again. "I thought you said nothing could be done."

Jensen moved to the bottom of my bed where my ankle was propped up. He took it gently in his hands and slid off my colorful patterned sock. I gritted my teeth at the touch and grimaced when I saw my ankle. It was at least three times its normal size. The blues and purples would have been beautiful anywhere but on my skin.

"I'm not one of them, Rhese," Jensen said softly. His eyes looked more hazel than green, but still captured my attention, making my heart flutter in only a way it did only when he looked at me.

Those words held power, and something dark lurked there. If I were like Jensen, if I were Ràej, that meant I wasn't one of them either. That meant I wasn't the same as Mark. I didn't really understand what that meant.

"I can't fix the injury," Jensen looked over his shoulder, "without someone noticing something happened. I can take away the rest."

"Okay." I nodded. My face felt like it was a furnace.

I couldn't tell which was more unbearable, the heat or the pain. "Please."

Jensen put one hand on either side of my gargantuan ankle. The pain seared like a hot iron through my foot. I felt more heat, like my foot was melting off my body. The heat spread up my body, and I was afraid I would start panting. I vaguely felt Jensen's hands leave my foot. He put his fingers on the sides of my face, and the intense heat rushed through my body and out. It felt like I pushed it out through every pore, a small explosion.

"Wow," I exhaled. I was no longer sweating. My face didn't feel flushed anymore. I could feel that my ankle was still sprained, but it no longer had the unbearable pain. Without that pain, I didn't feel dizzy or nauseous. My head was very clear.

"How do you feel?"

"Great!" I exclaimed. "I feel like a fog I didn't know was there has been lifted."

It was easy to sit up straight on my bed. I stretched my arms out and bent this way and that. Jensen sat next to me and smiled.

"I'm glad," he said. "Now, tell me what happened."

The words came flowing out of me. As extemporaneous as ever, I told him almost everything. In order for him to understand the experience with the Ràej Wolf completely, I needed to tell him about Telepathy class and how the wolf acted when Lenetta spoke to me. I needed to tell him about my continuous failures in Pinching class and my surprising success in Healing, which he told me was part of my Ràej power and not a lesser magic.

By the end of my half-hour anecdote, I told him about how everyone thought I used a Pebble to blast the wolf away. I knew I couldn't pinch, and many others knew that as well.

"What do I do?" I asked helplessly. "When Michelle told everyone, Mark had a very weird expression. Come to think of it, he's been acting odd since the announcement in the Great Hall. Since you."

"You will have to make people believe that you pinched tonight," Jensen said simply, ignoring the rest of my comment.

"How am I supposed to do that?"

"Say you got lucky." Jensen shrugged. "You tell people that it happened in the heat of the moment. If I were here, I could help train you to use your real power so it would look like you pinched a Pebble."

"Wait, wait." I stopped him. "What do you mean *if?* You're not staying?"

"Well." He looked up to the ceiling. "I don't know."

"Helpful," I muttered, giving him my best fake glare. He hit me with a throw pillow Aunt Chloe had embroidered for me.

"There is a lot happening right now."

I looked at Jensen slowly, up and down and across those broad shoulders. He looked tired. I forgot that we weren't children anymore. He was a few years older than me and was in the last year of his Investigator Internship. It was said to be rigorous training to prepare for the job of Official Investigator, comprised of course work and field work. Jensen had already received a job offer.

"What happened?" I probed gently. "The day you left with your uncle, where did you two go? What have you been doing this whole time?"

"I can't tell you much, Rhese." Jensen quirked his lips to one side and back as he thought. "No, I can't tell you much at all. I can tell you that a Ràej Wolf, or whatever they call it here, is not all it seems to be."

I took the pillow and hit him in the face with it. "Okay, fine," I huffed. "It doesn't seem like you're going to tell me anything tonight."

Jensen tilted his head and paused. He was listening to something I couldn't hear. I watched his face for a reaction, but it was blank.

"Natalie is taking a long time getting those Freeze Pebbles," he said loudly. I nodded slowly, wondering what he was doing.

"Yeah," I spoke evenly, raising my eyebrow at him.

"I rarely see those at the Academy. I'm not sure if she'll find any."

It had been an odd request. Freeze Pebbles were one of the first Pebbles we had practiced with because they were pretty harmless. They were tiny Pebbles and only made your skin feel cold for ten seconds, not that Official Loren would have cared if we froze our partner's entire arm. But glacier water would have been a better choice for this type of injury and easier for Natalie to get.

"Do you think she got lost?" Jensen asked, still using a slightly elevated voice.

"Doubt it." I shook my head. "She probably ran into Evan and forgot."

"Forgot?" Jensen's full attention was on me, ignoring whatever he'd thought he heard. "We are talking about Natalie, right? You could tell that girl to do something at a certain time of day a year from now and she would remember to do it."

I didn't have a response for this one. It was true. Natalie had always been the most responsible person I had known. If, Omneth forbid, she did forget something, she would probably cry for a day. Her self-esteem was based on how organized and punctual she was.

"Is Evan someone she's seeing?" Jensen pressed.

"Yes," I said happily. "He's the first man she's ever dated. You saw him at the beach. And at the ball. He stayed behind with Mark."

Jensen clicked his tongue and stood up. He paced back and forth a couple of times and looked around the room.

"I'm starting to see a picture, and it's not one I like." Jensen looked at me and said quietly, "I don't think either one of you should be seeing them. You, especially. I don't think I'm comfortable with you even talking to him."

Jensen was standing in front of me, looking down at me as I sat with my leg still propped up. I wished I could stand so I could run out of the room, letting the door slam behind me.

"What the Omneth, Jensen!" I shouted. "Just because you don't like who I date doesn't mean you have to tell me about it. You don't get to tell me who to date or who to talk to. And Natalie? She has her own big brother to watch over her."

"Oh, really?" Jensen challenged. It seemed like he was having a hard time keeping his voice low. "Is this the same big brother you dated behind her back because he told you not to tell anyone? The same man who slept with other women behind your back? The same man who I *told* you not to trust? The same man who is in prison for killing someone he slept with?"

I sat on the bed, lip trembling and fists clenched. His voice had grown to a shout. It was heartless and ruthless.

And all true. Jensen ran his hand through his hair and paced the length of the room again. He sat next to me and wiped his hand across his face.

"Rhese, I'm sorry," he said softly. "I stayed out of the way when it came to Nathan, but I knew what he was doing. It wasn't until Lucy was killed that I realized how close you were to danger. I'm not wrong often."

"He said the same thing about you," I retorted angrily.

"Who did?"

"Mark." I almost growled. I could feel my anger conquering my recent sadness. "When we were at the beach. He told me I'm not to talk to you."

Jensen tensed. "I'm sure he did," he scoffed. "Odd that he let me come up here with you."

It was odd. When we had left the beach, Mark hadn't wanted me to go. He kept seducing me with his eyes and his touch to keep me there with him. It was a jerk move, seeing as I was suffering from a tremendous amount of pain and thought I would faint. Why didn't I just leave? I hadn't wanted to go there in the first place.

He never pressured me. It was always a simple request, and he always persuaded me. Within seconds usually.

"I don't remember him saying it," I said slowly, still debating whether I should tell Jensen this, "but I'm sure

317

he intended me to be with Natalie. He probably thought you had something to do with your internship. He wanted me to go with Natalie."

I was sure about few things from the past few hours, but I was positive he'd wanted me to go with Natalie.

"Terhese, you have to listen to me." Jensen grabbed my hand, but I was more alerted by him saying my full name. "I can't explain everything now, but you have to stay away from Mark."

"What are you talking about?" I pleaded.

"It's time." Lenetta appeared over Jensen's shoulder and then flitted away and disappeared.

"Wh—" I started, but Jensen cut me off.

I heard a key turn in the door. Jensen swallowed and nodded at me and then released my hand.

Mark entered and stopped, clearly taken aback when he saw Jensen sitting at the edge of the bed. "Oh, Jensen. Where is Natalie?"

"She went to get Freezing Pebbles but still hasn't returned." Jensen feigned annoyance. "I'm glad you're back already because I have to go. It seems like her fever is subsiding, but she is still in a lot of pain. You rest up." Jensen chucked my chin, attracting Mark's glare to that action while he stole a last eye to eye with me. He was trying to tell me something. "I'll see you guys later."

Mark swooped in as soon as Jensen stood up. Mark

leaned over me and kissed me deeply, holding my hand in his. I was unprepared and gasped for air when he released me. It was nice having Jensen nurse me to health, but having Mark's hand in mine made all the pain seem like yesterday.

"She'll be fine now," Mark said curtly. He was sitting in my view of Jensen, and I had to push him to the side to say goodbye, but all I saw was Jensen closing the door behind him.

Bye, Jensen.

I'll see you soon, Terhese.

I almost jumped out of the bed.

"Woah, woah." Mark caught my shoulder, his face as startled as I felt. "Are you okay? We need to get you something for the pain."

"Yes, yes." I nodded. "Please."

Jensen? Can you hear me?

I closed my eyes, trying to focus on Jensen and our bond. It was hard, and it was making me sweat. This would only prove that I still felt sick, so why not try?

Jensen?

Yes, I can hear you. I have to go. I'll find you at the Fall Formal.

You'll be there?

I'll go for you.

Be safe.

See you soon.

I opened my eyes to see Mark hovering over me, staring at me.

"You okay?" he asked me again. "Looks like you drifted off somewhere and left me. You back?"

He gave a tight laugh, but I erased the goofy smile I must have been wearing.

"I'm sorry," I mumbled. "I'm just so tired. I should have gone to the sick wing."

Mark waved my suggestion away. "They wouldn't have done anything in the sick wing," he said. "Well, nothing I can't do."

Much to my surprise, Mark did have my bag, and he pulled out a length of fabric. It was about two inches wide and several feet long. He pulled out a little crock that was closed with a piece of twine.

"What is all that?" I asked, watching him unwind the fabric.

"Historically, it's used to tie you to the bed."

I froze.

He laughed. "Just joking."

I tried to laugh along but found myself looking for Lenetta, just in case.

Mark slid down the bed so he could assess my foot. He pulled the length of fabric towards him and started wrapping it around my foot and ankle. It was methodical and mesmerizing.

"That should help." Mark patted my leg and kissed the back of my hand. "I don't think you should put weight on it for a couple of weeks, but this will hold it straight and help it heal correctly."

The pressure felt both good and bad, but it felt more stable and comfortable.

"Why didn't you do this before?" I complained and hit him playfully on the shoulder. He grabbed my hand and kissed it again.

"Your Mr. Dontane may know about the side effects, but I know you aren't supposed to wrap a numbed appendage," Mark explained. "The risk is that you may do it too tight. Now, if I did it too tight, you would tell me or we would see your toes turn blue. If I did it while you were still numb, you wouldn't know if it were too tight. If the side effect theory is correct, you'd probably lose circulation completely once the numbing wore off if we did it wrap it too tightly," Mark said as an afterthought.

I didn't understand so many things about the world I was in. Everything Jensen said seemed to collide with what I grew up learning and what I was now learning. I wanted it to be simple. He'd been right about Nathan, though. It was hard to ignore that, but Mark was so different than Nathan. I thought he'd been jealous of Jensen, perhaps he'd felt threatened. With Jensen gone, he was as charming as ever.

Chapter 19

"Did I see Mark leave your room this morning?" Natalie asked me, looping her arm around mine.

I hid my face with my hands and gave a little scream. "Yes," I admitted. "But nothing happened. He stayed to make sure I was okay."

Natalie laughed. "Did he think you were going to die from a sprained ankle?"

As she said it, we rounded a corner and ran into a group of stopped students. I gritted my teeth as I stepped on my hurt foot, making it angle sideways.

"How is it that there are Pebbles for remedial tasks but not the healing of a sprain?" I asked Natalie.

"Well," Natalie was building up for a detailed answer, "the abilities of the Pebble are as great as the power put into them. Generally, a larger Pebble is able to hold more powerful magic. It also depends on the kind of soil the Pebble is made of. If the wrong soil is used—"

"Natalie," I cut her off. "You are reciting our study guide for Baking 101. I was asking a rhetorical question but was kind of hoping you were going to give me some knowledge from your Junior Healer Internship."

We both laughed and then concentrated on getting me down the stairs.

"Healing-wise," Natalie started again, "there is only so much magic can do. If there is a break, we have a Bone-Mend Pebble. You pinch it directly over the broken bone. When there is a sprain, that's just not as simple. Magic isn't a cure-all, but there are many ways it helps us, and we are finding new things all the time."

I knew Pebbles depended on size and use as well. Most Pebbles were used for household purposes. We only started learning about Fighting Pebbles and the other categories at the Academy, and most of the Pebbles we wouldn't learn about until we were interns, if we qualified.

It took us at least ten minutes longer than it normally did to get to the base of the stairs from our rooms. Mark was going to meet me in the Great Hall with crutches from the sick wing. All I needed to do was get to our table.

"So, what *did* happen?" Natalie squeezed my arm at the bottom of the stairs, urging me to fulfill her need of gossip. I smiled and blushed and tried to shush her response of giggles.

"Nothing, nothing," I bumped her shoulder with

mine as we walked into the Great Hall, "much."

"Hurry, hurry, tell me now," Natalie said as she helped me onto the bench at our table. "Evan is in line. We have a couple minutes."

"Okay, fine," I said. Secretly, I was bursting at the seams to tell her. "It was a very weird evening, as you can probably assume."

After Mark had wrapped my ankle, he'd opened the curtains at my window so we could look out. He pointed out some of the constellations we were supposed to have seen earlier that night. After he showed me all the constellations he could, he asked me what had happened with the wolf. I told Natalie what I told him, that I had somehow pinched a Pebble. When he asked me where I'd found the Pebble, I said it was just one I found outside in the courtyard. I didn't know what it was, but I had hoped it would be distracting at least.

I felt as guilty lying to Natalie as I had lying to Mark, if not more so. She had been the closest person to me throughout my life, and I had told her that I would never lie to her again. In the back of my mind, I wondered if she would forgive me for this.

"Okay, so you guys talked?" Natalie probed, motioning with her hand to hurry up. We both saw Evan piling food on his tray. I didn't have much time left to expel my newest experience.

"The talk just evolved." I smiled at the memory. He'd been holding my hand as we looked at the stars. When I told him about my fear and the wolf chasing us, he'd been resting his head against mine, gently stroking my arm. It was so gentle and tender.

He leaned over to close the curtains, but I told him I wanted to look at the stars longer. Before he lowered himself back down next to me, he leaned in and kissed me. It was a soft kiss that left me wanting more. I turned on my side so I could look at him, and he did the same. He pushed a straggling strand of hair behind my ear, then dragged his finger down my cheek, traced my collarbone, and rested on my shoulder.

One soft kiss led to the next, and he pulled me in close for a series of deep, passionate kisses. His hand was on my lower back, crawling up the back of my shirt. I couldn't help but think I should have changed from my ripped and torn outdoor clothing into my nightdress or anything else that was clean. It didn't matter.

Mark held me and rolled on top of me. His fingers touched my face, my neck, my waist, my thighs. I felt his biceps, his pecs, his abs...

"He said what?" Natalie let out a whispered shriek.

"Shh." I saw Evan coming from the line, and Mark had just entered the Great Hall with crutches for me. "Yes! He said he loved me."

"What did you say? What did you do?"

I hadn't known what to say. It seemed sudden to me. Instead of saying anything, I acknowledged it by pulling his face to mine and running my hands through his hair. I pushed my hips up towards him while we kissed. Then I'd lied.

"Oh, Omneth!" I cried and put a hand to my face.

"What's wrong?" he asked, concern written on his face.

"I forgot about my ankle," I whimpered, "and I just kicked it with my other foot."

At that moment, my injury was fortuitous. I never would have thought I would lie to get out of saying I loved someone, but it happened. So many thoughts were whirling around in my head that I couldn't say how I felt.

"No!" Natalie said. "You kicked your ankle and couldn't respond? You did have a weird night."

Evan stole Natalie's attention when he sat down. I hadn't told her that I had lied about kicking my hurt ankle, but I could tell her only so much these days.

"Hey beautiful." Mark kissed me before showing me the crutches. "Will these work?"

I stood up with his help and put one under each arm. They were by no means comfortable, but they were for utility only, and I hoped they would not be needed for long.

"I think so." I smiled and kissed his cheek. "Thank you for getting these for me. You should have seen Natalie and me going down the stairs. Getting to classes is going to be quite a feat."

"I have good news," Mark said. "I talked to the Master Healer in the sick wing. She said they don't have a Pebble, but they do have a potion or tonic or whatever."

"That sounds great!" I said. "What does it do? When can I take it?"

Maisy dropped down on the bench across from me. Her hair was frizzy, and her button-up dress was a button off.

"Maisy, what happened?" I asked, reaching out to touch her arm. She moved it away before I reached it.

"I'm having a..." She looked up at me. Her eyes were red and glossy like she had just stopped crying. "I'm just having a rough week."

I knew it was a trying time for students, with midterms coming up, but Maisy didn't struggle with any classes. She hadn't shown up to the beach last night though, and *everyone* had gone last night.

"Do you want to go to the library with me tonight?" I asked, noticing Natalie had turned her attention to us. "We can make it a group study session. Or we can spend a day this weekend."

"Yeah!" Natalie said excitedly. "We can have a girls'

day of studying with brain fuel and drinks."

I hadn't thought the idea of studying sounded fun, but it was growing on me fast.

"We can tag team our study guides, too," Shannon chimed in. I hadn't noticed she'd sat down until she spoke.

"Why can't we go?" Evan leaned across the table to ask us.

"No," Maisy said sharply. "I want my girls. None of you manboys to mess it up."

The eye contact that Maisy shared with Evan and Mark was almost concerning. I looked at Natalie, and she shared the same consternation. She gave me the eyebrow that meant we would talk about it when we were alone.

It had been decided. We girls would go to the library for the weekend and study until we dropped. The guys made a bet that we would drop first from drinking before anything else. We didn't let them get to us, though.

The morning of, I packed my book bag with papers, quills, ink, study guides, and notes from all my classes. Natalie had said she would bring snacks to munch on, and Shannon was going to bring wine. We hadn't found out what was wrong with Maisy yet, but we assured her that she didn't need to bring anything.

I told Lenetta she didn't need to come if she didn't want to and that she could go do whatever else she wanted to, but she insisted on coming. When I had asked her about the night in the Great Hall when she had talked to me telepathically, she would only tell me that it was a power of a fairy. I reminded her that she had given me a warning and that she had told me she would tell me more that night. Unfortunately, that was the night of the Ràej Wolf, my sprained ankle, and Jensen. She said it was nothing, but she rarely left my side anymore.

"You all ready for a super fun day of studying?" Natalie asked, as bright and perky as ever. She had set out a blueberry muffin for each of us: Maisy, Shannon, Michelle, Natalie, and me.

And Tilly.

I wanted to ask what she was doing there. Tilly and I had never been on the right track together. We didn't start on the right track, and we really just tried to avoid each other at all costs. It was hard and difficult, having mutual friends and classes together. Our story was more like a dangerous story that was half-written because the foreshadowing became too scary to finish the book.

"Natalie, you are too sweet." Tilly gave Natalie a hug. I stared at them. Super sweet and naive Natalie appreciated it, but I couldn't understand Tilly's motive. Had they actually become friends?

Shannon came around with cups. She said she had stowed one away in her bag each meal since we decided to do this. I wasn't sure where she got the wine from. It seemed everyone was able to find some sort of drink to bring but me. I think even Natalie had brought a bottle to the beach once or twice.

"What is this drink of heaven?" Tilly asked, putting her just-filled glass to her lips.

"We are drinking now?" I asked, watching the dark blue liquid fill my cup. It looked the same color as my bruised ankle had. Shortly after Mark had told me about the potion, he'd poured it into a cup in front of me. I was to take it twice a day for five days. Today was the third morning, and there was already a noticeable change in color and pain. When I asked what it was, he said it was a gross-tasting liquid that might make me dizzy, but it was supposed to reduce the swelling and quicken the healing process.

"Are you not able to drink without your man's say-so?" Tilly laughed and drained her goblet.

"I don't need anyone's say-so." I twirled the drink in front of me. "If that's the kind of man you're looking for though, I can point you in the right direction."

"Okay, okay, okay!" Natalie shouted, standing up with her hands raised. "I know you two aren't the best of friends, but you're both my friends. Can we put away our Pebbles today? And possibly tomorrow?"

I put my tongue between my molars and rolled it just

enough to feel it.

"I'll try my best," I said through my teeth.

Tilly poured herself another glass. "Natalie, I'll do anything for you." She smiled and clinked her glass with Natalie's and mine.

Natalie smiled and tasted her drink. I followed suit, mostly from necessity.

Shannon set the bottles on the table, and Michelle started unpacking her bag. I settled in, trying not to glare at Tilly or look at her at all. I took out my papers, quills, and ink pot and gave a study guide to each girl. We were splitting up subjects first, then we would share the guides and quiz each other the next day. Lenetta had already flown up to sit by a lit candle sconce.

"Okay." I stood up to describe the plan we had originally thought up. "I passed out a blank study guide for the different classes. These are for the general, first-year courses. Tilly, you may have only one or two of these classes, so I understand if you choose to leave us."

I watched Tilly from the side of my eye, hoping she would reconsider her decision. It was still bewildering to me that Natalie would invite her to our study group. Maybe she didn't know Tilly was one of the several who had been sleeping with her brother.

"Shannon, what is this?" Michelle asked as she stared into the dark liquid of her cup.

"It's blueberry wine." Shannon's eyes lit up as she said it. "My parents live a few miles from a blueberry patch. A *huge* blueberry patch. They harvest it each year and make wines, syrups, jams, you name it. My mom sends me a package once a month, but I came well-stocked too."

If it hadn't been blueberry wine, and if it hadn't been brought from Shannon's home, I think I could have held out on drinking at such an early time in the day. Contrary to what Tilly had said, I didn't need Mark's permission or approval, but I thought he would disapprove. I watched each girl finish their first cup of the deep blue liquid—Tilly finished her second—before I tasted it.

The sweet blueberry would overpower the taste of any alcohol. It filled my mouth and made me think of home. When I was a child, I would run around barefoot and bare-chested with Natalie, Nathan, and Jensen. We would run through the woods, trek up and down the Hill, splash in the lake, and fill ourselves on any berry we found. It made me think of Jensen.

"Compliments to the maker." Michelle smiled.

Shannon refilled all of our goblets, and we each pored over our study guide.

I gave myself the study guide for our Devils and Demons class. This library held secrets, and I was determined to find them. For everyone else, I tried to assign them their specialty or favorite class. Natalie, obviously, was given the study guide for Healing. I gave Michelle Astronomy, Maisy Pinching, Shannon Baking, and Tilly Cauldrons.

Though I had most of the information for my study guide, I wanted a reason to wander the library and look for more information. Like Natalie had said, it was a magnificent maze of dusty books that called to me. They begged me to touch them, open them, and smell their pages before running my fingers down their lines and reading their words.

Over here.

I had become attuned to Lenetta's voice in my head. The first few times it had happened, it had made me jump. Now, if we were alone outside my room, I would find myself listening for her, expecting her to talk to me.

I went to where I saw Lenetta, hovering in a dark alcove. Cautiously, I followed her through an unlit corridor. It was more like a dark tunnel. The light from the sconces in the other room didn't follow us far enough.

"I can't see." I stopped and turned around. "We need a candle."

"Follow me," Lenetta said. "I can see."

I blinked my eyes a few times and stared hard into the dark, barely making out the line of Lenetta's winged form. With my hands out in front of me, I continued forward. It was just a couple minutes until we were in a room.

The ceiling was low like the other rooms had been, but this one had a window in the side to let light in. Just enough light let me see where a candle sat on a table piled with books. The dust was years thick, but the fire starter should still be good. I squeezed the tool's two arms together and heard it scratching the flint. The arms were resistant at first, but a spark came after the fourth try.

"Hm." I fumbled with the angle of the candle and the striker. "Is there a torch in here? Or..."

I was going to tear a page from one of the books in front of me but didn't want to burn something that could be invaluable information, so I used a piece of paper from my bag. After crumbling the page into a tight ball, I squeezed the striker over it to let a couple of sparks land on the ridges. If I caught anything else on fire, this room looked like it would go up in flames, and me with it.

"There we go," I said, mostly to myself. I lit the candle with the page and dropped it on the floor, stomping out the fireball. "Okay, what should I be looking for in here?"

Lenetta sat on the handle of the chamberstick. Like a moth to light, she was to heat. "This room used to be where the Ràej secrets were stored." Lenetta pointed at the books. "There was a breach during the wars. Someone was able to get in, trying to steal journals and maps, but they weren't able to get out. The entryway we came through is shielded."

I watched Lenetta's giant eyes assess me. She paused as if she would say more, but the silence grew until I couldn't wait any longer.

"What do you mean shielded? Like at the beach?"

"No."

Sometimes, she was very helpful. Times like these, she was almost the opposite.

I took the chamberstick and walked around the little room. It was lined with bookshelves with just the one table in the middle. I leaned on the chair, ensuring it wouldn't buckle under me before pulling it out. The leg was stuck on something. Probably another stack of books; they seemed to be haphazardly stacked everywhere.

"Ahh!" I screamed and covered my mouth, hoping my voice wouldn't travel. I started whispering my terror. "Oh Omneth, oh Omneth, oh Omneth."

"That's Radik." Lenetta had flown off the chamberstick and was standing on the table. She was unperturbed by the human spine I had just grabbed or the rib cage I hit when I released it. I wasn't sure if I wanted to vomit or investigate it further.

"He's the one that couldn't get out?" I tried clarifying but got no response. "He died of starvation?"

"Probably died of dehydration."

"If this place is shielded," realization dawned on me and I thought I would panic, "then how do I get out?"

"It wasn't shielded against you."

She knew. I didn't know what to say or if I should say anything, but it seemed like Lenetta knew I was Ràej. If this room was supposed to hold Ràej secrets, it was obviously shielded against people who weren't Ràej. Was this a test? How long had she thought I was Ràej? Who would she tell?

I busied myself with blowing dust off the book covers, seeing what this man had been reading. The thought of Lenetta spying on me and turning on me had me on edge, though. It was hard to focus on what I was reading. *The Great War, The Fall of the Ràej, The Slate Kingdom...*

"Wait," I shook my head, shaking out my suspicions so I could concentrate. "This doesn't make sense."

If this castle had fallen at the beginning of the wars, there would be no book recounting the wars. I opened *The Great War* and flipped through the pages. The book was only a quarter full. The next book had only an intricate title page. The third book had a decently long prologue. The handwriting in all of the books was quite similar, with the same loops and swirls. I flipped each book open to the first page, and sure enough, Radik Bereins was the author of each book.

I couldn't take these books back with me and explain to anyone where I found them. If I was able to get into a secret, shielded room where a man had died while writing these, then I would definitely be questioned. It was hard not having anyone I could trust with this. The only person I could trust was never here. I would need to tell him when I saw him at the Fall Formal.

Though I didn't think I needed to worry about anyone else coming into this room, I stacked the three unfinished books and put them neatly in the back corner. I wanted to be able to find them easily the next time I came. It would be weird if I returned to my group empty-handed after all this time.

The books on the shelves didn't seem to have any organization. They were not arranged alphabetically, so finding a book titled the *Ràej Wolf* could take me hours. I browsed the titles until I grabbed something I thought would have anything to do with our Demons and Devils class. As I was about to extinguish the candle, I hesitated.

I dumped my bag out on the table and shoved *The Slate Kingdom* to the bottom, covering it with my sweater and then placing everything else carefully on top. The last thing I put in was the new book, *Arthur's Anecdote of Animals*. I capped the candle, effectively snuffing it out, and swung my bag over my shoulder.

"Let's go," I said, though Lenetta had already flown

ahead. The way in had been relatively straight, but I kept my hands out just in case.

"Wait here," Lenetta said as she flew ahead, through where the shielded entrance was. When I first saw her in this area, it had looked like she had merely been in the shadow of a wall. Then I saw that it was a dark corridor. I wondered if others saw just the wall.

After a couple of minutes, I started getting antsy. Was this a trap? Did she trick me into coming here?

Come out.

It was hard to put one foot in front of the next. I had heard rumors of what they did to Ràej supporters. They were tortured before they were killed. What would they do with someone who was Ràej?

Lenetta flew over my head. "What are you doing? We need to go before someone comes."

I nodded and followed her out this time. We were in one of the larger rooms with shelving from floor to ceiling. Alcoves lined the room here and there, little hallways that had doors that went to quiet study rooms, and all were lit by torches held in scones on the wall.

When I returned to the study room my group had chosen, they had finished two of the bottles Shannon had brought and were opening a third.

"Terhese!" Maisy shouted. "We were getting worried about you! Here, let me fill your cup. Where's your cup?"

Maisy and Shannon were laughing as they searched for my cup. I hadn't finished it, but it seemed someone else had. They grabbed one not being used and filled it to the brim. I had to set it on the table and slurp out the top bit of it in order to pick it up without spilling.

"What have you all been doing?" I asked, thinking I knew the answer already. Purple-blue stained the table and the floor, even some of the papers. It didn't look like any of the study guides had been started.

"We are bitching about men." Maisy gave me a sour smile and clinked her cup against mine, making both of them slosh their liquid. I didn't even know Maisy had been talking to anyone.

"Where is Natalie?" I looked around, but she seemed to be missing.

Michelle was curled up in a chair, holding her empty goblet like it was a precious object.

"She's right there. Open your..." Tilly had pointed to where Michelle was sitting but stopped. "Oh. Where is Natalie?"

"I'm sure she just went to get another book on healing." Michelle waved her hand as she spoke.

I wanted to help Maisy with what she was going through. I knew something critical had happened to her. She was always so composed, cheerful, and positive. The change that had overcome her so quickly was alarming, but I needed to pass my midterms. Splitting up the workload had seemed like a good idea in the beginning, but now it looked like a waste of time.

"Okay." I checked the messy table to make sure I hadn't left anything behind. "I'm going to go back to my room and rest up a bit. My ankle isn't feeling too great right now."

I knew if I told the girls they were not conducive to my grades and career at the Academy at that point in time, they would try to make me stay, and then I would stay and nothing would get done. I didn't have time to waste. I had six classes to study for.

"You're going to go find your boy toy, aren't you?" Tilly slurred.

I rolled my eyes and went to give Maisy a hug.

"When you are done studying today, let me know and we can have tea or something," I whispered into her hair.

"Thanks, Terhese," Maisy said in a teary voice.

"But which one is the real question." Tilly stood up and started following me out.

"What are you talking about?" I stopped short, making her bump into me.

"You know what I'm talking about!" she slurred. "You can't have evrone!"

I wondered how many bottles she had drunk by

herself.

"Bye, girls, I'm sure I'll see you tonight at dinner." I waved to glossy-eyed Maisy, flushed Shannon, and tired Michelle.

Tilly grabbed my wrist. "I know what you are, Terhese Neems," Tilly hissed.

If her eyes had been able to hold mine, they might have been shooting daggers at me. As it was, she was probably seeing two or three of me. I turned away from her and left the study room, walking as fast as my healing foot would allow me to down the corridor.

"You're a Ràej whore!"

I couldn't hold in my anger anymore. It was going to come down to us again. But this time, she'd called me Ràej rather than a Hillgirl. I felt my power stirring within; I felt the hair across my body lift up. Jensen had told me it was dangerous to use my power but that I could disguise it as a Pebble. I thought quickly of which Pebbles I had on me. The only ones I had were the little Sound Pebbles. The ones prone to catching skirts on fire when they weren't pinched right.

My hair felt like it was about to stand on end. I took a deep breath, centering myself, pulling in that energy, and focusing it. Tilly was teetering in front of me. I was holding the Pebble between my fingers in the pocket of my dress. Was that too easy? Should I just push her over instead?

"Nothing to say?" Tilly taunted. "I haven't figured out which one bedded you first."

I pinched the Sound Pebble and threw it. As I did, I released my anger through my hand in the form of fire. The Pebble broke in half and squeaked, throwing up its own little flame. No one would be the wiser that the flames on her dress didn't come from the same place. I was known for being the worst pincher, with some streaks of luck.

Tilly screamed and rolled around on the ground until the flames were out. Her dress was blackened and frayed at the bottom.

"What on Omneth is going on!" Ms. Primrose stood behind me, shouting down the hall. I closed my eyes and cursed under my breath.

"Good morning, Ms. Primrose." I turned and smiled, though I knew that wouldn't help anything. Tilly hadn't ratted me out last time, but I'd thought it was because she truly believed Jensen's story. If I didn't rat on her being too drunk to talk in the library, maybe we would get out of this.

"Again, what on Omneth is going on?" Ms. Primrose repeated. She was still a good twenty feet or more from me, which meant she was double that from Tilly. Could she see Tilly on the ground? If she did, I doubted she would see the Pebble fragments or Tilly's dress.

Neither of us said anything.

"Ms. Primrose, we're not sure what you're talking about." I feigned confusion. "I was just leaving our study group, and Tilly was trying to catch up with me when she slipped and fell. If you heard any commotion, that was probably what it was."

I held my breath, waiting for Tilly to say anything. She had to have realized she wasn't capable of talking to anyone of higher level at the Academy.

"Well?" Ms. Primrose said sharply. "Are you going to help her up?"

"Oh, of course!" I rushed down the hallway to Tilly and helped her stand. She wouldn't look at me, nor would she look at Ms. Primrose. Her eyes were determinedly staring at the floor.

"Get to where you're going." Ms. Primrose turned around and went back to her desk and the front entrance of the library. I thanked Omneth her desk was far enough away that she hadn't heard Tilly shouting at me.

As soon as she was out of eyesight, I dropped my arm from pretending to hold Tilly up. She glared at me and went back to the study room. I wondered if they had heard anything. What would Tilly tell them?

Chapter 20

Nothing seemed right anymore, and I was no longer in the right head space to study. I was going to take my book with me to the Great Hall and study amongst the several dozen other students who would be there studying, but I was too frustrated and overwhelmed. It seemed my secret was about to explode, and I didn't know what to do about it.

Jensen had told me that Mark was dangerous and I needed to stay away from him. But Mark had said I should stay away from Jensen. Tilly and Natalie are all chummy, and Tilly is spreading rumors about me and Jensen. Or whatever she was trying to do. What had she said? Something about being *bedded* by one of them?

"She called me a Ràej whore!" I threw my pillow at the window when I got to my room. "What is wrong with that girl? She always acts like I'm stealing something from her when really she's just mad because she's unable to steal it from me."

I laid my head on my hand with my ankle propped up, staring out the window. "Everyone is acting differently this week."

My door flew open, and I bolted up, thinking I was about to be taken for being Ràej. It was Natalie.

"What happened?" She set her bag down and sat on the bed next to me. "Are you okay?"

That was why I needed to lock my door. I looked over at my desk and realized Mark hadn't left my key behind.

"What do you mean?" I wasn't sure what Tilly possibly could have said to make me sound like the victim.

"I heard you two," Natalie said softly. "The other girls had too much wine. They were all in their own little world, but I was about to come out when you pinched. You just have to ignore her. Tilly is just jealous and tends to be a bitch."

"She's ruthless." I groaned, remembering how ruthless she really was. She dated the same man her cousin did. "I want to strangle her sometimes."

"I know." Natalie nibbled her bottom lip. "I thought it was rude when she used to call us Hillgirls."

"She called me a Ràej whore." A tear came to my eye. Astonished by the feel of it, I wiped it away.

"I hope no one else heard that. And," Natalie's shoulders fell down from her normally perfect posture, "I really hope she doesn't say that to anyone else."

"What aren't you saying?" I asked, confused by her demeanor.

"I'm not supposed to say anything, but I can't hide it from you." She looked up at the ceiling. "Even though you have never had a problem hiding things from me."

"I know, Nat, I'm sorry," I said, pulling my legs in and sitting next to her rather than lying down awkwardly beside her. "Is this about the night Jensen took me to my room?"

"Kind of." She crinkled her brow. "How did you know?"

"Well, you were supposed to come back and you never did."

"Oh, right." Natalie had a fringe of her dress in her hand and was wringing it like she wanted to get water out of it.

"So, where did you go?" I asked.

"You have to understand that Evan is the first man I've ever dated," she said, moving her hands to emphasize her point. "I want to do anything he says, and he's truly the sweetest man I've ever met. Not to say Mark is evil or anything..."

Natalie paused, looking at me with her head tilted.

Was she trying to imply Mark was something other than sweet?

"Are you trying to say something, Natalie?" I tried not snapping at her, but it had been a long few days. "Just spit it out. You know I don't like these games."

"I couldn't find Freeze Pebbles." She shrugged. "I was walking back in front of the Great Hall and heard Mark and Evan talking with some of the Officials who had been at the announcement."

Natalie had hoped to wait for Evan to come out, and then she would return to me with him. The few sentences she overheard had startled her.

"One of the Officials was talking to Mark and said they were running out of time for him to complete something. Mark said it was taking longer than he'd expected. The Official told him it wasn't a game and asked if he understood what happened if he failed."

Natalie had tried to peek into the Great Hall at this point to see who was talking. An ink pot fell from her bag, bouncing and rolling across the floor.

"I didn't know what to do, so I ran." Natalie was looking at her hands. "I didn't go back to the beach or to your room. I ran up the main stairs and headed for my room. Evan caught up with me. He always has a loose tongue when he's been drinking. He told me he was scared. He said he couldn't hide it from me because he knew I had been there listening."

"How did he know you were there?" I thought of the recent telepathy I'd been able to have with Jensen.

"They heard my ink pot drop, and Evan was sent to go check on the noise," Natalie explained. "I draw on the toppers of my ink pots. He knew it was mine when he found the rose drawn on the top."

"You always make things prettier." I smiled. "Why was Evan scared?"

"He said they had talked to Official Marin, who is big, brawny, and just mean. Evan said he was supposed to be helping Mark with something, but it's getting out of hand." Natalie's lip trembled. "I'm afraid it has something to do with you, Rhese."

This wasn't exactly what I was expecting to hear, but it wasn't too far off.

"Why would it have anything to do with me?" I asked slowly.

"Terhese, you have to swear to me right now." Natalie was using her serious voice, sitting up straighter and holding her pinky out to me, a tradition we'd never grown out of. "Swear on Aunt Chloe's life. Swear on Omneth!"

"Okay, okay." I grabbed her pinky with mine. "What am I swearing?"

"You swear you won't tell, of course." Natalie tried to

smile. That was usually what our promises were about.

"I have no one to tell but you, Natalie." I smiled. "I swear."

"They think you are Ràej!" Natalie blurted out. She put her hands on her face. "I know we can figure out how to prove it to them. But it sounds like they're trying to test you without letting others know."

It felt like my world was crashing in on itself. Was Lenetta really in on it then? Was the Ràej Wolf planned to force me to use my powers? Did this all stem from the Academy Ball, when I hadn't even known I had power yet?

"Rhese, you okay?" Natalie whispered.

"I don't know." I shook my head. "This means Mark doesn't love me like he said he did." I sucked my lips and chewed on the inside of my cheek.

"You said you didn't say it back. Do you love him?" Natalie asked.

"I don't know anything anymore." I fell back on my bed and covered my face with my arms. "Nothing is real."

"Don't tell him I told you." Natalie held up her finger in heedless warning. "Evan may not even remember he told me, but I couldn't not tell you. I just want you to be careful, especially with Tilly spreading rumors. We know you're not Ràej. I'll vouch for that with my life."

This turned my heart cold. What would happen to

the people I loved if I were found to be Ràej? Natalie would never talk to me if she found out I was Ràej and I hadn't told her. Maybe it would be safer to pretend I didn't know either.

"I know, Natalie," I decided to say. "You'll always be there for me."

◆

Though Natalie had told me her suspicions and what Evan had told her, I still saw Mark over the weekend before finals. Our original study group plan didn't work out, so I tried to stay in my room as much as possible to study. I flipped through the pages of *Arthur's Anecdote of Animals* when I needed a break from studying for classes, but *The Slate Kingdom* stayed hidden in my bag.

Mark came over to help me study or to bring me food. He didn't seem to be doing anything that would point to him thinking I was Ràej or doing anything to see if I was Ràej. It put me on edge, but I couldn't bring myself to believe it of Mark.

If someone had told me this about Nathan, I would have believed it. He was cold, insecure, and always wanted to be over people. It took no imagination to see him as someone who could do that.

With Mark spending most of the weekend in my room, I hadn't seen Lenetta much since the library. I wondered if she was reporting on me, telling someone I was able to get in and out of the shielded room. It didn't seem that the midterms would be too important for my future anymore, but I still wanted to do well.

"It's getting late," Mark said as I poured over Astrology constellations. "I have exams tomorrow as well, so I'm going to call it a night."

"I probably won't learn much more tonight either." I rubbed my eyes and looked at my short candle stub. Mark kissed my forehead.

"I probably should have asked you this before." Mark hesitated and I held my breath. Was he going to come forth and ask me if I was Ràej? "Will you go to the Fall Formal with me?"

I almost laughed with relief. He took it as great excitement.

"Yes." I smiled. "Of course I will."

I was beaming, ear to ear, and blushing. He took my hand and kissed my palm.

"I had hoped you would." He smiled my favorite smile. "I have to go, but I'll see you in the morning, my love."

We shared an intimate kiss, but I didn't say the word back. As soon as he was out of the room, I crawled into bed. I couldn't believe he could be plotting against me. I wouldn't believe it.

Midterms were exhausting. Each exam was three

hours, and I had two exams each day for three days. We had the rest of the week off, but that was really for students to have an opportunity to reschedule if they missed an exam or if they had a written excuse from the teacher to take it on another day.

I enjoyed the days off. I did no studying, no homework, and everything was relatively quiet with testing and studying going on. I had thought it would be a great week for the beach, but it turned out to be too cold. The winds were bringing winter on their tails.

Though I didn't think it was warm enough to traipse the beach, I put on a light jacket and boots so I could walk around. The first place I went was to the outer bailey where we had come out of the tunnels. It was impossible to see exactly where it was. The cobblestones had lain against each other so perfectly. As I was about to leave the area, I saw a little twig sticking out of the ground at an unnatural angle.

I went to my knees to further inspect the twig. It was there! The little stick had been caught in the hidden door. I wanted to lift it up, but I knew I would get in trouble for doing so. The other entrance, though, wouldn't be seen by anyone.

The Ràej Wolf wouldn't be stalking the gates to the Academy at all times, and we would probably never see it again, but I didn't know what could be out there. Tree goblins used to be plentiful in this forest. According to *What Walked Amongst Us*, tree goblins became extinct during the Great War, but *Arthur's Anecdote of Animals* said the purple solvent we used in baking came from the spit of tree goblins. They had to be on the mainland.

I ran down to the kitchens and grabbed some water, a few apples, hard cheese, and bread. By the time I had everything wrapped and tied in a cloth, I realized I couldn't carry this bundle while I was on crutches. My grand idea of chasing down long-lost creatures was doused. I brought my bundle of food to a table in the courtyard and started my own picnic.

Everyone else seemed to be preoccupied. The upperclassmen had their exams later in the week. Natalie was helping Evan study for his exams. Shannon had gone home for a short break to be with her family. I didn't know where Maisy was, but I knew Michelle was sick in bed. I ended up going back to my room so I could have Lenetta as company; she didn't like the cold weather.

Chapter 21

The time flew by once midterms were done, and the time for the Fall Formal had come. I was no longer on crutches, and I was looking forward to wearing the new dress Natalie had for me. We had suffered through the two-hour etiquette class with Official Kane and had learned very little.

Maisy returned to her normal self. She said it had just been stress over the exams. The group of us girls spent hours in my room trying new hair styles and makeup. I was the only one who didn't have a roommate, so I had the extra space to use.

After talking to Natalie about what Evan had said, she had stopped inviting Tilly to do things. I was grateful she had chosen me over Tilly, but I was scared she was going to be angry with me no matter what I chose to do. I wanted to talk to Jensen. I needed advice.

I wasn't sure what Mark had been talking to the

Official about, but it couldn't have been about me. He was sweeter and as charming as ever, and he seemed more excited about the Fall Formal than I was. I was still a little wary with him. It was just odd that Lenetta wouldn't stay around him.

When the night of the Fall Formal finally arrived, the castle was alight with activity and excitement. Decorations were on every floor and in every room. Different colored and scented candles were lit on every windowsill. Pumpkins and scarecrows were set up in common areas and in the Great Hall. Orange, red, and bronze leafed garlands wrapped down the banisters and hung over doorways.

"I'm more excited than I was for the Academy Ball!" Natalie danced around my room. She had a bag full of colors and tints for our faces and hair. I wore rouge on my cheeks and fig on my lips. Natalie fancied the coral pink lip color. She said the hair color was for special occasions, but I didn't understand what occasion would warrant it.

After our faces were painted, she pulled out a long, curling wand. "Where's the hot plate? Or do you have a candle?"

I grabbed the hot plate Aunt Chloe had sent me with. When it was hot, Natalie curled my hair, piece by piece. I watched it fall in big waves. She did her own in tighter curls. Her hair was able to hold the curls better. Natalie said she knew this from years of experience with doing my hair.

"You are my one and only hairdresser." I laughed.

When our hair and makeup was done, we looked in the mirror. I had wanted to wear the same dress I had worn for the Academy Ball, but Natalie asked me if I'd learned anything in etiquette class. I took that as meaning I needed a new dress.

"I don't have another one, though." I had cringed.

"I'll lend you one." Natalie smiled.

It had taken half a day for me to pick a dress for the Fall Formal. In actuality, it took Maisy, Shannon, Michelle, and Natalie half a day to pick a dress for me. I would try on something from one of the other girls, and it would be slightly too big, but they all said they could hem it or stitch it to make it fit. Or we would have a conversation of which shoes I would wear.

"She can't wear flats to a ball!" Natalie exclaimed, as if it were a crime.

"If she wears her heels with this dress, it'll look all wrong." Maisy shook her head.

I was patient, pretending to be a pincushion. It was something I was used to. Aunt Chloe would use me like a mannequin to mend or sew new clothing. Natalie dressed me up for any holiday I allowed her to. After I'd tried on several dresses, possibly all of the dresses they had brought, they picked one.

It had a deep maroon fabric, with three-quarter sleeves that had cinched ruffles at the elbow. The chest was similar to the back of a corset, low cut with the strings tying at the bottom, all in a much darker maroon. The dress was long enough for me to wear heels and have it barely sweep the ground. It was more flashy than the last dress I'd worn. The girls told me all formals were elegant and if you didn't feel like a princess, then you weren't dressed up enough.

I felt like a princess.

When we were ready, we joined the rest of the girls attending the ball. They were going down the main stairs, one by one. The men all stood at the bottom of the stairs, waiting to watch their date descend. It was like a dance in itself. As soon as a girl reached the last step, there were lips to kiss her cheek and an arm to guide her into the Great Hall.

"I'm nervous," Natalie whispered to me. We were standing at the top of the staircase, awaiting our turn.

"Me too." I laughed nervously.

"I just hope they have drinks." The voice made me lift my lip in a disgruntled way. Tilly was right behind me. She must have snuck in front of Michelle and Maisy.

The line moved, and I didn't respond to her comment. As soon as Natalie was halfway down the stairs,

I followed. It was difficult going down these three flights of stairs in heels. When I saw Mark at the bottom, I kept my eyes on him, focusing on not tripping. My nerves had plastered a smile on my face. I wondered how he was feeling; his smile was stunning.

"Gorgeous." He kissed my cheek and took my hand.

"Thank you, kind sir," I said, using a lesson from my etiquette class. We laughed and walked into the Great Hall.

I had thought there would be more decorations, but it was as the girls said it would be: elegant. Simple twinkle lights scattered through the room looked like little Light Pebbles. We'd had dinner hours ago, so the only tables in the Great Hall were in the corners or the long one in the front with the drinks. Officials had placed themselves around the room, too. The women were in black or gold, and the men were in black. Even the magistrate was there.

Mark looked great in black. I was glad he didn't go for a fashion statement in blue, like Maisy's date did, because my dress went very well with him. I'd never seen Maisy's date before, and I wanted to go meet him, but then I saw Jensen walk in.

He didn't have a girl on his arm, and I felt oddly happy. His black clothing was less formal that what Mark was wearing, but it was still elegant. Simple and elegant.

"What's got your attention?" Mark asked, turning to

see why I had craned my neck. "Of course."

Before Mark could get more irritated, Jensen left. I was a little hurt he didn't come to say hello. I could have sworn he saw me. Maybe he did have a date.

"You want a dance? Or a drink?" Mark walked me over to the drink table. He poured me a cup of something and shoved it into my hand. "Here."

"Thanks," I said, begrudgingly. "Let's go see Maisy. I haven't met her date before."

"Okay, you go over there." Mark finished his drink and poured another. "I'll be right back."

"What?" But he'd already turned and was walking towards the doors. "Mark, wait!"

He stormed out with his newly filled cup. I looked for Maisy, but it looked like she was having an intimate conversation with her date against the wall. Natalie should have been in here, too, but the room was filling up fast. It seemed I was the only one without a partner. Definitely, the only one whose date had just left her.

Rhese.

Jensen? I picked up my dress and hurried out of the room. He must be close by. *Where are you?*

I'm in your room.

Jensen was trying really hard not to be seen. I made sure Mark wasn't around before I went up the stairs as quickly as I could with the heels. When I got to my door,

I smoothed down my dress, fluffed my hair, and slowed my breathing before going in.

"Why didn't you—" I stopped when I saw Mark. Trying to recover from this unexpected visitor, I closed the door and turned around with a smile. "What are you doing up here?"

Jensen, where are you? I'm in my room and you're not here.

Oh, I'm here all right.

"But I'm not Jensen," Mark said out loud.

It took me a second to realize what was happening. My heart beat faster and I didn't know what to say.

"I'm sorry." Mark stood up and walked towards me. "Are you not happy to see me? Were you excited to see Jensen here instead? Seeing another man behind my back?"

"No, no." I shook my head. "It's not like that at all."

"I know, Terhese." Mark nodded. He didn't seem angry, but he didn't seem like he was in a pleasant mood either. "I believe you. It is unfortunate, though, that you couldn't just tell me you loved me. How hard is it to get you to love someone?"

"What?" I was caught off guard. "What do you mean? Mark, we haven't been dating very long. I love being with you."

"Not the point." Mark shook his head. "Come here."

I was hesitant, but I walked towards him. My red dress swung at my ankles, the slit Shannon had cut revealing my leg up to the knee when I walked. Mark grabbed my hand and spun me around. He pulled me close and kissed me hard, one hand on my lower back, holding me to him. When I tried to push away, he put his fingers in my hair and tugged just enough to hurt.

"Mark," I pushed his chest harder and moved my head, "stop."

"This could have been so much easier." Mark pulled me back to him. His hand traveled farther down my back until he found my bottom. After he gave it a squeeze, he lifted me and carried me the few steps to my bed. He pushed me down onto the bed and crawled on top of me, holding down each wrist.

"No! Mark, stop!" I screamed. He pulled out a length of fabric from his pocket, kissed me deeply, and wrapped it around my wrists so my fists faced each other. I knew this wrong, but I couldn't fight him. "What's happening?"

I felt tears welling up again.

"Don't fret, Rhesey." He mocked me with the name Nathan had called me, the name I hated. How did he even know that name? He pushed my arms above my head. "You really want to know what's going on?"

"Yes," I whimpered. "This can't be you."

"Oh, it's me all right." Mark laughed. He kissed my

cheek and nibbled my ear. "You won't remember any of this once you're mine."

"Once I'm yours?" My voice was almost a squeak. I was becoming truly frightened. "What do you mean?"

"Come on, Terhese! Use that brain of yours," Mark taunted, tracing a finger down my leg and to my open-toed heel. "This is a scandalous ensemble for a ball, don't you think?"

I thought of what Natalie had said she overheard.

"I'm a Binder, Terhese!"

That name I remembered. Jensen's uncle had told me about them. It had been a quick and vague recollection of how the Ràej War started, but he said they had left Omneth. My expression was too easy for him to read.

"Oh, you have heard of us. You probably haven't heard the real story," he said triumphantly, a gleam in his eye. "In short, we never left Omneth.

"The Slates were a cover name for us. Technically, we don't have our own magic, but we are able to use people with magic, and we use them well. We created Pebbles so we could carry magic from others with us." Mark laughed. "By the look on your face, that is not what you were expecting."

"What does this have to do with me?" I struggled to stay calm, not wanting to show him how scared I was.

"My sweet, sweet love." Mark kissed my forehead, as gentle as ever, and bent down to whisper into my ear. "I've known you were Ràej from the first time I touched you."

Touch. Fear washed over me. From the moment we met, he'd held my hand or kissed me.

"We Bind temporarily through skin-to-skin contact. The more contact we have, the longer the Bond can last. There are two ways, though, that you are Bound forever." Mark leaned on his arm and brushed my bare shoulder with his fingertips. "If you fall in love with your Binder or if he beds you."

He paused and rolled his eyes. "I wonder, if that dolt Nathan had known you were Ràej, if he would have worked harder at Binding you."

"What?" I felt sick to stomach.

"Oh, yes," Mark traced my cheek with his finger. "Of all the girls Nathan Bound, you were the only one he couldn't get. I made sure to be the first man you met at the Academy, the first man to touch you. And when I felt your Ràej blood that first time, it gave me a high."

He laughed. "I would have stolen you from him even if he hadn't gone to prison," Mark said solemnly. "I'm smarter. And I'm much stronger than he is." He adjusted his weight and unbuckled his belt.

Pieces of this giant messed up puzzle were coming together, and I realized what he was about to do. My anger sparked and I felt hot.

"I'll admit, you've been so *hard*!" Mark snarled. "The touching, the kissing, and you still won't Bind to me. I almost had you until Jensen came back. They say he's not Ràej, but I don't believe it. What do you think?"

I stared at Mark, and betrayal washed over me. All the pleasant feelings were gone. He tried kissing me again, as if that would make me fall in love with him. I bit his unwanted tongue and felt his hand crash against my face, making my whole head turn to the side.

"Bitch!" he shouted. "See? Even now. Why can't I Bind you?"

The metallic taste of blood filled my mouth. I licked it and looked back at him, hoping he could see the anger in my eyes. If I wasn't worried about him hearing me, I would call for Lenetta. Then again, I wasn't sure which side she was on.

"I didn't mean to hurt you." Mark wiped the blood off with his finger and popped it into his mouth. "Blood of the Ràej. I've heard rumors about the power it can give you. But that's not my mission today."

Mark pulled my dress, ripping it from the knee up to the hip. I saw him unbutton his pants, and I squirmed and fought against the fabric binding he'd used to tie me to the bed. When I screamed, his hand covered my mouth forcibly, and he kissed my forehead.

"Shh." His eyes were darker than before, pupils enveloping the iris, scaring me even more. "The easier you make this, the quicker it'll be done. Accept my touch. Accept this!"

I felt his body against mine and heard myself cry out. He had me poisoned with his will. I knew I should want to fight harder, but I couldn't. He pulled my dress up and moved my thighs apart. I held my breath and searched for my strength.

"Good," he said gently. "You won't even remember not wanting this in a few minutes."

The panic settled in. My heart was hammering so fast I thought I was going to hyperventilate. I felt his fingers, always cold, on my inner thigh, and I jerked. Mark hushed me like I was a skittish horse he was trying to break. That's exactly what he was doing by Binding. He was trying to break me, to own me. His kind had wiped out the entire Ràej Kingdom. I wasn't going to let it happen to me.

I focused all the willpower I had left on pushing my power towards my hands. If I could have my hands free, I would be able to do a lot more. With every extra touch or kiss from him, it became harder to focus on what I wanted to do. At the same time, I became more frustrated, humiliated, and determined.

"Terhese, this is happening now," Mark whispered, getting into his final position. "It'll only hurt for a second.

Accept the Binding."

"No!" I screamed. Feeling it was my last chance, I released my power in any way possible. It felt similar to what I had done at the Academy Ball. Power flew from me, pushing Mark off me with a force so strong he hit the ceiling before falling back down.

I was still tied to the bed, but I was able to move my head so Mark didn't land on it and knock me out. He was holding his head where it had hit the ceiling. My willpower was back. He had nothing over me. I used this time to reach up and untie the knot that held me. I just needed to unwrap each hand.

I stood up from the bed and struggled with the fabric. When I had one hand free, Mark grabbed the trailing fabric and pulled me back towards him.

"NO!" he roared. "You are not getting away. I will *not* fail!"

Mark pushed me to my back on the ground and knelt over me, holding my flailing hands down and away. I gave him a second to think he was winning so I could slip a high heel off my foot. I was going to have to use it at the perfect timing. He must have realized his touch was no longer affecting me and he had only one option. When he fumbled with my dress again, I headbutted him.

Fuck!

"Damn it, Terhese!" Mark shouted. Then I hit him

in the head with the heel of my shoe. He grabbed the shoe from me and threw it across the room. I put my hands on his chest and pushed him, but this time he was propelled by two smoldering balls of fire.

I grabbed my bag and ran out the door and into the hall. It was deserted, with everyone being at the Fall Formal in the Great Hall. I had one shoe on, but I wasn't sure if I had enough time to squeeze out of the straps. I ran as well as I could until I heard Mark shouting after me. In a hopeless effort, I swung my arm out as I turned to look at him. Another force of power rushed towards him, knocking him off his feet.

seconds I had gained, I stopped to pull my other shoe off. Maisy was standing at the top of the staircase when I turned around, her dress and hair perfectly in place.

"Maisy, help me," I begged. "I need you to hide me. I can't explain right now, but please."

I watched Maisy's face go from worried to uncertain, then sad. "I'm so sorry, Rhese," she said, pulling a Pebble from the pouch at her wrist. "I didn't know it was you."

"What?" I shook my head.

She Pinched the Pebble towards me, but I waved it to the ground before it released anything. Maisy's face turned to astonishment after that. She took another Pebble from her pouch, and I heard Mark shouting from behind me.

"I'm sorry, too," I said.

I threw my hands towards Maisy, throwing her back against the wall, and she crumpled on the floor. There wasn't time to cry, just run. I didn't know how I was going to get out; the only option was blocked by dozens of ballgowns.

I chanced a glance over my shoulder and saw Mark getting closer. The castle was too confusing for me to try to outwit him. I ran down the main stairs, hoping I could find Jensen. The dress was too long to make it down the stairs quickly, and Mark was going two or three at a time. When I reached the bottom, Mark jumped over the banister and landed in front of me. He grabbed a girl's wrist from behind him and pulled her forward.

"Ouch! Mark, let go." Natalie squirmed, trying to pry his fingers off. She looked up at Evan who was standing between me and her. "Evan, tell your drunk friend to let go of me."

I wasn't sure what was about to happen, but I felt nauseous. Was he going to tell Natalie? Was he going to tell everyone?

The crowd around us was dead silent. No one was asking questions or trying to help. Natalie looked more confused than I had ever seen her. She couldn't stop looking at her unresponsive boyfriend.

"Rhese?" she pleaded. "What's going on?"

I didn't want to lie to her anymore, but I didn't know how to tell her the truth.

"Accept it, Terhese," Mark said, pulling a sheathed dagger from his pocket. He pulled it up against his leg, slipping the covering off to reveal the sharpened blade. "This is happening *tonight.*"

"Accept what?" Natalie's voice had gone high. "What the *fuck* is happening!"

"Hold this." Mark put the knife in Natalie's hand but still held her other wrist tightly. He had control.

"Mark." Evan took a step toward his friend. "Man, what are you doing?"

"Get back."

Mark's eyes were darting from Evan to me. He looked unstable. I couldn't understand why no one was doing anything. They should be alerting the Officials if nothing else.

"Last chance, Terhese."

"Never," I enunciated slowly for him.

"Have it your way."

Natalie plunged the dagger into her own stomach. She screamed and fell to her knees, both hands holding the dagger, blood running out over her pale pink dress. I ran to catch her and help her to lie on her back. Evan punched Mark until he was on the ground, and then he ran over to Natalie and took her into his arms. I saw her mouth relax. The light in her eyes was quickly fading.

"There is no one here that would help a Ràej. We set up these academies all over Omneth so we can train Ràej killers." Mark smirked, raising his hands to point out all the bystanders.

The dagger fell from Natalie's hand, and my heart broke. It hurt more than telepathy with Shannon, more than my sprained ankle, and more than the post-Numbing Pebble. I fell to my knees and shrieked, then lifted my hands to my face and sobbed.

"Crying won't help you."

Despair, anger, hate. My sobs turned into a banshee-like bawl. My emotions needed to be let out, so I screamed. I could hear the wind outside the castle mimic me. Rain poured down, distracting the students to look outside. The more emotions I released, the more powerful I felt.

I stood up slowly. Lightning cracked with thunder hot on its heels. Mark didn't look fazed; he looked like he'd lost his mind. I took a deep breath and felt everything around me. Then I stomped and threw my fisted hands towards the ground, lifted my head, and screamed.

It was the most liberating feeling. I pushed out all that anger and sadness, betrayal and loss. With it, I blew the wall of the Keep into the courtyard and everyone off their feet. Some students were blown outside, stuck in the rubble outside and, what looked to be, a hurricane brewing. I couldn't see Mark, but this disruption made people from the ballroom come see what was happening. It was mostly Officials, ready to fight.

"Terhese, run!" Jensen shouted. He didn't give me time to figure out where I was supposed to run before he threw power at the ground under the Officials. The stones rumbled and fell to whatever room was below, then the structure of the Keep started to collapse. "RUN!"

He grabbed my arm this time and pulled me out from the crumbling Keep. We didn't stop. My bare feet were stepping on broken stones, but Jensen was pulling me behind him. We were running towards the mainland. I hoped he would have a carriage somewhere, but I didn't see one. When we reached the end of the island, Jensen turned around and shoved his hands towards the main gate. I watched the force of power hit the top of the barricade, breaking the contraption, and making it fall closed.

"What do we now?" I whimpered. My dress was torn and my bare feet were bleeding from several cuts.

"Trust me." Jensen picked me up and threw me over the edge of the causeway.